"*The Unbearable Lightness of Being* is both a love story and a novel of ideas. . . . Witty, seductive, serious. . . also full of feeling and enormously experienced in the tricky interplay of sex and politics. . . . One of the finest and most consistently interesting novelists in Europe or America, [Kundera] has a powerful tale to tell."

—Richard Locke, *The Washington Post Book World*

"Few contemporary writers have succeeded as Kundera has in combining a cool, elegant, formal objectivity with warm, intimate (almost embarrassingly intimate) pictures of the imperfect realities of adult love. Kundera's heroes may be Don Juans, but they are shy, apologetic ones; his women are intensely physical beings, but they are also as quirkily intelligent and stubbornly independent as his men."

—Edmund White, *The Nation*

"Let me say it simply: *The Unbearable Lightness of Being* is one of the greatest novels of the twentieth century, and with its publication Kundera has firmly established himself as the world's greatest living writer."

—John Podhoretz, *The Washington Times*

"Outstanding . . . Burning compassion, extraordinary intelligence, and dazzling artistry."

—Thomas DiPietro, *Commonweal*

"A work of large scale and complexity, symphonically arranged . . . political and philosophical, erotic and spiritual, funny and profound. . . . There is no wiser observer now writing of the multifarious relations of men and women. . . . Kundera's intelligence is both speculative and playful. *The Unbearable Lightness of Being* is his best novel yet."

—Frances Taliaferro, *The Wall Street Journal*

"Mr. Kundera's novel, composed in the spirit of the late quartets of Beethoven, is concerned with the opposing elements of freedom and necessity among a quartet of entangled lovers."

—*The New Yorker*

"Encyclopaedic and epigrammatic, profound and playful, Kundera explores the intersection of the sublime and the ridiculous to give us an important chapter in the moral history of our time."

—Judges' citation, 1984 *Los Angeles Times* Book Prize

"With cunning, wit and elegiac sadness, Milan Kundera, the celebrated Czechoslovak émigré writer, expresses the trap the world has become."

—*New York Times Book Review* citation, 15 Best Books of 1984

## Also by Milan Kundera

THE JOKE

LAUGHABLE LOVES

LIFE IS ELSEWHERE

THE FAREWELL PARTY

THE BOOK OF LAUGHTER AND FORGETTING

JACQUES AND HIS MASTER

THE ART OF THE NOVEL

IMMORTALITY

MILAN KUNDERA

# The Unbearable Lightness of Being

Translated from the Czech by Michael Henry Heim

HarperPerennial
*A Division of* HarperCollins*Publishers*

Portions of this work originally appeared, in somewhat different form, in *The New Yorker.*

A hardcover edition of this book was published in 1984 by Harper & Row, Publishers, Inc.



First Harper Colophon edition published 1985. Reissued in Perennial Library edition 1987. Reissued in HarperPerennial edition 1991.

---

Library of Congress Cataloging in Publication Data

Kundera, Milan.
The unbearable lightness of being.

"Perennial Library"

I. Heim, Michael Henry. II. Title.
PG5039.21.U6U5 1987 891.8'635 83-48363
ISBN 0-06-091465-3 (pbk.)

---

92 93 94 95 MPC 20 19 18 17 16 15 14 13

# CONTENTS

# PART ONE

# Lightness and Weight

# 1

The idea of eternal return is a mysterious one, and Nietzsche has often perplexed other philosophers with it: to think that everything recurs as we once experienced it, and that the recurrence itself recurs ad infinitum! What does this mad myth signify?

Putting it negatively, the myth of eternal return states that a life which disappears once and for all, which does not return, is like a shadow, without weight, dead in advance, and whether it was horrible, beautiful, or sublime, its horror, sublimity, and beauty mean nothing. We need take no more note of it than of a war between two African kingdoms in the fourteenth century, a war that altered nothing in the destiny of the world, even if a hundred thousand blacks perished in excruciating torment.

Will the war between two African kingdoms in the fourteenth century itself be altered if it recurs again and again, in eternal return?

It will: it will become a solid mass, permanently protuberant, its inanity irreparable.

If the French Revolution were to recur eternally, French historians would be less proud of Robespierre. But because they deal with something that will not return, the bloody years of the Revolution have turned into mere words, theories, and discussions, have become lighter than feathers, frightening no one. There is an infinite difference between a Robespierre who occurs only once in history and a Robespierre who eternally returns, chopping off French heads.

Let us therefore agree that the idea of eternal return implies a perspective from which things appear other than as we know them: they appear without the mitigating circumstance of their transitory nature. This mitigating circumstance prevents us from coming to a verdict. For how can we condemn something that is ephemeral, in transit? In the sunset of dissolution, everything is illuminated by the aura of nostalgia, even the guillotine.

Not long ago, I caught myself experiencing a most incredible sensation. Leafing through a book on Hitler, I was touched by some of his portraits: they reminded me of my childhood. I grew up during the war; several members of my family perished in Hitler's concentration camps; but what were their deaths compared with the memories of a lost period in my life, a period that would never return?

This reconciliation with Hitler reveals the profound moral perversity of a world that rests essentially on the nonexistence of return, for in this world everything is pardoned in advance and therefore everything cynically permitted.

# 2

If every second of our lives recurs an infinite number of times, we are nailed to eternity as Jesus Christ was nailed to the cross. It is a terrifying prospect. In the world of eternal return the weight of unbearable responsibility lies heavy on every move we make. That is why Nietzsche called the idea of eternal return the heaviest of burdens (*das schwerste Gewicht*).

If eternal return is the heaviest of burdens, then our lives can stand out against it in all their splendid lightness.

But is heaviness truly deplorable and lightness splendid?

The heaviest of burdens crushes us, we sink beneath it, it pins us to the ground. But in the love poetry of every age, the woman longs to be weighed down by the man's body. The heaviest of burdens is therefore simultaneously an image of life's most intense fulfillment. The heavier the burden, the closer our lives come to the earth, the more real and truthful they become.

Conversely, the absolute absence of a burden causes man to be lighter than air, to soar into the heights, take leave of the earth and his earthly being, and become only half real, his movements as free as they are insignificant.

What then shall we choose? Weight or lightness?

Parmenides posed this very question in the sixth century before Christ. He saw the world divided into pairs of opposites: light/darkness, fineness/coarseness, warmth/cold, being/non-being. One half of the opposition he called positive (light, fineness, warmth, being), the other negative. We might find this division into positive and negative poles childishly simple except for one difficulty: which one is positive, weight or lightness?

Parmenides responded: lightness is positive, weight negative.

Was he correct or not? That is the question. The only certainty is: the lightness/weight opposition is the most mysterious, most ambiguous of all.

# 3

I have been thinking about Tomas for many years. But only in the light of these reflections did I see him clearly. I saw him standing at the window of his flat and looking across the courtyard at the opposite walls, not knowing what to do.

He had first met Tereza about three weeks earlier in a small Czech town. They had spent scarcely an hour together. She had accompanied him to the station and waited with him until he boarded the train. Ten days later she paid him a visit. They made love the day she arrived. That night she came down with a fever and stayed a whole week in his flat with the flu.

He had come to feel an inexplicable love for this all but complete stranger; she seemed a child to him, a child someone had put in a bulrush basket daubed with pitch and sent downstream for Tomas to fetch at the riverbank of his bed.

She stayed with him a week, until she was well again, then went back to her town, some hundred and twenty-five miles from Prague. And then came the time I have just spoken of and see as the key to his life: Standing by the window, he looked out over the courtyard at the walls opposite him and deliberated.

Should he call her back to Prague for good? He feared the responsibility. If he invited her to come, then come she would, and offer him up her life.

Or should he refrain from approaching her? Then she would remain a waitress in a hotel restaurant of a provincial town and he would never see her again.

Did he want her to come or did he not?

He looked out over the courtyard at the opposite walls, seeking an answer.

He kept recalling her lying on his bed; she reminded him of no one in his former life. She was neither mistress nor wife. She was a child whom he had taken from a bulrush basket that had been daubed with pitch and sent to the riverbank of his bed. She fell asleep. He knelt down next to her. Her feverous breath quickened and she gave out a weak moan. He pressed his face to hers and whispered calming words into her sleep. After a while he felt her breath return to normal and her face rise unconsciously to meet his. He smelled the delicate aroma of her fever and breathed it in, as if trying to glut himself with the intimacy of her body. And all at once he fancied she had been with him for many years and was dying. He had a sudden clear feeling that he would not survive her death. He would lie down beside her and want to die with her. He pressed his face into the pillow beside her head and kept it there for a long time.

Now he was standing at the window trying to call that moment to account. What could it have been if not love declaring itself to him?

But was it love? The feeling of wanting to die beside her was clearly exaggerated: he had seen her only once before in his life! Was it simply the hysteria of a man who, aware deep down of his inaptitude for love, felt the self-deluding need to simulate it? His unconscious was so cowardly that the best partner it could choose for its little comedy was this miserable provincial waitress with practically no chance at all to enter his life!

Looking out over the courtyard at the dirty walls, he realized he had no idea whether it was hysteria or love.

And he was distressed that in a situation where a real man would instantly have known how to act, he was vacillating and therefore depriving the most beautiful moments he had ever experienced (kneeling at her bed and thinking he would not survive her death) of their meaning.

He remained annoyed with himself until he realized that not knowing what he wanted was actually quite natural.

We can never know what to want, because, living only one life, we can neither compare it with our previous lives nor perfect it in our lives to come.

Was it better to be with Tereza or to remain alone?

There is no means of testing which decision is better, because there is no basis for comparison. We live everything as it comes, without warning, like an actor going on cold. And what can life be worth if the first rehearsal for life is life itself? That is why life is always like a sketch. No, "sketch" is not quite the word, because a sketch is an outline of something, the groundwork for a picture, whereas the sketch that is our life is a sketch for nothing, an outline with no picture.

*Einmal ist keinmal,* says Tomas to himself. What happens but once, says the German adage, might as well not have happened at all. If we have only one life to live, we might as well not have lived at all.

# 4

But then one day at the hospital, during a break between operations, a nurse called him to the telephone. He heard Tereza's voice coming from the receiver. She had phoned him from the railway station. He was overjoyed. Unfortunately, he had something on that evening and could not invite her to his place until the next day. The moment he hung up, he reproached himself for not telling her to go straight there. He had time enough to cancel his plans, after all! He tried to imagine what Tereza would do in Prague during the thirty-six long hours before they were to meet, and had half a mind to jump into his car and drive through the streets looking for her.

She arrived the next evening, a handbag dangling from her shoulder, looking more elegant than before. She had a thick book under her arm. It was *Anna Karenina.* She seemed in a good mood, even a little boisterous, and tried to make him think she had just happened to drop in, things had just worked out that way: she was in Prague on business, perhaps (at this point she became rather vague) to find a job.

Later, as they lay naked and spent side by side on the bed, he asked her where she was staying. It was night by then, and he offered to drive her there. Embarrassed, she answered that she still had to find a hotel and had left her suitcase at the station.

Only two days ago, he had feared that if he invited her to Prague she would offer him up her life. When she told him her suitcase was at the station, he immediately realized that the suitcase contained her life and that she had left it at the station only until she could offer it up to him.

The two of them got into his car, which was parked in front of the house, and drove to the station. There he claimed the suitcase (it was large and enormously heavy) and took it and her home.

How had he come to make such a sudden decision when for nearly a fortnight he had wavered so much that he could not even bring himself to send a postcard asking her how she was?

He himself was surprised. He had acted against his principles. Ten years earlier, when he had divorced his wife, he celebrated the event the way others celebrate a marriage. He understood he was not born to live side by side with any woman and could be fully himself only as a bachelor. He tried to design his life in such a way that no woman could move in with a suitcase. That was why his flat had only the one bed. Even though it was wide enough, Tomas would tell his mistresses that he was unable to fall asleep with anyone next to him, and drive them home after midnight. And so it was not the flu that kept him from sleeping with Tereza on her first visit. The first night he had slept in his large armchair, and the rest of that week he drove each night to the hospital, where he had a cot in his office.

But this time he fell asleep by her side. When he woke up the next morning, he found Tereza, who was still asleep, holding his hand. Could they have been hand in hand all night? It was hard to believe.

And while she breathed the deep breath of sleep and held his hand (firmly: he was unable to disengage it from her grip), the enormously heavy suitcase stood by the bed.

He refrained from loosening his hand from her grip for fear of waking her, and turned carefully on his side to observe her better.

Again it occurred to him that Tereza was a child put in a pitch-daubed bulrush basket and sent downstream. He couldn't very well let a basket with a child in it float down a stormy river! If the Pharaoh's daughter hadn't snatched the basket carrying little Moses from the waves, there would have been no Old Testament, no civilization as we now know it! How many ancient myths begin with the rescue of an abandoned child! If Polybus hadn't taken in the young Oedipus, Sophocles wouldn't have written his most beautiful tragedy!

Tomas did not realize at the time that metaphors are dangerous. Metaphors are not to be trifled with. A single metaphor can give birth to love.

## 5

He lived a scant two years with his wife, and they had a son. At the divorce proceedings, the judge awarded the infant to its mother and ordered Tomas to pay a third of his salary for its support. He also granted him the right to visit the boy every other week.

But each time Tomas was supposed to see him, the boy's mother found an excuse to keep him away. He soon realized that bringing them expensive gifts would make things a good deal easier, that he was expected to bribe the mother for the son's love. He saw a future of quixotic attempts to inculcate his views in the boy, views opposed in every way to the mother's. The very thought of it exhausted him. When, one Sunday, the boy's mother again canceled a scheduled visit, Tomas decided on the spur of the moment never to see him again.

Why should he feel more for that child, to whom he was bound by nothing but a single improvident night, than for any other? He would be scrupulous about paying support; he just didn't want anybody making him fight for his son in the name of paternal sentiments!

Needless to say, he found no sympathizers. His own parents condemned him roundly: if Tomas refused to take an interest in his son, then they, Tomas's parents, would no longer take an interest in theirs. They made a great show of maintaining good relations with their daughter-in-law and trumpeted their exemplary stance and sense of justice.

Thus in practically no time he managed to rid himself of wife, son, mother, and father. The only thing they bequeathed to him was a fear of women. Tomas desired but feared them. Needing to create a compromise between fear and desire, he devised what he called "erotic friendship." He would tell his mistresses: the only relationship that can make both partners happy is one in which sentimentality has no place and neither partner makes any claim on the life and freedom of the other.

To ensure that erotic friendship never grew into the aggression of love, he would meet each of his long-term mistresses only at intervals. He considered this method flawless and propagated it among his friends: "The important thing is to abide by the rule of threes. Either you see a woman three times in quick succession and then never again, or you maintain relations over the years but make sure that the rendezvous are at least three weeks apart."

The rule of threes enabled Tomas to keep intact his liaisons with some women while continuing to engage in short-term affairs with many others. He was not always understood. The woman who understood him best was Sabina. She was a painter. "The reason I like you," she would say to him, "is you're the complete opposite of kitsch. In the kingdom of kitsch you would be a monster."

It was Sabina he turned to when he needed to find a job for Tereza in Prague. Following the unwritten rules of erotic friendship, Sabina promised to do everything in her power, and before long she had in fact located a place for Tereza in the darkroom of an illustrated weekly. Although her new job did not require any particular qualifications, it raised her status from waitress to member of the press. When Sabina herself introduced Tereza to everyone on the weekly, Tomas knew he had never had a better friend as a mistress than Sabina.

## *6*

The unwritten contract of erotic friendship stipulated that Tomas should exclude all love from his life. The moment he violated that clause of the contract, his other mistresses would assume inferior status and become ripe for insurrection.

Accordingly, he rented a room for Tereza and her heavy suitcase. He wanted to be able to watch over her, protect her, enjoy her presence, but felt no need to change his way of life. He did not want word to get out that Tereza was sleeping at his place: spending the night together was the corpus delicti of love.

He never spent the night with the others. It was easy enough if he was at their place: he could leave whenever he pleased. It was worse when they were at his and he had to explain that come midnight he would have to drive them home because he was an insomniac and found it impossible to fall asleep in close proximity to another person. Though it was not far from the truth, he never dared tell them the whole truth: after making love he had an uncontrollable craving to be by himself; waking in the middle of the night at the side of an alien body was distasteful to him, rising in the morning with an intruder repellent; he had no desire to be overheard brushing his teeth in the bathroom, nor was he enticed by the thought of an intimate breakfast.

That is why he was so surprised to wake up and find Tereza squeezing his hand tightly. Lying there looking at her, he could not quite understand what had happened. But as he ran through the previous few hours in his mind, he began to sense an aura of hitherto unknown happiness emanating from them.

From that time on they both looked forward to sleeping together. I might even say that the goal of their lovemaking was not so much pleasure as the sleep that followed it. She especially was affected. Whenever she stayed overnight in her rented room (which quickly became only an alibi for Tomas), she was unable to fall asleep; in his arms she would fall asleep no matter how wrought up she might have been. He would whisper impromptu fairy tales about her, or gibberish, words he repeated monotonously, words soothing or comical, which turned into vague visions lulling her through the first dreams of the night. He had complete control over her sleep: she dozed off at the second he chose.

While they slept, she held him as on the first night, keeping a firm grip on wrist, finger, or ankle. If he wanted to move without waking her, he had to resort to artifice. After freeing his finger (wrist, ankle) from her clutches, a process which, since she guarded him carefully even in her sleep, never failed to rouse her partially, he would calm her by slipping an object into her hand (a rolled-up pajama top, a slipper, a book), which she then gripped as tightly as if it were a part of his body.

Once, when he had just lulled her to sleep but she had gone no farther than dream's antechamber and was therefore still responsive to him, he said to her, "Good-bye, I'm going now." "Where?" she asked in her sleep. "Away," he answered sternly. "Then I'm going with you," she said, sitting up in bed. "No, you can't. I'm going away for good," he said, going out into the hall. She stood up and followed him out, squinting. She was naked beneath her short nightdress. Her face was blank, expressionless, but she moved energetically. He walked through the hall of the flat into the hall of the building (the hall shared by all the occupants), closing the door in her face. She flung it open and continued to follow him, convinced in her sleep that he meant to leave her for good and she had to stop him. He walked down the stairs to the first landing and waited for her there. She went down after him, took him by the hand, and led him back to bed.

Tomas came to this conclusion: Making love with a woman and sleeping with a woman are two separate passions, not merely different but opposite. Love does not make itself felt in the desire for copulation (a desire that extends to an infinite number of women) but in the desire for shared sleep (a desire limited to one woman).

## 7

In the middle of the night she started moaning in her sleep. Tomas woke her up, but when she saw his face she said, with hatred in her voice, "Get away from me! Get away from me!" Then she told him her dream: The two of them and Sabina had been in a big room together. There was a bed in the middle of the room. It was like a platform in the theater. Tomas ordered her to stand in the corner while he made love to Sabina. The sight of it caused Tereza intolerable suffering. Hoping to alleviate the pain in her heart by pains of the flesh, she jabbed needles under her fingernails. "It hurt so much," she said, squeezing her hands into fists as if they actually were wounded.

He pressed her to him, and she gradually (trembling violently for a long time) fell asleep in his arms.

Thinking about the dream the next day, he remembered something. He opened a desk drawer and took out a packet of letters Sabina had written to him. He was not long in finding the following passage: "I want to make love to you in my studio. It will be like a stage surrounded by people. The audience won't be allowed up close, but they won't be able to take their eyes off us. . . ."

The worst of it was that the letter was dated. It was quite recent, written long after Tereza had moved in with Tomas.

"So you've been rummaging in my letters!"

She did not deny it. "Throw me out, then!"

But he did not throw her out. He could picture her pressed against the wall of Sabina's studio jabbing needles up under her nails. He took her fingers between his hands and stroked them, brought them to his lips and kissed them, as if they still had drops of blood on them.

But from that time on, everything seemed to conspire against him. Not a day went by without her learning something about his secret life.

At first he denied it all. Then, when the evidence became too blatant, he argued that his polygamous way of life did not in the least run counter to his love for her. He was inconsistent: first he disavowed his infidelities, then he tried to justify them.

Once he was saying good-bye after making a date with a woman on the phone, when from the next room came a strange sound like the chattering of teeth.

By chance she had come home without his realizing it. She was pouring something from a medicine bottle down her throat, and her hand shook so badly the glass bottle clicked against her teeth.

He pounced on her as if trying to save her from drowning. The bottle fell to the floor, spotting the carpet with valerian drops. She put up a good fight, and he had to keep her in a straitjacket-like hold for a quarter of an hour before he could calm her.

He knew he was in an unjustifiable situation, based as it was on complete inequality.

One evening, before she discovered his correspondence with Sabina, they had gone to a bar with some friends to celebrate Tereza's new job. She had been promoted at the weekly from darkroom technician to staff photographer. Because he had never been much for dancing, one of his younger colleagues took over. They made a splendid couple on the dance floor, and Tomas found her more beautiful than ever. He looked on in amazement at the split-second precision and deference with which Tereza anticipated her partner's will. The dance seemed to him a declaration that her devotion, her ardent desire to satisfy his every whim, was not necessarily bound to his person, that if she hadn't met Tomas, she would have been ready to respond to the call of any other man she might have met instead. He had no difficulty imagining Tereza and his young colleague as lovers. And the ease with which he arrived at this fiction wounded him. He realized that Tereza's body was perfectly thinkable coupled with any male body, and the thought put him in a foul mood. Not until late that night, at home, did he admit to her he was jealous.

This absurd jealousy, grounded as it was in mere hypotheses, proved that he considered her fidelity an unconditional postulate of their relationship. How then could he begrudge her her jealousy of his very real mistresses?

# 8

During the day, she tried (though with only partial success) to believe what Tomas told her and to be as cheerful as she had been before. But her jealousy thus tamed by day burst forth all the more savagely in her dreams, each of which ended in a wail he could silence only by waking her.

Her dreams recurred like themes and variations or television series. For example, she repeatedly dreamed of cats jumping at her face and digging their claws into her skin. We need not look far for an interpretation: in Czech slang the word "cat" means a pretty woman. Tereza saw herself threatened by women, all women. All women were potential mistresses for Tomas, and she feared them all.

In another cycle she was being sent to her death. Once, when he woke her as she screamed in terror in the dead of night, she told him about it. "I was at a large indoor swimming pool. There were about twenty of us. All women. We were naked and had to march around the pool. There was a basket hanging from the ceiling and a man standing in the basket. The man wore a broad-brimmed hat shading his face, but I could see it was you. You kept giving us orders. Shouting at us. We had to sing as we marched, sing and do kneebends. If one of us did a bad kneebend, you would shoot her with a pistol and she would fall dead into the pool. Which made everybody laugh and sing even louder. You never took your eyes off us, and the minute we did something wrong, you would shoot. The pool was full of corpses floating just below the surface. And I knew I lacked the strength to do the next kneebend and you were going to shoot me!"

In a third cycle she was dead.

Lying in a hearse as big as a furniture van, she was surrounded by dead women. There were so many of them that the back door would not close and several legs dangled out.

"But I'm not dead!" Tereza cried. "I can still feel!"

"So can we," the corpses laughed.

They laughed the same laugh as the live women who used to tell her cheerfully it was perfectly normal that one day she would have bad teeth, faulty ovaries, and wrinkles, because they all had bad teeth, faulty ovaries, and wrinkles. Laughing the same laugh, they told her that she was dead and it was perfectly all right!

Suddenly she felt a need to urinate. "You see," she cried. "I need to pee. That's proof positive I'm not dead!"

But they only laughed again. "Needing to pee is perfectly normal!" they said. "You'll go on feeling that kind of thing for a long time yet. Like a person who has an arm cut off and keeps feeling it's there. We may not have a drop of pee left in us, but we keep needing to pee."

Tereza huddled against Tomas in bed. "And the way they talked to me! Like old friends, people who'd known me forever. I was appalled at the thought of having to stay with them forever."

## 9

All languages that derive from Latin form the word "compassion" by combining the prefix meaning "with" (*com-*) and the root meaning "suffering" (Late Latin, *passio*). In other languages—Czech, Polish, German, and Swedish, for instance—this word is translated by a noun formed of an equivalent prefix combined with the word that means "feeling" (Czech, *sou-cit;* Polish, *współ-czucie;* German, *Mit-gefühl;* Swedish, *med-känsla*).

In languages that derive from Latin, "compassion" means: we cannot look on coolly as others suffer; or, we sympathize with those who suffer. Another word with approximately the same meaning, "pity" (French, *pitié;* Italian, *pietà;* etc.), connotes a certain condescension towards the sufferer. "To take pity on a woman" means that we are better off than she, that we stoop to her level, lower ourselves.

That is why the word "compassion" generally inspires suspicion; it designates what is considered an inferior, second-rate sentiment that has little to do with love. To love someone out of compassion means not really to love.

In languages that form the word "compassion" not from the root "suffering" but from the root "feeling," the word is used in approximately the same way, but to contend that it designates a bad or inferior sentiment is difficult. The secret strength of its etymology floods the word with another light and gives it a broader meaning: to have compassion (co-feeling) means not only to be able to live with the other's misfortune but also to feel with him any emotion—joy, anxiety, happiness, pain. This kind of compassion (in the sense of *soucit, współczucie, Mitgefühl, medkänsla*) therefore signifies the maximal capacity of affective imagination, the art of emotional telepathy. In the hierarchy of sentiments, then, it is supreme.

By revealing to Tomas her dream about jabbing needles under her fingernails, Tereza unwittingly revealed that she had gone through his desk. If Tereza had been any other woman, Tomas would never have spoken to her again. Aware of that, Tereza said to him, "Throw me out!" But instead of throwing her out, he seized her hand and kissed the tips of her fingers, because at that moment he himself felt the pain under her fingernails as surely as if the nerves of her fingers led straight to his own brain.

Anyone who has failed to benefit from the Devil's gift of compassion (co-feeling) will condemn Tereza coldly for her deed, because privacy is sacred and drawers containing intimate correspondence are not to be opened. But because compassion was Tomas's fate (or curse), he felt that he himself had knelt before the open desk drawer, unable to tear his eyes from Sabina's letter. He understood Tereza, and not only was he incapable of being angry with her, he loved her all the more.

## 10

Her gestures grew abrupt and unsteady. Two years had elapsed since she discovered he was unfaithful, and things had grown worse. There was no way out.

Was he genuinely incapable of abandoning his erotic friendships? He was. It would have torn him apart. He lacked the strength to control his taste for other women. Besides, he failed to see the need. No one knew better than he how little his exploits threatened Tereza. Why then give them up? He saw no more reason for that than to deny himself soccer matches.

But was it still a matter of pleasure? Even as he set out to visit another woman, he found her distasteful and promised himself he would not see her again. He constantly had Tereza's image before his eyes, and the only way he could erase it was by quickly getting drunk. Ever since meeting Tereza, he had been unable to make love to other women without alcohol! But alcohol on his breath was a sure sign to Tereza of infidelity.

He was caught in a trap: even on his way to see them, he found them distasteful, but one day without them and he was back on the phone, eager to make contact.

He still felt most comfortable with Sabina. He knew she was discreet and would not divulge their rendezvous. Her studio greeted him like a memento of his past, his idyllic bachelor past.

Perhaps he himself did not realize how much he had changed: he was now afraid to come home late, because Tereza would be waiting up for him. Then one day Sabina caught him glancing at his watch during intercourse and trying to hasten its conclusion.

Afterwards, still naked and lazily walking across the studio, she stopped before an easel with a half-finished painting and watched him sidelong as he threw on his clothes.

When he was fully dressed except for one bare foot, he looked around the room, and then got down on all fours to continue the search under a table.

"You seem to be turning into the theme of all my paintings," she said. "The meeting of two worlds. A double exposure. Showing through the outline of Tomas the libertine, incredibly, the face of a romantic lover. Or, the other way, through a Tristan, always thinking of his Tereza, I see the beautiful, betrayed world of the libertine."

Tomas straightened up and, distractedly, listened to Sabina's words.

"What are you looking for?" she asked.

"A sock."

She searched all over the room with him, and again he got down on all fours to look under the table.

"Your sock isn't anywhere to be seen," said Sabina. "You must have come without it."

"How could I have come without it?" cried Tomas, looking at his watch. "I wasn't wearing only one sock when I came, was I?"

"It's not out of the question. You've been very absent-minded lately. Always rushing somewhere, looking at your watch. It wouldn't surprise me in the least if you forgot to put on a sock."

He was just about to put his shoe on his bare foot. "It's cold out," Sabina said. "I'll lend you one of my stockings."

She handed him a long, white, fashionable, wide-net stocking.

He knew very well she was getting back at him for glancing at his watch while making love to her. She had hidden his sock somewhere. It was indeed cold out, and he had no choice but to take her up on the offer. He went home wearing a sock on one foot and a wide-net stocking rolled down over his ankle on the other.

He was in a bind: in his mistresses' eyes, he bore the stigma of his love for Tereza; in Tereza's eyes, the stigma of his exploits with the mistresses.

## 11

To assuage Tereza's sufferings, he married her (they could finally give up the room, which she had not lived in for quite some time) and gave her a puppy.

It was born to a Saint Bernard owned by a colleague. The sire was a neighbor's German shepherd. No one wanted the little mongrels, and his colleague was loath to kill them.

Looking over the puppies, Tomas knew that the ones he rejected would have to die. He felt like the president of the republic standing before four prisoners condemned to death and empowered to pardon only one of them. At last he made his choice: a bitch whose body seemed reminiscent of the German shepherd and whose head belonged to its Saint Bernard mother. He took it home to Tereza, who picked it up and pressed it to her breast. The puppy immediately peed on her blouse.

Then they tried to come up with a name for it. Tomas wanted the name to be a clear indication that the dog was Tereza's, and he thought of the book she was clutching under her arm when she arrived unannounced in Prague. He suggested they call the puppy Tolstoy.

"It can't be Tolstoy," Tereza said. "It's a girl. How about Anna Karenina?"

"It can't be Anna Karenina," said Tomas. "No woman could possibly have so funny a face. It's much more like Karenin. Yes, Anna's husband. That's just how I've always pictured him."

"But won't calling her Karenin affect her sexuality?"

"It is entirely possible," said Tomas, "that a female dog addressed continually by a male name will develop lesbian tendencies."

Strangely enough, Tomas's words came true. Though bitches are usually more affectionate to their masters than to their mistresses, Karenin proved an exception, deciding that he was in love with Tereza. Tomas was grateful to him for it. He would stroke the puppy's head and say, "Well done, Karenin! That's just what I wanted you for. Since I can't cope with her by myself, you must help me."

But even with Karenin's help Tomas failed to make her happy. He became aware of his failure some years later, on approximately the tenth day after his country was occupied by Russian tanks. It was August 1968, and Tomas was receiving daily phone calls from a hospital in Zurich. The director there, a physician who had struck up a friendship with Tomas at an international conference, was worried about him and kept offering him a job.

# 12

If Tomas rejected the Swiss doctor's offer without a second thought, it was for Tereza's sake. He assumed she would not want to leave. She had spent the whole first week of the occupation in a kind of trance almost resembling happiness. After roaming the streets with her camera, she would hand the rolls of film to foreign journalists, who actually fought over them. Once, when she went too far and took a close-up of an officer pointing his revolver at a group of people, she was arrested and kept overnight at Russian military headquarters. There they threatened to shoot her, but no sooner did they let her go than she was back in the streets with her camera.

That is why Tomas was surprised when on the tenth day of the occupation she said to him, "Why is it you don't want to go to Switzerland?"

"Why should I?"

"They could make it hard for you here."

"They can make it hard for anybody," replied Tomas with a wave of the hand. "What about you? Could you live abroad?"

"Why not?"

"You've been out there risking your life for this country. How can you be so nonchalant about leaving it?"

"Now that Dubcek is back, things have changed," said Tereza.

It was true: the general euphoria lasted no longer than the first week. The representatives of the country had been hauled away like criminals by the Russian army, no one knew where they were, everyone feared for the men's lives, and hatred for the Russians drugged people like alcohol. It was a drunken carnival of hate. Czech towns were decorated with thousands of hand-painted posters bearing ironic texts, epigrams, poems, and cartoons of Brezhnev and his soldiers, jeered at by one and all as a circus of illiterates. But no carnival can go on forever. In the meantime, the Russians had forced the Czech representatives to sign a compromise agreement in Moscow. When Dubcek returned with them to Prague, he gave a speech over the radio. He was so devastated after his six-day detention he could hardly talk; he kept stuttering and gasping for breath, making long pauses between sentences, pauses lasting nearly thirty seconds.

The compromise saved the country from the worst: the executions and mass deportations to Siberia that had terrified everyone. But one thing was clear: the country would have to bow to the conqueror. For ever and ever, it will stutter, stammer, gasp for air like Alexander Dubcek. The carnival was over. Workaday humiliation had begun.

Tereza had explained all this to Tomas and he knew that it was true. But he also knew that underneath it all hid still another, more fundamental truth, the reason why she wanted to leave Prague: she had never really been happy before.

The days she walked through the streets of Prague taking pictures of Russian soldiers and looking danger in the face were the best of her life. They were the only time when the television series of her dreams had been interrupted and she had enjoyed a few happy nights. The Russians had brought equilibrium to her in their tanks, and now that the carnival was over, she feared her nights again and wanted to escape them. She now knew there were conditions under which she could feel strong and fulfilled, and she longed to go off into the world and seek those conditions somewhere else.

"It doesn't bother you that Sabina has also emigrated to Switzerland?" Tomas asked.

"Geneva isn't Zurich," said Tereza. "She'll be much less of a difficulty there than she was in Prague."

A person who longs to leave the place where he lives is an unhappy person. That is why Tomas accepted Tereza's wish to emigrate as the culprit accepts his sentence, and one day he and Tereza and Karenin found themselves in the largest city in Switzerland.

## 13

He bought a bed for their empty flat (they had no money yet for other furniture) and threw himself into his work with the frenzy of a man of forty beginning a new life.

He made several telephone calls to Geneva. A show of Sabina's work had opened there by chance a week after the Russian invasion, and in a wave of sympathy for her tiny country, Geneva's patrons of the arts bought up all her paintings.

"Thanks to the Russians, I'm a rich woman," she said, laughing into the telephone. She invited Tomas to come and see her new studio, and assured him it did not differ greatly from the one he had known in Prague.

He would have been only too glad to visit her, but was unable to find an excuse to explain his absence to Tereza. And so Sabina came to Zurich. She stayed at a hotel. Tomas went to see her after work. He phoned first from the reception desk, then went upstairs. When she opened the door, she stood before him on her beautiful long legs wearing nothing but panties and bra. And a black bowler hat. She stood there staring, mute and motionless. Tomas did the same. Suddenly he realized how touched he was. He removed the bowler from her head and placed it on the bedside table. Then they made love without saying a word.

Leaving the hotel for his flat (which by now had acquired table, chairs, couch, and carpet), he thought happily that he carried his way of living with him as a snail carries his house. Tereza and Sabina represented the two poles of his life, separate and irreconcilable, yet equally appealing.

But the fact that he carried his life-support system with him everywhere like a part of his body meant that Tereza went on having her dreams.

They had been in Zurich for six or seven months when he came home late one evening to find a letter on the table telling him she had left for Prague. She had left because she lacked the strength to live abroad. She knew she was supposed to bolster him up, but did not know how to go about it. She had been silly enough to think that going abroad would change her. She thought that after what she had been through during the invasion she would stop being petty and grow up, grow wise and strong, but she had overestimated herself. She was weighing him down and would do so no longer. She had drawn the necessary conclusions before it was too late. And she apologized for taking Karenin with her.

He took some sleeping pills but still did not close his eyes until morning. Luckily it was Saturday and he could stay at home. For the hundred and fiftieth time he went over the situation: the borders between his country and the rest of the world were no longer open. No telegrams or telephone calls could bring her back. The authorities would never let her travel abroad. Her departure was staggeringly definitive.

# 14

The realization that he was utterly powerless was like the blow of a sledgehammer, yet it was curiously calming as well. No one was forcing him into a decision. He felt no need to stare at the walls of the houses across the courtyard and ponder whether to live with her or not. Tereza had made the decision herself.

He went to a restaurant for lunch. He was depressed, but as he ate, his original desperation waned, lost its strength, and soon all that was left was melancholy. Looking back on the years he had spent with her, he came to feel that their story could have had no better ending. If someone had invented the story, this is how he would have had to end it.

One day Tereza came to him uninvited. One day she left the same way. She came with a heavy suitcase. She left with a heavy suitcase.

He paid the bill, left the restaurant, and started walking through the streets, his melancholy growing more and more beautiful. He had spent seven years of life with Tereza, and now he realized that those years were more attractive in retrospect than they were when he was living them.

His love for Tereza was beautiful, but it was also tiring: he had constantly had to hide things from her, sham, dissemble, make amends, buck her up, calm her down, give her evidence of his feelings, play the defendant to her jealousy, her suffering, and her dreams, feel guilty, make excuses and apologies. Now what was tiring had disappeared and only the beauty remained.

Saturday found him for the first time strolling alone through Zurich, breathing in the heady smell of his freedom. New adventures hid around each corner. The future was again a secret. He was on his way back to the bachelor life, the life he had once felt destined for, the life that would let him be what he actually was.

For seven years he had lived bound to her, his every step subject to her scrutiny. She might as well have chained iron balls to his ankles. Suddenly his step was much lighter. He soared. He had entered Parmenides' magic field: he was enjoying the sweet lightness of being.

(Did he feel like phoning Sabina in Geneva? Contacting one or another of the women he had met during his several months in Zurich? No, not in the least. Perhaps he sensed that any woman would make his memory of Tereza unbearably painful.)

## 15

This curious melancholic fascination lasted until Sunday evening. On Monday, everything changed. Tereza forced her way into his thoughts: he imagined her sitting there writing her farewell letter; he felt her hands trembling; he saw her lugging her heavy suitcase in one hand and leading Karenin on his leash with the other; he pictured her unlocking their Prague flat, and suffered the utter abandonment breathing her in the face as she opened the door.

During those two beautiful days of melancholy, his compassion (that curse of emotional telepathy) had taken a holiday. It had slept the sound Sunday sleep of a miner who, after a hard week's work, needs to gather strength for his Monday shift.

Instead of the patients he was treating, Tomas saw Tereza. He tried to remind himself, Don't think about her! Don't think about her! He said to himself, I'm sick with compassion. It's good that she's gone and that I'll never see her again, though it's not Tereza I need to be free of—it's that sickness, compassion, which I thought I was immune to until she infected me with it.

On Saturday and Sunday, he felt the sweet lightness of being rise up to him out of the depths of the future. On Monday, he was hit by a weight the likes of which he had never known. The tons of steel of the Russian tanks were nothing compared with it. For there is nothing heavier than compassion. Not even one's own pain weighs so heavy as the pain one feels with someone, for someone, a pain intensified by the imagination and prolonged by a hundred echoes.

He kept warning himself not to give in to compassion, and compassion listened with bowed head and a seemingly guilty conscience. Compassion knew it was being presumptuous, yet it quietly stood its ground, and on the fifth day after her departure Tomas informed the director of his hospital (the man who had phoned him daily in Prague after the Russian invasion) that he had to return at once. He was ashamed. He knew that the move would appear irresponsible, inexcusable to the man. He thought to unbosom himself and tell him the story of Tereza and the letter she had left on the table for him. But in the end he did not. From the Swiss doctor's point of view Tereza's move could only appear hysterical and abhorrent. And Tomas refused to allow anyone an opportunity to think ill of her.

The director of the hospital was in fact offended.

Tomas shrugged his shoulders and said, "*Es muss sein. Es muss sein.*"

It was an allusion. The last movement of Beethoven's last quartet is based on the following two motifs:

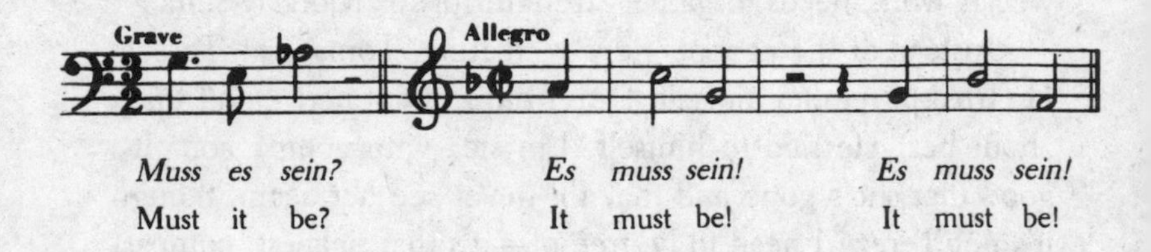


To make the meaning of the words absolutely clear, Beethoven introduced the movement with a phrase, "*Der schwer gefasste Entschluss,*" which is commonly translated as "the difficult resolution."

This allusion to Beethoven was actually Tomas's first step back to Tereza, because she was the one who had induced him to buy records of the Beethoven quartets and sonatas.

The allusion was even more pertinent than he had thought because the Swiss doctor was a great music lover. Smiling serenely, he asked, in the melody of Beethoven's motif, *"Muss es sein?"*

*"Ja, es muss sein!"* Tomas said again.

# 16

Unlike Parmenides, Beethoven apparently viewed weight as something positive. Since the German word *schwer* means both "difficult" and "heavy," Beethoven's "difficult resolution" may also be construed as a "heavy" or "weighty resolution." The weighty resolution is at one with the voice of Fate (*"Es muss sein!"*); necessity, weight, and value are three concepts inextricably bound: only necessity is heavy, and only what is heavy has value.

This is a conviction born of Beethoven's music, and although we cannot ignore the possibility (or even probability) that it owes its origins more to Beethoven's commentators than to Beethoven himself, we all more or less share it: we believe that the greatness of man stems from the fact that he *bears* his fate as Atlas bore the heavens on his shoulders. Beethoven's hero is a lifter of metaphysical weights.

Tomas approached the Swiss border. I imagine a gloomy, shock-headed Beethoven, in person, conducting the local firemen's brass band in a farewell to emigration, an *"Es Muss Sein"* march.

Then Tomas crossed the Czech border and was welcomed by columns of Russian tanks. He had to stop his car and wait a half hour before they passed. A terrifying soldier in the black uniform of the armored forces stood at the crossroads directing traffic as if every road in the country belonged to him and him alone.

*"Es muss sein!"* Tomas repeated to himself, but then he began to doubt. Did it really have to be?

Yes, it was unbearable for him to stay in Zurich imagining Tereza living on her own in Prague.

But how long would he have been tortured by compassion? All his life? A year? Or a month? Or only a week?

How could he have known? How could he have gauged it?

Any schoolboy can do experiments in the physics laboratory to test various scientific hypotheses. But man, because he has only one life to live, cannot conduct experiments to test whether to follow his passion (compassion) or not.

It was with these thoughts in mind that he opened the door to his flat. Karenin made the homecoming easier by jumping up on him and licking his face. The desire to fall into Tereza's arms (he could still feel it while getting into his car in Zurich) had completely disintegrated. He fancied himself standing opposite her in the midst of a snowy plain, the two of them shivering from the cold.

## 17

From the very beginning of the occupation, Russian military airplanes had flown over Prague all night long. Tomas, no longer accustomed to the noise, was unable to fall asleep.

Twisting and turning beside the slumbering Tereza, he recalled something she had told him a long time before in the course of an insignificant conversation. They had been talking about his friend Z. when she announced, "If I hadn't met you, I'd certainly have fallen in love with him."

Even then, her words had left Tomas in a strange state of melancholy, and now he realized it was only a matter of chance that Tereza loved him and not his friend Z. Apart from her consummated love for Tomas, there were, in the realm of possibility, an infinite number of unconsummated loves for other men.

We all reject out of hand the idea that the love of our life may be something light or weightless; we presume our love is what must be, that without it our life would no longer be the same; we feel that Beethoven himself, gloomy and awe-inspiring, is playing the *"Es muss sein!"* to our own great love.

Tomas often thought of Tereza's remark about his friend Z. and came to the conclusion that the love story of his life exemplified not *"Es muss sein!"* (It must be so), but rather *"Es könnte auch anders sein"* (It could just as well be otherwise).

Seven years earlier, a complex neurological case *happened* to have been discovered at the hospital in Tereza's town. They called in the chief surgeon of Tomas's hospital in Prague for consultation, but the chief surgeon of Tomas's hospital *happened* to be suffering from sciatica, and because he could not move he sent Tomas to the provincial hospital in his place. The town had several hotels, but Tomas *happened* to be given a room in the one where Tereza was employed. He *happened* to have had enough free time before his train left to stop at the hotel restaurant. Tereza *happened* to be on duty, and *happened* to be serving Tomas's table. It had taken six chance happenings to push Tomas towards Tereza, as if he had little inclination to go to her on his own.

He had gone back to Prague because of her. So fateful a decision resting on so fortuitous a love, a love that would not even have existed had it not been for the chief surgeon's sciatica seven years earlier. And that woman, that personification of absolute fortuity, now again lay asleep beside him, breathing deeply.

It was late at night. His stomach started acting up as it tended to do in times of psychic stress.

Once or twice her breathing turned into mild snores. Tomas felt no compassion. All he felt was the pressure in his stomach and the despair of having returned.

# PART TWO

# Soul and Body

# 1

It would be senseless for the author to try to convince the reader that his characters once actually lived. They were not born of a mother's womb; they were born of a stimulating phrase or two or from a basic situation. Tomas was born of the saying "*Einmal ist keinmal.*" Tereza was born of the rumbling of a stomach.

The first time she went to Tomas's flat, her insides began to rumble. And no wonder: she had had nothing to eat since breakfast but a quick sandwich on the platform before boarding the train. She had concentrated on the daring journey ahead of her and forgotten about food. But when we ignore the body, we are more easily victimized by it. She felt terrible standing there in front of Tomas listening to her belly speak out. She felt like crying. Fortunately, after the first ten seconds Tomas put his arms around her and made her forget her ventral voices.

# 2

Tereza was therefore born of a situation which brutally reveals the irreconcilable duality of body and soul, that fundamental human experience.

A long time ago, man would listen in amazement to the sound of regular beats in his chest, never suspecting what they were. He was unable to identify himself with so alien and unfamiliar an object as the body. The body was a cage, and inside that cage was something which looked, listened, feared, thought, and marveled; that something, that remainder left over after the body had been accounted for, was the soul.

Today, of course, the body is no longer unfamiliar: we know that the beating in our chest is the heart and that the nose is the nozzle of a hose sticking out of the body to take oxygen to the lungs. The face is nothing but an instrument panel registering all the body mechanisms: digestion, sight, hearing, respiration, thought.

Ever since man has learned to give each part of the body a name, the body has given him less trouble. He has also learned that the soul is nothing more than the gray matter of the brain in action. The old duality of body and soul has become shrouded in scientific terminology, and we can laugh at it as merely an obsolete prejudice.

But just make someone who has fallen in love listen to his stomach rumble, and the unity of body and soul, that lyrical illusion of the age of science, instantly fades away.

# 3

Tereza tried to see herself through her body. That is why, from girlhood on, she would stand before the mirror so often. And because she was afraid her mother would catch her at it, every peek into the mirror had a tinge of secret vice.

It was not vanity that drew her to the mirror; it was amazement at seeing her own "I." She forgot she was looking at the instrument panel of her body mechanisms; she thought she saw her soul shining through the features of her face. She forgot that the nose was merely the nozzle of a hose that took oxygen to the lungs; she saw it as the true expression of her nature.

Staring at herself for long stretches of time, she was occasionally upset at the sight of her mother's features in her face. She would stare all the more doggedly at her image in an attempt to wish them away and keep only what was hers alone. Each time she succeeded was a time of intoxication: her soul would rise to the surface of her body like a crew charging up from the bowels of a ship, spreading out over the deck, waving at the sky and singing in jubilation.

# 4

She took after her mother, and not only physically. I sometimes have the feeling that her entire life was merely a continuation of her mother's, much as the course of a ball on the billiard table is merely the continuation of the player's arm movement.

Where and when did it begin, the movement that later turned into Tereza's life?

Perhaps at the time when Tereza's grandfather, a Prague businessman, began extolling the beauty of his daughter, Tereza's mother, for all to hear. When she was three or four, he would tell her she was the image of Raphael's madonna. Tereza's four-year-old mother never forgot it. When as an adolescent she sat at her desk in school, she would not listen to the teachers; she would think about which paintings she was like.

Then came the time for her to marry. She had nine suitors. They all knelt round her in a circle. Standing in the middle like a princess, she did not know which one to choose: one was the handsomest, another the wittiest, the third was the richest, the fourth the most athletic, the fifth from the best family, the sixth recited verse, the seventh traveled widely, the eighth played the violin, and the ninth was the most manly. But they all knelt in the same way, they all had the same calluses on their knees.

The reason she finally chose the ninth was not so much that he was the most manly of all as that when she whispered "Be careful, very careful" to him during their lovemaking he was purposely careless, and she had to marry him after failing to find a doctor willing to perform an abortion. And so Tereza was born. Numerous relatives gathered from all corners of the country to lean over the pram and talk baby talk. Tereza's mother talked no baby talk. She did not talk at all. She thought about the eight other suitors, all of whom seemed better than the ninth.

Like her daughter, Tereza's mother frequently looked in the mirror. One day she discovered wrinkles near her eyes and decided her marriage made no sense. At about that time she met an unmanly man who had several charges of fraud on his record, not to mention two failed marriages. Now she hated those suitors with their callused knees. She had a passionate desire to be the one to kneel for a change. She went down on her knees before her new swindler friend and left her husband and Tereza to fend for themselves.

The most manly of men became the most downcast. He became so downcast that nothing meant anything to him anymore. He said openly what was on his mind, and the Communist police, shocked by his rash statements, arrested him, brought him to trial, and sentenced him to a long term in prison. They closed up his flat and sent Tereza to stay with her mother.

The most downcast of men died after a short spell behind bars, and Tereza and her mother went to live in a small town near the mountains with her mother's swindler. The swindler worked in an office, her mother in a shop. Her mother also gave birth to three more children. Then she looked in the mirror again and discovered she was old and ugly.

## 5

When she realized she had lost everything, she initiated a search for the culprit. Anyone would do: her first husband, manly and unloved, who had failed to heed her whispered warning; her second husband, unmanly and much loved, who had dragged her away from Prague to a small town and kept her in a state of permanent jealousy by going through one woman after another. But she was powerless against either. The only person who belonged to her and had no means of escape, the hostage who could do penance for all the culprits, was Tereza.

Indeed, was she not the principal culprit determining her mother's fate? She, the absurd encounter of the sperm of the most manly of men and the egg of the most beautiful of women? Yes, it was in that fateful second, which was named Tereza, that the botched long-distance race, her mother's life, had begun.

Tereza's mother never stopped reminding her that being a mother meant sacrificing everything. Her words had the ring of truth, backed as they were by the experience of a woman who had lost everything because of her child. Tereza would listen and believe that being a mother was the highest value in life and that being a mother was a great sacrifice. If a mother was Sacrifice personified, then a daughter was Guilt, with no possibility of redress.

## 6

Of course, Tereza did not know the story of the night when her mother whispered "Be careful" into the ear of her father. Her guilty conscience was as vague as original sin. But she did what she could to rid herself of it. Her mother took her out of school at the age of fifteen, and Tereza went to work as a waitress, handing over all her earnings. She was willing to do anything to gain her mother's love. She ran the household, took care of her siblings, and spent all day Sunday cleaning house and doing the family wash. It was a pity, because she was the brightest in her class. She yearned for something higher, but in the small town there was nothing higher for her. Whenever she did the clothes, she kept a book next to the tub. As she turned the pages, the wash water dripped all over them.

At home, there was no such thing as shame. Her mother marched about the flat in her underwear, sometimes braless and sometimes, on summer days, stark naked. Her stepfather did not walk about naked, but he did go into the bathroom every time Tereza was in the bath. Once she locked herself in and her mother was furious. "Who do you think you are, anyway? Do you think he's going to bite off a piece of your beauty?"

(This confrontation shows clearly that hatred for her daughter outweighed suspicion of her husband. Her daughter's guilt was infinite and included the husband's infidelities. Tereza's desire to be emancipated and insist on her rights—like the right to lock herself in the bathroom—was more objectionable to Tereza's mother than the possibility of her husband's taking a prurient interest in Tereza.)

Once her mother decided to go naked in the winter when the lights were on. Tereza quickly ran to pull the curtains so that no one could see her from across the street. She heard her mother's laughter behind her. The following day her mother had some friends over: a neighbor, a woman she worked with, a local schoolmistress, and two or three other women in the habit of getting together regularly. Tereza and the sixteen-year-old son of one of them came in at one point to say hello, and her mother immediately took advantage of their presence to tell how Tereza had tried to protect her mother's modesty. She laughed, and all the women laughed with her. "Tereza can't reconcile herself to the idea that the human body pisses and farts," she said. Tereza turned bright red, but her mother would not stop. "What's so terrible about that?" and in answer to her own question she broke wind loudly. All the women laughed again.

# 7

Tereza's mother blew her nose noisily, talked to people in public about her sex life, and enjoyed demonstrating her false teeth. She was remarkably skillful at loosening them with her tongue, and in the midst of a broad smile would cause the uppers to drop down over the lowers in such a way as to give her face a sinister expression.

Her behavior was but a single grand gesture, a casting off of youth and beauty. In the days when she had had nine suitors kneeling round her in a circle, she guarded her nakedness apprehensively, as though trying to express the value of her body in terms of the modesty she accorded it. Now she had not only lost that modesty, she had radically broken with it, ceremoniously using her new immodesty to draw a dividing line through her life and proclaim that youth and beauty were overrated and worthless.

Tereza appears to me a continuation of the gesture by which her mother cast off her life as a young beauty, cast it far behind her.

(And if Tereza has a nervous way of moving, if her gestures lack a certain easy grace, we must not be surprised: her mother's grand, wild, and self-destructive gesture has left an indelible imprint on her.)

# 8

Tereza's mother demanded justice. She wanted to see the culprit penalized. That is why she insisted her daughter remain with her in the world of immodesty, where youth and beauty mean nothing, where the world is nothing but a vast concentration camp of bodies, one like the next, with souls invisible.

Now we can better understand the meaning of Tereza's secret vice, her long looks and frequent glances in the mirror. It was a battle with her mother. It was a longing to be a body unlike other bodies, to find that the surface of her face reflected the crew of the soul charging up from below. It was not an easy task: her soul—her sad, timid, self-effacing soul—lay concealed in the depths of her bowels and was ashamed to show itself.

So it was the day she first met Tomas. Weaving its way through the drunks in the hotel restaurant, her body sagged under the weight of the beers on the tray, and her soul lay somewhere at the level of the stomach or pancreas. Then Tomas called to her. That call meant a great deal, because it came from someone who knew neither her mother nor the drunks with their daily stereotypically scabrous remarks. His outsider status raised him above the rest.

Something else raised him above the others as well: he had an open book on his table. No one had ever opened a book in that restaurant before. In Tereza's eyes, books were the emblems of a secret brotherhood. For she had but a single weapon against the world of crudity surrounding her: the books she took out of the municipal library, and above all, the novels. She had read any number of them, from Fielding to Thomas Mann. They not only offered the possibility of an imaginary escape from a life she found unsatisfying; they also had a meaning for her as physical objects: she loved to walk down the street with a book under her arm. It had the same significance for her as an elegant cane for the dandy a century ago. It differentiated her from others.

(Comparing the book to the elegant cane of the dandy is not absolutely precise. A dandy's cane did more than make him different; it made him modern and up to date. The book made Tereza different, but old-fashioned. Of course, she was too young to see how old-fashioned she looked to others. The young men walking by with transistor radios pressed to their ears seemed silly to her. It never occurred to her that they were modern.)

And so the man who called to her was simultaneously a stranger and a member of the secret brotherhood. He called to her in a kind voice, and Tereza felt her soul rushing up to the surface through her blood vessels and pores to show itself to him.

## 9

After Tomas had returned to Prague from Zurich, he began to feel uneasy at the thought that his acquaintance with Tereza was the result of six improbable fortuities.

But is not an event in fact more significant and noteworthy the greater the number of fortuities necessary to bring it about?

Chance and chance alone has a message for us. Everything that occurs out of necessity, everything expected, repeated day in and day out, is mute. Only chance can speak to us. We read its message much as gypsies read the images made by coffee grounds at the bottom of a cup.

Tomas appeared to Tereza in the hotel restaurant as chance in the absolute. There he sat, poring over an open book, when suddenly he raised his eyes to her, smiled, and said, "A cognac, please."

At that moment, the radio happened to be playing music. On her way behind the counter to pour the cognac, Tereza turned the volume up. She recognized Beethoven. She had known his music from the time a string quartet from Prague had visited their town. Tereza (who, as we know, yearned for "something higher") went to the concert. The hall was nearly empty. The only other people in the audience were the local pharmacist and his wife. And although the quartet of musicians on stage faced only a trio of spectators down below, they were kind enough not to cancel the concert, and gave a private performance of the last three Beethoven quartets.

Then the pharmacist invited the musicians to dinner and asked the girl in the audience to come along with them. From then on, Beethoven became her image of the world on the other side, the world she yearned for. Rounding the counter with Tomas's cognac, she tried to read chance's message: How was it possible that at the very moment she was taking an order of cognac to a stranger she found attractive, at that very moment she heard Beethoven?

Necessity knows no magic formulae—they are all left to chance. If a love is to be unforgettable, fortuities must immediately start fluttering down to it like birds to Francis of Assisi's shoulders.

# 10

He called her back to pay for the cognac. He closed his book (the emblem of the secret brotherhood), and she thought of asking him what he was reading.

"Can you have it charged to my room?" he asked.

"Yes," she said. "What number are you in?"

He showed her his key, which was attached to a piece of wood with a red six drawn on it.

"That's odd," she said. "Six."

"What's so odd about that?" he asked.

She had suddenly recalled that the house where they had lived in Prague before her parents were divorced was number six. But she answered something else (which we may credit to her wiles): "You're in room six and my shift ends at six."

"Well, my train leaves at seven," said the stranger.

She did not know how to respond, so she gave him the bill for his signature and took it over to the reception desk. When she finished work, the stranger was no longer at his table. Had he understood her discreet message? She left the restaurant in a state of excitement.

Opposite the hotel was a barren little park, as wretched as only the park of a dirty little town can be, but for Tereza it had always been an island of beauty: it had grass, four poplars, benches, a weeping willow, and a few forsythia bushes.

He was sitting on a yellow bench that afforded a clear view of the restaurant entrance. The very same bench she had sat on the day before with a book in her lap! She knew then (the birds of fortuity had begun alighting on her shoulders) that this stranger was her fate. He called out to her, invited her to sit next to him. (The crew of her soul rushed up to the deck of her body.) Then she walked him to the station, and he gave her his card as a farewell gesture. "If ever you should happen to come to Prague . . ."

# 11

Much more than the card he slipped her at the last minute, it was the call of all those fortuities (the book, Beethoven, the number six, the yellow park bench) which gave her the courage to leave home and change her fate. It may well be those few fortuities (quite modest, by the way, even drab, just what one would expect from so lackluster a town) which set her love in motion and provided her with a source of energy she had not yet exhausted at the end of her days.

Our day-to-day life is bombarded with fortuities or, to be more precise, with the accidental meetings of people and events we call coincidences. "Co-incidence" means that two events unexpectedly happen at the same time, they meet: Tomas appears in the hotel restaurant at the same time the radio is playing Beethoven. We do not even notice the great majority of such coincidences. If the seat Tomas occupied had been occupied instead by the local butcher, Tereza never would have noticed that the radio was playing Beethoven (though the meeting of Beethoven and the butcher would also have been an interesting coincidence). But her nascent love inflamed her sense of beauty, and she would never forget that music. Whenever she heard it, she would be touched. Everything going on around her at that moment would be haloed by the music and take on its beauty.

Early in the novel that Tereza clutched under her arm when she went to visit Tomas, Anna meets Vronsky in curious circumstances: they are at the railway station when someone is run over by a train. At the end of the novel, Anna throws herself under a train. This symmetrical composition—the same motif appears at the beginning and at the end—may seem quite "novelistic" to you, and I am willing to agree, but only on condition that you refrain from reading such notions as "fictive," "fabricated," and "untrue to life" into the word "novelistic." Because human lives are composed in precisely such a fashion.

They are composed like music. Guided by his sense of beauty, an individual transforms a fortuitous occurrence (Beethoven's music, death under a train) into a motif, which then assumes a permanent place in the composition of the individual's life. Anna could have chosen another way to take her life. But the motif of death and the railway station, unforgettably bound to the birth of love, enticed her in her hour of despair with its dark beauty. Without realizing it, the individual composes his life according to the laws of beauty even in times of greatest distress.

It is wrong, then, to chide the novel for being fascinated by mysterious coincidences (like the meeting of Anna, Vronsky, the railway station, and death or the meeting of Beethoven, Tomas, Tereza, and the cognac), but it is right to chide man for being blind to such coincidences in his daily life. For he thereby deprives his life of a dimension of beauty.

# 12

Impelled by the birds of fortuity fluttering down on her shoulders, she took a week's leave and, without a word to her mother, boarded the train to Prague. During the journey, she made frequent trips to the toilet to look in the mirror and beg her soul not to abandon the deck of her body for a moment on this most crucial day of her life. Scrutinizing herself on one such trip, she had a sudden scare: she felt a scratch in her throat. Could she be coming down with something on this most crucial day of her life?

But there was no turning back. So she phoned him from the station, and the moment he opened the door, her stomach started rumbling terribly. She was mortified. She felt as though she were carrying her mother in her stomach and her mother had guffawed to spoil her meeting with Tomas.

For the first few seconds, she was afraid he would throw her out because of the crude noises she was making, but then he put his arms around her. She was grateful to him for ignoring her rumbles, and kissed him passionately, her eyes misting. Before the first minute was up, they were making love. She screamed while making love. She had a fever by then. She had come down with the flu. The nozzle of the hose supplying oxygen to the lungs was stuffed and red.

When she traveled to Prague a second time, it was with a heavy suitcase. She had packed all her things, determined never again to return to the small town. He had invited her to come to his place the following evening. That night, she had slept in a cheap hotel. In the morning, she carried her heavy suitcase to the station, left it there, and roamed the streets of Prague the whole day with *Anna Karenina* under her arm. Not even after she rang the doorbell and he opened the door would she part with it. It was like a ticket into Tomas's world. She realized that she had nothing but that miserable ticket, and the thought brought her nearly to tears. To keep from crying, she talked too much and too loudly, and she laughed. And again he took her in his arms almost at once and they made love. She had entered a mist in which nothing could be seen and only her scream could be heard.

## 13

It was no sigh, no moan; it was a real scream. She screamed so hard that Tomas had to turn his head away from her face, afraid that her voice so close to his ear would rupture his eardrum. The scream was not an expression of sensuality. Sensuality is the total mobilization of the senses: an individual observes his partner intently, straining to catch every sound. But her scream aimed at crippling the senses, preventing all seeing and hearing. What was screaming in fact was the naive idealism of her love trying to banish all contradictions, banish the duality of body and soul, banish perhaps even time.

Were her eyes closed? No, but they were not looking anywhere. She kept them fixed on the void of the ceiling. At times she twisted her head violently from side to side.

When the scream died down, she fell asleep at his side, clutching his hand. She held his hand all night.

Even at the age of eight she would fall asleep by pressing one hand into the other and making believe she was holding the hand of the man whom she loved, the man of her life. So if in her sleep she pressed Tomas's hand with such tenacity, we can understand why: she had been training for it since childhood.

# 14

A young woman forced to keep drunks supplied with beer and siblings with clean underwear—instead of being allowed to pursue "something higher"—stores up great reserves of vitality, a vitality never dreamed of by university students yawning over their books. Tereza had read a good deal more than they, and learned a good deal more about life, but she would never realize it. The difference between the university graduate and the autodidact lies not so much in the extent of knowledge as in the extent of vitality and self-confidence. The élan with which Tereza flung herself into her new Prague existence was both frenzied and precarious. She seemed to be expecting someone to come up to her any day and say, "What are you doing here? Go back where you belong!" All her eagerness for life hung by a thread: Tomas's voice. For it was Tomas's voice that had once coaxed forth her timorous soul from its hiding place in her bowels.

Tereza had a job in a darkroom, but it was not enough for her. She wanted to take pictures, not develop them. Tomas's friend Sabina lent her three or four monographs of famous photographers, then invited her to a café and explained over the open books what made each of the pictures interesting. Tereza listened with silent concentration, the kind few professors ever glimpse on their students' faces.

Thanks to Sabina, she came to understand the ties between photography and painting, and she made Tomas take her to every exhibit that opened in Prague. Before long, she was placing her own pictures in the illustrated weekly where she worked, and finally she left the darkroom for the staff of professional photographers.

On the evening of that day, she and Tomas went out to a bar with friends to celebrate her promotion. Everyone danced. Tomas began to mope. Back at home, after some prodding from Tereza, he admitted that he had been jealous watching her dance with a colleague of his.

"You mean you were really jealous?" she asked him ten times or more, incredulously, as though someone had just informed her she had been awarded a Nobel Prize.

Then she put her arm around his waist and began dancing across the room. The step she used was not the one she had shown off in the bar. It was more like a village polka, a wild romp that sent her legs flying in the air and her torso bouncing all over the room, with Tomas in tow.

Before long, unfortunately, she began to be jealous herself, and Tomas saw her jealousy not as a Nobel Prize, but as a burden, a burden he would be saddled with until not long before his death.

# 15

While she marched around the pool naked with a large group of other naked women, Tomas stood over them in a basket hanging from the pool's arched roof, shouting at them, making them sing and do kneebends. The moment one of them did a faulty kneebend, he would shoot her.

Let me return to this dream. Its horror did not begin with Tomas's first pistol shot; it was horrifying from the outset. Marching naked in formation with a group of naked women was for Tereza the quintessential image of horror. When she lived at home, her mother forbade her to lock the bathroom door. What she meant by her injunction was: Your body is just like all other bodies; you have no right to shame; you have no reason to hide something that exists in millions of identical copies. In her mother's world all bodies were the same and marched behind one another in formation. Since childhood, Tereza had seen nudity as a sign of concentration camp uniformity, a sign of humiliation.

There was yet another horror at the very beginning of the dream: all the women had to sing! Not only were their bodies identical, identically worthless, not only were their bodies mere resounding soulless mechanisms—the women rejoiced over it! Theirs was the joyful solidarity of the soulless. The women were pleased at having thrown off the ballast of the soul—that laughable conceit, that illusion of uniqueness—to become one like the next. Tereza sang with them, but did not rejoice. She sang because she was afraid that if she did not sing the women would kill her.

But what was the meaning of the fact that Tomas shot at them, toppling one after another into the pool, dead?

The women, overjoyed by their sameness, their lack of diversity, were, in fact, celebrating their imminent demise, which would render their sameness absolute. So Tomas's shots were merely the joyful climax to their morbid march. After every report of his pistol, they burst into joyous laughter, and as each corpse sank beneath the surface, they sang even louder.

But why was Tomas the one doing the shooting? And why was he out to shoot Tereza with the rest of them?

Because he was the one who sent Tereza to join them. That was what the dream was meant to tell Tomas, what Tereza was unable to tell him herself. She had come to him to escape her mother's world, a world where all bodies were equal. She had come to him to make her body unique, irreplaceable. But he, too, had drawn an equal sign between her and the rest of them: he kissed them all alike, stroked them alike, made no, absolutely no distinction between Tereza's body and the other bodies. He had sent her back into the world she tried to escape, sent her to march naked with the other naked women.

## 16

She would dream three series of dreams in succession: the first was of cats going berserk and referred to the sufferings she had gone through in her lifetime; the second was images of her execution and came in countless variations; the third was of her life after death, when humiliation turned into a never-ending state.

The dreams left nothing to be deciphered. The accusation they leveled at Tomas was so clear that his only reaction was to hang his head and stroke her hand without a word.

The dreams were eloquent, but they were also beautiful. That aspect seems to have escaped Freud in his theory of dreams. Dreaming is not merely an act of communication (or coded communication, if you like); it is also an aesthetic activity, a game of the imagination, a game that is a value in itself. Our dreams prove that to imagine—to dream about things that have not happened—is among mankind's deepest needs. Herein lies the danger. If dreams were not beautiful, they would quickly be forgotten. But Tereza kept coming back to her dreams, running through them in her mind, turning them into legends. Tomas lived under the hypnotic spell cast by the excruciating beauty of Tereza's dreams.

"Dear Tereza, sweet Tereza, what am I losing you to?" he once said to her as they sat face to face in a wine cellar. "Every night you dream of death as if you really wished to quit this world. . . ."

It was day; reason and will power were back in place. A drop of red wine ran slowly down her glass as she answered. "There's nothing I can do about it, Tomas. Oh, I understand. I know you love me. I know your infidelities are no great tragedy . . ."

She looked at him with love in her eyes, but she feared the night ahead, feared her dreams. Her life was split. Both day and night were competing for her.

## 17

Anyone whose goal is "something higher" must expect some day to suffer vertigo. What is vertigo? Fear of falling? Then why do we feel it even when the observation tower comes equipped with a sturdy handrail? No, vertigo is something other than the fear of falling. It is the voice of the emptiness below us which tempts and lures us, it is the desire to fall, against which, terrified, we defend ourselves.

The naked women marching around the swimming pool, the corpses in the hearse rejoicing that she, too, was dead—these were the "down below" she had feared and fled once before but which mysteriously beckoned her. These were her vertigo: she heard a sweet (almost joyous) summons to renounce her fate and soul. The solidarity of the soulless calling her. And in times of weakness, she was ready to heed the call and return to her mother. She was ready to dismiss the crew of her soul from the deck of her body; ready to descend to a place among her mother's friends and laugh when one of them broke wind noisily; ready to march around the pool naked with them and sing.

## 18

True, Tereza fought with her mother until the day she left home, but let us not forget that she never stopped loving her. She would have done anything for her if her mother had asked in a loving voice. The only reason she found the strength to leave was that she never heard that voice.

When Tereza's mother realized that her aggressiveness no longer had any power over her daughter, she started writing her querulous letters, complaining about her husband, her boss, her health, her children, and assuring Tereza she was the only person left in her life. Tereza thought that at last, after twenty years, she was hearing the voice of her mother's love, and felt like going back. All the more because she felt so weak, so debilitated by Tomas's infidelities. They exposed her powerlessness, which in turn led to vertigo, the insuperable longing to fall.

One day her mother phoned to say she had cancer and only a few months to live. The news transformed into rebellion Tereza's despair at Tomas's infidelities. She had betrayed her mother, she told herself reproachfully, and for a man who did not love her. She was willing to forget everything her mother had done to torture her. She was in a position to understand her now; they were in the same situation: her mother loved her stepfather just as Tereza loved Tomas, and her stepfather tortured her mother with his infidelities just as Tomas galled her with his. The cause of her mother's malice was that she had suffered so.

Tereza told Tomas that her mother was ill and that she would be taking a week off to go and see her. Her voice was full of spite.

Sensing that the real reason calling her back to her mother was vertigo, Tomas opposed the trip. He rang up the hospital in the small town. Meticulous records of the incidence of cancer were kept throughout the country, so he had no trouble finding out that Tereza's mother had never been suspected of having the disease nor had she even seen a doctor for over a year.

Tereza obeyed Tomas and did not go to visit her mother. Several hours after the decision she fell in the street and injured her knee. She began to teeter as she walked, fell almost daily, bumped into things or, at the very least, dropped objects.

She was in the grip of an insuperable longing to fall. She lived in a constant state of vertigo.

"Pick me up," is the message of a person who keeps falling. Tomas kept picking her up, patiently.

# 19

"I want to make love to you in my studio. It will be like a stage surrounded by people. The audience won't be allowed up close, but they won't be able to take their eyes off us. . . ."

As time passed, the image lost some of its original cruelty and began to excite Tereza. She would whisper the details to him while they made love.

Then it occurred to her that there might be a way to avoid the condemnation she saw in Tomas's infidelities: all he had to do was take her along, take her with him when he went to see his mistresses! Maybe then her body would again become the first and only among all others. Her body would become his second, his assistant, his alter ego.

"I'll undress them for you, give them a bath, bring them in to you . . ." she would whisper to him as they pressed together. She yearned for the two of them to merge into a hermaphrodite. Then the other women's bodies would be their playthings.

# 20

Oh, to be the alter ego of his polygamous life! Tomas refused to understand, but she could not get it out of her head, and tried to cultivate her friendship with Sabina. Tereza began by offering to do a series of photographs of Sabina.

Sabina invited Tereza to her studio, and at last she saw the spacious room and its centerpiece: the large, square, platform-like bed.

"I feel awful that you've never been here before," said Sabina, as she showed her the pictures leaning against the wall. She even pulled out an old canvas, of a steelworks under construction, which she had done during her school days, a period when the strictest realism had been required of all students (art that was not realistic was said to sap the foundations of socialism). In the spirit of the wager of the times, she had tried to be stricter than her teachers and had painted in a style concealing the brush strokes and closely resembling color photography.

"Here is a painting I happened to drip red paint on. At first I was terribly upset, but then I started enjoying it. The trickle looked like a crack; it turned the building site into a battered old backdrop, a backdrop with a building site painted on it. I began playing with the crack, filling it out, wondering what might be visible behind it. And that's how I began my first cycle of paintings. I called it "Behind the Scenes." Of course, I couldn't show them to anybody. I'd have been kicked out of the Academy. On the surface, there was always an impeccably realistic world, but underneath, behind the backdrop's cracked canvas, lurked something different, something mysterious or abstract."

After pausing for a moment, she added, "On the surface, an intelligible lie; underneath, the unintelligible truth."

Tereza listened to her with the remarkable concentration that few professors ever see on the face of a student and began to perceive that all Sabina's paintings, past and present, did indeed treat the same idea, that they all featured the confluence of two themes, two worlds, that they were all double exposures, so to speak. A landscape showing an old-fashioned table lamp shining through it. An idyllic still life of apples, nuts, and a tiny, candle-lit Christmas tree showing a hand ripping through the canvas.

She felt a rush of admiration for Sabina, and because Sabina treated her as a friend it was an admiration free of fear and suspicion and quickly turned into friendship.

She nearly forgot she had come to take photographs. Sabina had to remind her. Tereza finally looked away from the paintings only to see the bed set in the middle of the room like a platform.

## 21

Next to the bed stood a small table, and on the table the model of a human head, the kind hairdressers put wigs on. Sabina's wig stand sported a bowler hat rather than a wig. "It used to belong to my grandfather," she said with a smile.

It was the kind of hat—black, hard, round—that Tereza had seen only on the screen, the kind of hat Chaplin wore. She smiled back, picked it up, and after studying it for a time, said, "Would you like me to take your picture in it?"

Sabina laughed for a long time at the idea. Tereza put down the bowler hat, picked up her camera, and started taking pictures.

When she had been at it for almost an hour, she suddenly said, "What would you say to some nude shots?"

"Nude shots?" Sabina laughed.

"Yes," said Tereza, repeating her proposal more boldly, "nude shots."

"That calls for a drink," said Sabina, and opened a bottle of wine.

Tereza felt her body going weak; she was suddenly tongue-tied. Sabina, meanwhile, strode back and forth, wine in hand, going on about her grandfather, who'd been the mayor of a small town; Sabina had never known him; all he'd left behind was this bowler hat and a picture showing a raised platform with several small-town dignitaries on it; one of them was Grandfather; it wasn't at all clear what they were doing up there on the platform; maybe they were officiating at some ceremony, unveiling a monument to a fellow dignitary who had also once worn a bowler hat at public ceremonies.

Sabina went on and on about the bowler hat and her grandfather until, emptying her third glass, she said "I'll be right back" and disappeared into the bathroom.

She came out in her bathrobe. Tereza picked up her camera and put it to her eye. Sabina threw open the robe.

# 22

The camera served Tereza as both a mechanical eye through which to observe Tomas's mistress and a veil by which to conceal her face from her.

It took Sabina some time before she could bring herself to slip out of the robe entirely. The situation she found herself in was proving a bit more difficult than she had expected. After several minutes of posing, she went up to Tereza and said, "Now it's my turn to take your picture. Strip!"

Sabina had heard the command "Strip!" so many times from Tomas that it was engraved in her memory. Thus, Tomas's mistress had just given Tomas's command to Tomas's wife. The two women were joined by the same magic word. That was Tomas's way of unexpectedly turning an innocent conversation with a woman into an erotic situation. Instead of stroking, flattering, pleading, he would issue a command, issue it abruptly, unexpectedly, softly yet firmly and authoritatively, and at a distance: at such moments he never touched the woman he was addressing. He often used it on Tereza as well, and even though he said it softly, even though he whispered it, it was a command, and obeying never failed to arouse her. Hearing the word now made her desire to obey even stronger, because doing a stranger's bidding is a special madness, a madness all the more heady in this case because the command came not from a man but from a woman.

Sabina took the camera from her, and Tereza took off her clothes. There she stood before Sabina naked and disarmed. Literally *disarmed:* deprived of the apparatus she had been using to cover her face and aim at Sabina like a weapon. She was completely at the mercy of Tomas's mistress. This beautiful submission intoxicated Tereza. She wished that the moments she stood naked opposite Sabina would never end.

I think that Sabina, too, felt the strange enchantment of the situation: her lover's wife standing oddly compliant and timorous before her. But after clicking the shutter two or three times, almost frightened by the enchantment and eager to dispel it, she burst into loud laughter.

Tereza followed suit, and the two of them got dressed.

# 23

All previous crimes of the Russian empire had been committed under the cover of a discreet shadow. The deportation of a million Lithuanians, the murder of hundreds of thousands of Poles, the liquidation of the Crimean Tatars remain in our memory, but no photographic documentation exists; sooner or later they will therefore be proclaimed as fabrications. Not so the 1968 invasion of Czechoslovakia, of which both stills and motion pictures are stored in archives throughout the world.

Czech photographers and cameramen were acutely aware that they were the ones who could best do the only thing left to do: preserve the face of violence for the distant future. Seven days in a row, Tereza roamed the streets, photographing Russian soldiers and officers in compromising situations. The Russians did not know what to do. They had been carefully briefed about how to behave if someone fired at them or threw stones, but they had received no directives about what to do when someone aimed a lens.

She shot roll after roll and gave about half of them, undeveloped, to foreign journalists (the borders were still open, and reporters passing through were grateful for any kind of document). Many of her photographs turned up in the Western press. They were pictures of tanks, of threatening fists, of houses destroyed, of corpses covered with bloodstained red-white-and-blue Czech flags, of young men on motorcycles racing full speed around the tanks and waving Czech flags on long staffs, of young girls in unbelievably short skirts provoking the miserable sexually famished Russian soldiers by kissing random passersby before their eyes. As I have said, the Russian invasion was not only a tragedy; it was a carnival of hate filled with a curious (and no longer explicable) euphoria.

# 24

She took some fifty prints with her to Switzerland, prints she had made herself with all the care and skill she could muster. She offered them to a high-circulation illustrated magazine. The editor gave her a kind reception (all Czechs still wore the halo of their misfortune, and the good Swiss were touched); he offered her a seat, looked through the prints, praised them, and explained that because a certain time had elapsed since the events, they hadn't the slightest chance ("not that they aren't very beautiful!") of being published.

"But it's not over yet in Prague!" she protested, and tried to explain to him in her bad German that at this very moment, even with the country occupied, with everything against them, workers' councils were forming in the factories, the students were going out on strike demanding the departure of the Russians, and the whole country was saying aloud what it thought. "That's what's so unbelievable! And nobody here cares anymore."

The editor was glad when an energetic woman came into the office and interrupted the conversation. The woman handed him a folder and said, "Here's the nudist beach article."

The editor was delicate enough to fear that a Czech who photographed tanks would find pictures of naked people on a beach frivolous. He laid the folder at the far end of the desk and quickly said to the woman, "How would you like to meet a Czech colleague of yours? She's brought me some marvelous pictures."

The woman shook Tereza's hand and picked up her photographs. "Have a look at mine in the meantime," she said.

Tereza leaned over to the folder and took out the pictures.

Almost apologetically the editor said to Tereza, "Of course

they're completely different from your pictures."

"Not at all," said Tereza. "They're the same."

Neither the editor nor the photographer understood her, and even I find it difficult to explain what she had in mind when she compared a nude beach to the Russian invasion. Looking through the pictures, she stopped for a time at one that showed a family of four standing in a circle: a naked mother leaning over her children, her giant tits hanging low like a goat's or cow's, and the husband leaning the same way on the other side, his penis and scrotum looking very much like an udder in miniature.

"You don't like them, do you?" asked the editor.

"They're good photographs."

"She's shocked by the subject matter," said the woman. "I can tell just by looking at you that you've never set foot on a nude beach."

"No," said Tereza.

The editor smiled. "You see how easy it is to guess where you're from? The Communist countries are awfully puritanical."

"There's nothing wrong with the naked body," the woman said with maternal affection. "It's normal. And everything normal is beautiful!"

The image of her mother marching through the flat naked flashed through Tereza's mind. She could still hear the laughter behind her back when she ran and pulled the curtains to stop the neighbors from seeing her naked mother.

# 25

The woman photographer invited Tereza to the magazine's cafeteria for a cup of coffee. "Those pictures of yours, they're very interesting. I couldn't help noticing what a terrific sense of the female body you have. You know what I mean. The girls with the provocative poses!"

"The ones kissing passersby in front of the Russian tanks?"

"Yes. You'd be a top-notch fashion photographer, you know? You'd have to get yourself a model first, someone like you who's looking for a break. Then you could make a portfolio of photographs and show them to the agencies. It would take some time before you made a name for yourself, naturally, but I can do one thing for you here and now: introduce you to the editor in charge of our garden section. He might need some shots of cactuses and roses and things."

"Thank you very much," Tereza said sincerely, because it was clear that the woman sitting opposite her was full of good will.

But then she said to herself, Why take pictures of cactuses? She had no desire to go through in Zurich what she'd been through in Prague: battles over job and career, over every picture published. She had never been ambitious out of vanity. All she had ever wanted was to escape from her mother's world. Yes, she saw it with absolute clarity: no matter how enthusiastic she was about taking pictures, she could just as easily have turned her enthusiasm to any other endeavor. Photography was nothing but a way of getting at "something higher" and living beside Tomas.

She said, "My husband is a doctor. He can support me. I don't need to take pictures."

The woman photographer replied, "I don't see how you

can give it up after the beautiful work you've done."

Yes, the pictures of the invasion were something else again. She had not done them for Tomas. She had done them out of passion. But not passion for photography. She had done them out of passionate hatred. The situation would never recur. And these photographs, which she had made out of passion, were the ones nobody wanted because they were out of date. Only cactuses had perennial appeal. And cactuses were of no interest to her.

She said, "You're too kind, really, but I'd rather stay at home. I don't need a job."

The woman said, "But will you be fulfilled sitting at home?"

Tereza said, "More fulfilled than by taking pictures of cactuses."

The woman said, "Even if you take pictures of cactuses, you're leading *your* life. If you live only for your husband, you have no life of your own."

All of a sudden Tereza felt annoyed: "My husband is my life, not cactuses."

The woman photographer responded in kind: "You mean you think of yourself as happy?"

Tereza, still annoyed, said, "Of course I'm happy!"

The woman said, "The only kind of woman who can say that is very . . ." She stopped short.

Tereza finished it for her: " . . . limited. That's what you mean, isn't it?"

The woman regained control of herself and said, "Not limited. Anachronistic."

"You're right," said Tereza wistfully. "That's just what my husband says about me."

# 26

But Tomas spent days on end at the hospital, and she was at home alone. At least she had Karenin and could take him on long walks! Home again, she would pore over her German and French grammars. But she felt sad and had trouble concentrating. She kept coming back to the speech Dubcek had given over the radio after his return from Moscow. Although she had completely forgotten what he said, she could still hear his quavering voice. She thought about how foreign soldiers had arrested him, the head of an independent state, in his own country, held him for four days somewhere in the Ukrainian mountains, informed him he was to be executed—as, a decade before, they had executed his Hungarian counterpart Imre Nagy—then packed him off to Moscow, ordered him to have a bath and shave, to change his clothes and put on a tie, apprised him of the decision to commute his execution, instructed him to consider himself head of state once more, sat him at a table opposite Brezhnev, and forced him to act.

He returned, humiliated, to address his humiliated nation. He was so humiliated he could not even speak. Tereza would never forget those awful pauses in the middle of his sentences. Was he that exhausted? Ill? Had they drugged him? Or was it only despair? If nothing was to remain of Dubcek, then at least those awful long pauses when he seemed unable to breathe, when he gasped for air before a whole nation glued to its radios, at least those pauses would remain. Those pauses contained all the horror that had befallen their country.

It was the seventh day of the invasion. She heard the speech in the editorial offices of a newspaper that had been transformed overnight into an organ of the resistance. Everyone present hated Dubcek at that moment. They reproached him for compromising; they felt humiliated by his humiliation; his weakness offended them.

Thinking in Zurich of those days, she no longer felt any aversion to the man. The word "weak" no longer sounded like a verdict. Any man confronted with superior strength is weak, even if he has an athletic body like Dubcek's. The very weakness that at the time had seemed unbearable and repulsive, the weakness that had driven Tereza and Tomas from the country, suddenly attracted her. She realized that she belonged among the weak, in the camp of the weak, in the country of the weak, and that she had to be faithful to them precisely because they were weak and gasped for breath in the middle of sentences.

She felt attracted by their weakness as by vertigo. She felt attracted by it because she felt weak herself. Again she began to feel jealous and again her hands shook. When Tomas noticed it, he did what he usually did: he took her hands in his and tried to calm them by pressing hard. She tore them away from him.

"What's the matter?" he asked.

"Nothing."

"What do you want me to do for you?"

"I want you to be old. Ten years older. Twenty years older!"

What she meant was: I want you to be weak. As weak as I am.

# 27

Karenin was not overjoyed by the move to Switzerland. Karenin hated change. Dog time cannot be plotted along a straight line; it does not move on and on, from one thing to the next. It moves in a circle like the hands of a clock, which—they, too, unwilling to dash madly ahead—turn round and round the face, day in and day out following the same path. In Prague, when Tomas and Tereza bought a new chair or moved a flower pot, Karenin would look on in displeasure. It disturbed his sense of time. It was as though they were trying to dupe the hands of the clock by changing the numbers on its face.

Nonetheless, he soon managed to reestablish the old order and old rituals in the Zurich flat. As in Prague, he would jump up on their bed and welcome them to the day, accompany Tereza on her morning shopping jaunt, and make certain he got the other walks coming to him as well.

He was the timepiece of their lives. In periods of despair, she would remind herself she had to hold on because of him, because he was weaker than she, weaker perhaps even than Dubcek and their abandoned homeland.

One day when they came back from a walk, the phone was ringing. She picked up the receiver and asked who it was.

It was a woman's voice speaking German and asking for Tomas. It was an impatient voice, and Tereza felt there was a hint of derision in it. When she said that Tomas wasn't there and she didn't know when he'd be back, the woman on the other end of the line started laughing and, without saying goodbye, hung up.

Tereza knew it did not mean a thing. It could have been a nurse from the hospital, a patient, a secretary, anyone. But still she was upset and unable to concentrate on anything. It was then that she realized she had lost the last bit of strength she had had at home: she was absolutely incapable of tolerating this absolutely insignificant incident.

Being in a foreign country means walking a tightrope high above the ground without the net afforded a person by the country where he has his family, colleagues, and friends, and where he can easily say what he has to say in a language he has known from childhood. In Prague she was dependent on Tomas only when it came to the heart; here she was dependent on him for everything. What would happen to her here if he abandoned her? Would she have to live her whole life in fear of losing him?

She told herself: Their acquaintance had been based on an error from the start. The copy of *Anna Karenina* under her arm amounted to false papers; it had given Tomas the wrong idea. In spite of their love, they had made each other's life a hell. The fact that they loved each other was merely proof that the fault lay not in themselves, in their behavior or inconstancy of feeling, but rather in their incompatibility: he was strong and she was weak. She was like Dubcek, who made a thirty-second pause in the middle of a sentence; she was like her country, which stuttered, gasped for breath, could not speak.

But when the strong were too weak to hurt the weak, the weak had to be strong enough to leave.

And having told herself all this, she pressed her face against Karenin's furry head and said, "Sorry, Karenin. It looks as though you're going to have to move again."

# 28

Sitting crushed into a corner of the train compartment with her heavy suitcase above her head and Karenin squeezed against her legs, she kept thinking about the cook at the hotel restaurant where she had worked when she lived with her mother. The cook would take every opportunity to give her a slap on the behind, and never tired of asking her in front of everyone when she would give in and go to bed with him. It was odd that he was the one who came to mind. He had always been the prime example of everything she loathed. And now all she could think of was looking him up and telling him, "You used to say you wanted to sleep with me. Well, here I am."

She longed to do something that would prevent her from turning back to Tomas. She longed to destroy brutally the past seven years of her life. It was vertigo. A heady, insuperable longing to fall.

We might also call vertigo the intoxication of the weak. Aware of his weakness, a man decides to give in rather than stand up to it. He is drunk with weakness, wishes to grow even weaker, wishes to fall down in the middle of the main square in front of everybody, wishes to be down, lower than down.

She tried to talk herself into settling outside of Prague and giving up her profession as a photographer. She would go back to the small town from which Tomas's voice had once lured her.

But once in Prague, she found she had to spend some time taking care of various practical matters, and began putting off her departure.

On the fifth day, Tomas suddenly turned up. Karenin jumped all over him, so it was a while before they had to make any overtures to each other.

They felt they were standing on a snow-covered plain, shivering with cold.

Then they moved together like lovers who had never kissed before.

"Has everything been all right?" he asked.

"Yes," she answered.

"Have you been to the magazine?"

"I've given them a call."

"Well?"

"Nothing yet. I've been waiting."

"For what?"

She made no response. She could not tell him that she had been waiting for him.

## 29

Now we return to a moment we already know about. Tomas was desperately unhappy and had a bad stomachache. He did not fall asleep until very late at night.

Soon thereafter Tereza awoke. (There were Russian airplanes circling over Prague, and it was impossible to sleep for the noise.) Her first thought was that he had come back because of her; because of her, he had changed his destiny. Now he would no longer be responsible for her; now she was responsible for him.

The responsibility, she felt, seemed to require more strength than she could muster.

But all at once she recalled that just before he had appeared at the door of their flat the day before, the church bells had chimed six o'clock. On the day they first met, her shift had ended at six. She saw him sitting there in front of her on the yellow bench and heard the bells in the belfry chime six.

No, it was not superstition, it was a sense of beauty that cured her of her depression and imbued her with a new will to live. The birds of fortuity had alighted once more on her shoulders. There were tears in her eyes, and she was unutterably happy to hear him breathing at her side.

# PART THREE

# Words Misunderstood

# 1

Geneva is a city of fountains large and small, of parks where music once rang out from the bandstands. Even the university is hidden among trees. Franz had just finished his afternoon lecture. As he left the building, the sprinklers were spouting jets of water over the lawn and he was in a capital mood. He was on his way to see his mistress. She lived only a few streets away.

He often stopped in for a visit, but only as a friend, never as a lover. If he made love to her in her Geneva studio, he would be going from one woman to the other, from wife to mistress and back in a single day, and because in Geneva husband and wife sleep together in the French style, in the same bed, he would be going from the bed of one woman to the bed of another in the space of several hours. And that, he felt, would humiliate both mistress and wife and, in the end, himself as well.

The love he bore this woman, with whom he had fallen in

love several months before, was so precious to him that he tried to create an independent space for her in his life, a restricted zone of purity. He was often invited to lecture at foreign universities, and now he accepted all offers. But because they were not enough to satisfy his new-found wanderlust, he took to inventing congresses and symposia as a means of justifying the new absences to his wife. His mistress, who had a flexible schedule, accompanied him on all speaking engagements, real and imagined. So it was that within a short span of time he introduced her to many European cities and an American one.

"How would you like to go to Palermo ten days from now?" asked Franz.

"I prefer Geneva," she answered. She was standing in front of her easel examining a work in progress.

"How can you live without seeing Palermo?" asked Franz in an attempt at levity.

"I have seen Palermo," she said.

"You have?" he said with a hint of jealousy.

"A friend of mine once sent me a postcard from there. It's taped up over the toilet. Haven't you noticed?"

Then she told him a story. "Once upon a time, in the early part of the century, there lived a poet. He was so old he had to be taken on walks by his amanuensis. 'Master,' his amanuensis said one day, 'look what's up in the sky! It's the first airplane ever to fly over the city!' 'I have my own picture of it,' said the poet to his amanuensis, without raising his eyes from the ground. Well, I have my own picture of Palermo. It has the same hotels and cars as all cities. And my studio always has new and different pictures."

Franz was sad. He had grown so accustomed to linking their love life to foreign travel that his "Let's go to Palermo!" was an unambiguous erotic message and her "I prefer Geneva" could have only one meaning: his mistress no longer desired him.

How could he be so unsure of himself with her? She had not given him the slightest cause for worry! In fact, she was the one who had taken the erotic initiative shortly after they met. He was a good-looking man; he was at the peak of his scholarly career; he was even feared by his colleagues for the arrogance and tenacity he displayed during professional meetings and colloquia. Then why did he worry daily that his mistress was about to leave him?

The only explanation I can suggest is that for Franz, love was not an extension of public life but its antithesis. It meant a longing to put himself at the mercy of his partner. He who gives himself up like a prisoner of war must give up his weapons as well. And deprived in advance of defense against a possible blow, he cannot help wondering when the blow will fall. That is why I can say that for Franz, love meant the constant expectation of a blow.

While Franz attended to his anguish, his mistress put down her brush and went into the next room. She returned with a bottle of wine. She opened it without a word and poured out two glasses.

Immediately he felt relieved and slightly ridiculous. The "I prefer Geneva" did not mean she refused to make love; quite the contrary, it meant she was tired of limiting their lovemaking to foreign cities.

She raised her glass and emptied it in one swig. Franz did the same. He was naturally overjoyed that her refusal to go to Palermo was actually a call to love, but he was a bit sorry as well: his mistress seemed determined to violate the zone of purity he had introduced into their relationship; she had failed to understand his apprehensive attempts to save their love from banality and separate it radically from his conjugal home.

The ban on making love with his painter-mistress in Geneva was actually a self-inflicted punishment for having married another woman. He felt it as a kind of guilt or defect. Even though his conjugal sex life was hardly worth mentioning, he and his wife still slept in the same bed, awoke in the middle of the night to each other's heavy breathing, and inhaled the smells of each other's body. True, he would rather have slept by himself, but the marriage bed is still the symbol of the marriage bond, and symbols, as we know, are inviolable.

Each time he lay down next to his wife in that bed, he thought of his mistress imagining him lying down next to his wife in that bed, and each time he thought of her he felt ashamed. That was why he wished to separate the bed he slept in with his wife as far as possible in space from the bed he made love in with his mistress.

His painter-mistress poured herself another glass of wine, drank it down, and then, still silent and with a curious nonchalance, as if completely unaware of Franz's presence, slowly removed her blouse. She was behaving like an acting student whose improvisation assignment is to make the class believe she is alone in a room and no one can see her.

Standing there in her skirt and bra, she suddenly (as if recalling only then that she was not alone in the room) fixed Franz with a long stare.

That stare bewildered him; he could not understand it. All lovers unconsciously establish their own rules of the game, which from the outset admit no transgression. The stare she had just fixed on him fell outside their rules; it had nothing in common with the looks and gestures that usually preceded their lovemaking. It was neither provocative nor flirtatious, simply interrogative. The problem was, Franz had not the slightest notion what it was asking.

Next she stepped out of her skirt and, taking Franz by the hand, turned him in the direction of a large mirror propped against the wall. Without letting go of his hand, she looked into the mirror with the same long questioning stare, training it first on herself, then on him.

Near the mirror stood a wig stand with an old black bowler hat on it. She bent over, picked up the hat, and put it on her head. The image in the mirror was instantaneously transformed: suddenly it was a woman in her undergarments, a beautiful, distant, indifferent woman with a terribly out-of-place bowler hat on her head, holding the hand of a man in a gray suit and a tie.

Again he had to smile at how poorly he understood his mistress. When she took her clothes off, it wasn't so much erotic provocation as an odd little caper, a happening à deux. His smile beamed understanding and consent.

He waited for his mistress to respond in kind, but she did not. Without letting go of his hand, she stood staring into the mirror, first at herself, then at him.

The time for the happening had come and gone. Franz was beginning to feel that the caper (which, in and of itself, he was happy to think of as charming) had dragged on too long. So he gently took the brim of the bowler hat between two fingers, lifted it off Sabina's head with a smile, and laid it back on the wig stand. It was as though he were erasing the mustache a naughty child had drawn on a picture of the Virgin Mary.

For several more seconds she remained motionless, staring at herself in the mirror. Then Franz covered her with tender kisses and asked her once more to go with him in ten days to Palermo. This time she said yes unquestioningly, and he left.

He was in an excellent mood again. Geneva, which he had cursed all his life as the metropolis of boredom, now seemed beautiful and full of adventure. Outside in the street, he looked back up at the studio's broad window. It was late spring and hot. All the windows were shaded with striped awnings. Franz walked to the park. At its far end, the golden cupolas of the Orthodox church rose up like two gilded cannonballs kept from imminent collapse and suspended in the air by some invisible power. Everything was beautiful. Then he went down to the embankment and took the public transport boat to the north bank of the lake, where he lived.

# 2

Sabina was now by herself. She went back to the mirror, still in her underwear. She put the bowler hat back on her head and had a long look at herself. She was amazed at the number of years she had spent pursuing one lost moment.

Once, during a visit to her studio many years before, the bowler hat had caught Tomas's fancy. He had set it on his head and looked at himself in the large mirror which, as in the Geneva studio, leaned against the wall. He wanted to see what he would have looked like as a nineteenth-century mayor. When Sabina started undressing, he put the hat on her head. There they stood in front of the mirror (they always stood in front of the mirror while she undressed), watching themselves. She stripped to her underwear, but still had the hat on her head. And all at once she realized they were both excited by what they saw in the mirror.

What could have excited them so? A moment before, the hat on her head had seemed nothing but a joke. Was excitement really a mere step away from laughter?

Yes. When they looked at each other in the mirror that time, all she saw for the first few seconds was a comic situation. But suddenly the comic became veiled by excitement: the bowler hat no longer signified a joke; it signified violence; violence against Sabina, against her dignity as a woman. She saw her bare legs and thin panties with her pubic triangle showing through. The lingerie enhanced the charm of her femininity, while the hard masculine hat denied it, violated and ridiculed it. The fact that Tomas stood beside her fully dressed meant that the essence of what they both saw was far from good clean fun (if it had been fun he was after, he, too, would have had to strip and don a bowler hat); it was humiliation. But instead of spurning it, she proudly, provocatively played it for all it was worth, as if submitting of her own will to public rape; and suddenly, unable to wait any longer, she pulled Tomas down to the floor. The bowler hat rolled under the table, and they began thrashing about on the rug at the foot of the mirror.

But let us return to the bowler hat:

First, it was a vague reminder of a forgotten grandfather, the mayor of a small Bohemian town during the nineteenth century.

Second, it was a memento of her father. After the funeral her brother appropriated all their parents' property, and she, refusing out of sovereign contempt to fight for her rights, announced sarcastically that she was taking the bowler hat as her sole inheritance.

Third, it was a prop for her love games with Tomas.

Fourth, it was a sign of her originality, which she consciously cultivated. She could not take much with her when she emigrated, and taking this bulky, impractical thing meant giving up other, more practical ones.

Fifth, now that she was abroad, the hat was a sentimental object. When she went to visit Tomas in Zurich, she took it along and had it on her head when he opened the hotel-room door. But then something she had not reckoned with happened: the hat, no longer jaunty or sexy, turned into a monument to time past. They were both touched. They made love as they never had before. This was no occasion for obscene games. For this meeting was not a continuation of their erotic rendezvous, each of which had been an opportunity to think up some new little vice; it was a recapitulation of time, a hymn to their common past, a sentimental summary of an unsentimental story that was disappearing in the distance.

The bowler hat was a motif in the musical composition that was Sabina's life. It returned again and again, each time with a different meaning, and all the meanings flowed through the bowler hat like water through a riverbed. I might call it Heraclitus' ("You can't step twice into the same river") riverbed: the bowler hat was a bed through which each time Sabina saw another river flow, another *semantic river:* each time the same object would give rise to a new meaning, though all former meanings would resonate (like an echo, like a parade of echoes) together with the new one. Each new experience would resound, each time enriching the harmony. The reason why Tomas and Sabina were touched by the sight of the bowler hat in a Zurich hotel and made love almost in tears was that its black presence was not merely a reminder of their love games but also a memento of Sabina's father and of her grandfather, who lived in a century without airplanes and cars.

Now, perhaps, we are in a better position to understand the abyss separating Sabina and Franz: he listened eagerly to the story of her life and she was equally eager to hear the story of his, but although they had a clear understanding of the logical meaning of the words they exchanged, they failed to hear the semantic susurrus of the river flowing through them.

And so when she put on the bowler hat in his presence, Franz felt uncomfortable, as if someone had spoken to him in a language he did not know. It was neither obscene nor sentimental, merely an incomprehensible gesture. What made him feel uncomfortable was its very lack of meaning.

While people are fairly young and the musical composition of their lives is still in its opening bars, they can go about writing it together and exchange motifs (the way Tomas and Sabina exchanged the motif of the bowler hat), but if they meet when they are older, like Franz and Sabina, their musical compositions are more or less complete, and every motif, every object, every word means something different to each of them.

If I were to make a record of all Sabina and Franz's conversations, I could compile a long lexicon of their misunderstandings. Let us be content, instead, with a short dictionary.

# 3

## A Short Dictionary of Misunderstood Words

### WOMAN

Being a woman is a fate Sabina did not choose. What we have not chosen we cannot consider either our merit or our failure. Sabina believed that she had to assume the correct attitude to her unchosen fate. To rebel against being born a woman seemed as foolish to her as to take pride in it.

During one of their first times together, Franz announced to her, in an oddly emphatic way, "Sabina, you are a *woman.*" She could not understand why he accentuated the obvious with the solemnity of a Columbus who has just sighted land. Not until later did she understand that the word "woman," on which he had placed such uncommon emphasis, did not, in his eyes, signify one of the two human sexes; it represented a *value.* Not every woman was worthy of being called a woman.

But if Sabina was, in Franz's eyes, a *woman,* then what was his wife, Marie-Claude? More than twenty years earlier, several months after Franz met Marie-Claude, she had threatened to take her life if he abandoned her. Franz was bewitched by the threat. He was not particularly fond of Marie-Claude, but he was very much taken with her love. He felt himself unworthy of so great a love, and felt he owed her a low bow.

He bowed so low that he married her. And even though Marie-Claude never recaptured the emotional intensity that accompanied her suicide threat, in his heart he kept its memory alive with the thought that he must never hurt her and always respect the woman in her.

It is an interesting formulation. Not "respect Marie-Claude," but "respect the woman in Marie-Claude."

But if Marie-Claude is herself a woman, then who is that other woman hiding in her, the one he must always respect? The Platonic ideal of a woman, perhaps?

No. His mother. It never would have occurred to him to say he respected the woman in his mother. He worshipped his mother and not some woman inside her. His mother and the Platonic ideal of womanhood were one and the same.

When he was twelve, she suddenly found herself alone, abandoned by Franz's father. The boy suspected something serious had happened, but his mother muted the drama with mild, insipid words so as not to upset him. The day his father left, Franz and his mother went into town together, and as they left home Franz noticed that her shoes did not match. He was in a quandary: he wanted to point out her mistake, but was afraid he would hurt her. So during the two hours they spent walking through the city together he kept his eyes fixed on her feet. It was then he had his first inkling of what it means to suffer.

### FIDELITY AND BETRAYAL

He loved her from the time he was a child until the time he accompanied her to the cemetery; he loved her in his memories as well. That is what made him feel that fidelity deserved pride of place among the virtues: fidelity gave a unity to lives that would otherwise splinter into thousands of split-second impressions.

Franz often spoke about his mother to Sabina, perhaps even with a certain unconscious ulterior motive: he assumed that Sabina would be charmed by his ability to be faithful, that it would win her over.

What he did not know was that Sabina was charmed more by betrayal than by fidelity. The word "fidelity" reminded her of her father, a small-town puritan, who spent his Sundays painting away at canvases of woodland sunsets and roses in vases. Thanks to him, she started drawing as a child. When she was fourteen, she fell in love with a boy her age. Her father was so frightened that he would not let her out of the house by herself for a year. One day, he showed her some Picasso reproductions and made fun of them. If she couldn't love her fourteen-year-old schoolboy, she could at least love cubism. After completing school, she went off to Prague with the euphoric feeling that now at last she could betray her home.

Betrayal. From tender youth we are told by father and teacher that betrayal is the most heinous offense imaginable. But what is betrayal? Betrayal means breaking ranks. Betrayal means breaking ranks and going off into the unknown. Sabina knew of nothing more magnificent than going off into the unknown.

Though a student at the Academy of Fine Arts, she was not allowed to paint like Picasso. It was the period when so-called socialist realism was prescribed and the school manufactured portraits of Communist statesmen. Her longing to betray her father remained unsatisfied: Communism was merely another father, a father equally strict and limited, a father who forbade her love (the times were puritanical) and Picasso, too. And if she married a second-rate actor, it was only because he had a reputation for being eccentric and was unacceptable to both fathers.

Then her mother died. The day following her return to Prague from the funeral, she received a telegram saying that her father had taken his life out of grief.

Suddenly she felt pangs of conscience: Was it really so terrible that her father had painted vases filled with roses and hated Picasso? Was it really so reprehensible that he was afraid of his fourteen-year-old daughter's coming home pregnant? Was it really so laughable that he could not go on living without his wife?

And again she felt a longing to betray: betray her own betrayal. She announced to her husband (whom she now considered a difficult drunk rather than an eccentric) that she was leaving him.

But if we betray B., for whom we betrayed A., it does not necessarily follow that we have placated A. The life of a divorcée-painter did not in the least resemble the life of the parents she had betrayed. The first betrayal is irreparable. It calls forth a chain reaction of further betrayals, each of which takes us farther and farther away from the point of our original betrayal.

### MUSIC

For Franz music was the art that comes closest to Dionysian beauty in the sense of intoxication. No one can get really drunk on a novel or a painting, but who can help getting drunk on Beethoven's Ninth, Bartok's Sonata for Two Pianos and Percussion, or the Beatles' White Album? Franz made no distinction between "classical" music and "pop." He found the distinction old-fashioned and hypocritical. He loved rock as much as Mozart.

He considered music a liberating force: it liberated him

from loneliness, introversion, the dust of the library; it opened the door of his body and allowed his soul to step out into the world to make friends. He loved to dance and regretted that Sabina did not share his passion.

They were sitting together at a restaurant, and loud music with a heavy beat poured out of a nearby speaker as they ate.

"It's a vicious circle," Sabina said. "People are going deaf because music is played louder and louder. But because they're going deaf, it has to be played louder still."

"Don't you like music?" Franz asked.

"No," said Sabina, and then added, "though in a different era . . ." She was thinking of the days of Johann Sebastian Bach, when music was like a rose blooming on a boundless snow-covered plain of silence.

Noise masked as music had pursued her since early childhood. During her years at the Academy of Fine Arts, students had been required to spend whole summer vacations at a youth camp. They lived in common quarters and worked together on a steelworks construction site. Music roared out of loudspeakers on the site from five in the morning to nine at night. She felt like crying, but the music was cheerful, and there was nowhere to hide, not in the latrine or under the bedclothes: everything was in range of the speakers. The music was like a pack of hounds that had been sicked on her.

At the time, she had thought that only in the Communist world could such musical barbarism reign supreme. Abroad, she discovered that the transformation of music into noise was a planetary process by which mankind was entering the historical phase of total ugliness. The total ugliness to come had made itself felt first as omnipresent acoustical ugliness: cars, motorcycles, electric guitars, drills, loudspeakers, sirens. The omnipresence of visual ugliness would soon follow.

After dinner, they went upstairs to their room and made

love, and as Franz fell asleep his thoughts began to lose coherence. He recalled the noisy music at dinner and said to himself, "Noise has one advantage. It drowns out words." And suddenly he realized that all his life he had done nothing but talk, write, lecture, concoct sentences, search for formulations and amend them, so in the end no words were precise, their meanings were obliterated, their content lost, they turned into trash, chaff, dust, sand; prowling through his brain, tearing at his head, they were his insomnia, his illness. And what he yearned for at that moment, vaguely but with all his might, was unbounded music, absolute sound, a pleasant and happy all-encompassing, overpowering, window-rattling din to engulf, once and for all, the pain, the futility, the vanity of words. Music was the negation of sentences, music was the anti-word! He yearned for one long embrace with Sabina, yearned never to say another sentence, another word, to let his orgasm fuse with the orgiastic thunder of music. And lulled by that blissful imaginary uproar, he fell asleep.

### LIGHT AND DARKNESS

Living for Sabina meant seeing. Seeing is limited by two borders: strong light, which blinds, and total darkness. Perhaps that was what motivated Sabina's distaste for all extremism. Extremes mean borders beyond which life ends, and a passion for extremism, in art and in politics, is a veiled longing for death.

In Franz the word "light" did not evoke the picture of a landscape basking in the soft glow of day; it evoked the source of light itself: the sun, a light bulb, a spotlight. Franz's associations were familiar metaphors: the sun of righteousness, the lambent flame of the intellect, and so on.

Darkness attracted him as much as light. He knew that these days turning out the light before making love was considered laughable, and so he always left a small lamp burning over the bed. At the moment he penetrated Sabina, however, he closed his eyes. The pleasure suffusing his body called for darkness. That darkness was pure, perfect, thoughtless, visionless; that darkness was without end, without borders; that darkness was the infinite we each carry within us. (Yes, if you're looking for infinity, just close your eyes!)

And at the moment he felt pleasure suffusing his body, Franz himself disintegrated and dissolved into the infinity of his darkness, himself becoming infinite. But the larger a man grows in his own inner darkness, the more his outer form diminishes. A man with closed eyes is a wreck of a man. Then, Sabina found the sight of Franz distasteful, and to avoid looking at him she too closed her eyes. But for her, darkness did not mean infinity; for her, it meant a disagreement with what she saw, the negation of what was seen, the refusal to see.

## 4

Sabina once allowed herself to be taken along to a gathering of fellow émigrés. As usual, they were hashing over whether they should or should not have taken up arms against the Russians. In the safety of emigration, they all naturally came out in favor of fighting. Sabina said: "Then why don't you go back and fight?"

That was not the thing to say. A man with artificially waved gray hair pointed a long index finger at her. "That's no way to talk. You're all responsible for what happened. You, too. How did you oppose the Communist regime? All you did was paint pictures. . . ."

Assessing the populace, checking up on it, is a principal and never-ending social activity in Communist countries. If a painter is to have an exhibition, an ordinary citizen to receive a visa to a country with a sea coast, a soccer player to join the national team, then a vast array of recommendations and reports must be garnered (from the concierge, colleagues, the police, the local Party organization, the pertinent trade union) and added up, weighed, and summarized by special officials. These reports have nothing to do with artistic talent, kicking ability, or maladies that respond well to salt sea air; they deal with one thing only: the "citizen's political profile" (in other words, what the citizen says, what he thinks, how he behaves, how he acquits himself at meetings or May Day parades). Because everything (day-to-day existence, promotion at work, vacations) depends on the outcome of the assessment process, everyone (whether he wants to play soccer for the national team, have an exhibition, or spend his holidays at the seaside) must behave in such a way as to deserve a favorable assessment.

That was what ran through Sabina's mind as she listened to the gray-haired man speak. He didn't care whether his fellow-countrymen were good kickers or painters (none of the Czechs at the émigré gathering ever showed any interest in what Sabina painted); he cared whether they had opposed Communism actively or just passively, really and truly or just for appearances' sake, from the very beginning or just since emigration.

Because she was a painter, she had an eye for detail and a memory for the physical characteristics of the people in Prague who had a passion for assessing others. All of them had index fingers slightly longer than their middle fingers and pointed them at whomever they happened to be talking to. In fact, President Novotny, who had ruled the country for the fourteen years preceding 1968, sported the very same barber-induced gray waves and had the longest index finger of all the inhabitants of Central Europe.

When the distinguished émigré heard from the lips of a painter whose pictures he had never seen that he resembled Communist President Novotny, he turned scarlet, then white, then scarlet again, then white once more; he tried to say something, did not succeed, and fell silent. Everyone else kept silent until Sabina stood up and left.

It made her unhappy, and down in the street she asked herself why she should bother to maintain contact with Czechs. What bound her to them? The landscape? If each of them were asked to say what the name of his native country evoked in him, the images that came to mind would be so different as to rule out all possibility of unity.

Or the culture? But what was that? Music? Dvorak and Janacek? Yes. But what if a Czech had no feeling for music? Then the essence of being Czech vanished into thin air.

Or great men? Jan Hus? None of the people in that room had ever read a line of his works. The only thing they were all able to understand was the flames, the glory of the flames when he was burned at the stake, the glory of the ashes, so for them the essence of being Czech came down to ashes and nothing more. The only things that held them together were their defeats and the reproaches they addressed to one another.

She was walking fast. She was more disturbed by her own thoughts than by her break with the émigrés. She knew she was being unfair. There were other Czechs, after all, people quite different from the man with the long index finger. The embarrassed silence that followed her little speech did not by any means indicate they were all against her. No, they were probably bewildered by the sudden hatred, the lack of understanding they were all subjected to in emigration. Then why wasn't she sorry for them? Why didn't she see them for the woeful and abandoned creatures they were?

We know why. After she betrayed her father, life opened up before her, a long road of betrayals, each one attracting her as vice and victory. She *would not* keep ranks! She *refused* to keep ranks—always with the same people, with the same speeches! That was why she was so stirred by her own injustice. But it was not an unpleasant feeling; quite the contrary, Sabina had the impression she had just scored a victory and someone invisible was applauding her for it.

Then suddenly the intoxication gave way to anguish: The road had to end somewhere! Sooner or later she would have to put an end to her betrayals! Sooner or later she would have to stop herself!

It was evening and she was hurrying through the railway station. The train to Amsterdam was in. She found her coach. Guided by a friendly guard, she opened the door to her compartment and found Franz sitting on a couchette. He rose to greet her; she threw her arms around him and smothered him with kisses.

She had an overwhelming desire to tell him, like the most banal of women, Don't let me go, hold me tight, make me your plaything, your slave, be strong! But they were words she could not say.

The only thing she said when he released her from his embrace was, "You don't know how happy I am to be with you." That was the most her reserved nature allowed her to express.

# 5

## A Short Dictionary of Misunderstood Words (*continued*)

### PARADES

People in Italy or France have it easy. When their parents force them to go to church, they get back at them by joining the Party (Communist, Maoist, Trotskyist, etc.). Sabina, however, was first sent to church by her father, then forced by him to attend meetings of the Communist Youth League. He was afraid of what would happen if she stayed away.

When she marched in the obligatory May Day parades, she could never keep in step, and the girl behind her would shout at her and purposely tread on her heels. When the time came to sing, she never knew the words of the songs and would merely open and close her mouth. But the other girls would notice and report her. From her youth on, she hated parades.

Franz had studied in Paris, and because he was extraordinarily gifted his scholarly career was assured from the time he was twenty. At twenty, he knew he would live out his life within the confines of his university office, one or two libraries, and two or three lecture halls. The idea of such a life made him feel suffocated. He yearned to step out of his life the way one steps out of a house into the street.

And so as long as he lived in Paris, he took part in every possible demonstration. How nice it was to celebrate something, demand something, protest against something; to be out in the open, to be with others. The parades filing down the Boulevard Saint-Germain or from the Place de la République to the Bastille fascinated him. He saw the marching, shouting crowd as the image of Europe and its history. Europe was the Grand March. The march from revolution to revolution, from struggle to struggle, ever onward.

I might put it another way: Franz felt his book life to be unreal. He yearned for real life, for the touch of people walking side by side with him, for their shouts. It never occurred to him that what he considered unreal (the work he did in the solitude of the office or library) was in fact his real life, whereas the parades he imagined to be reality were nothing but theater, dance, carnival—in other words, a dream.

During her studies, Sabina lived in a dormitory. On May Day all the students had to report early in the morning for the parade. Student officials would comb the building to ensure that no one was missing. Sabina hid in the lavatory. Not until long after the building was empty would she go back to her room. It was quieter than anywhere she could remember. The only sound was the parade music echoing in the distance. It was as though she had found refuge inside a shell and the only sound she could hear was the sea of an inimical world.

A year or two after emigrating, she happened to be in Paris on the anniversary of the Russian invasion of her country. A protest march had been scheduled, and she felt driven to take part. Fists raised high, the young Frenchmen shouted out slogans condemning Soviet imperialism. She liked the slogans, but to her surprise she found herself unable to shout along with them. She lasted no more than a few minutes in the parade.

When she told her French friends about it, they were amazed. "You mean you don't want to fight the occupation of your country?" She would have liked to tell them that behind Communism, Fascism, behind all occupations and invasions lurks a more basic, pervasive evil and that the image of that evil was a parade of people marching by with raised fists and shouting identical syllables in unison. But she knew she would never be able to make them understand. Embarrassed, she changed the subject.

THE BEAUTY OF NEW YORK

Franz and Sabina would walk the streets of New York for hours at a time. The view changed with each step, as if they were following a winding mountain path surrounded by breathtaking scenery: a young man kneeling in the middle of the sidewalk praying; a few steps away, a beautiful black woman leaning against a tree; a man in a black suit directing an invisible orchestra while crossing the street; a fountain spurting water and a group of construction workers sitting on the rim eating lunch; strange iron ladders running up and down buildings with ugly red façades, so ugly that they were beautiful; and next door, a huge glass skyscraper backed by another, itself topped by a small Arabian pleasure-dome with turrets, galleries, and gilded columns.

She was reminded of her paintings. There, too, incongruous things came together: a steelworks construction site superimposed on a kerosene lamp; an old-fashioned lamp with a painted-glass shade shattered into tiny splinters and rising up over a desolate landscape of marshland.

Franz said, "Beauty in the European sense has always had a premeditated quality to it. We've always had an aesthetic intention and a long-range plan. That's what enabled Western man to spend decades building a Gothic cathedral or a Renaissance piazza. The beauty of New York rests on a completely different base. It's unintentional. It arose independent of human design, like a stalagmitic cavern. Forms which are in themselves quite ugly turn up fortuitously, without design, in such incredible surroundings that they sparkle with a sudden wondrous poetry."

Sabina said, "Unintentional beauty. Yes. Another way of putting it might be 'beauty by mistake.' Before beauty disappears entirely from the earth, it will go on existing for a while by mistake. 'Beauty by mistake'—the final phase in the history of beauty."

And she recalled her first mature painting, which came into being because some red paint had dripped on it by mistake. Yes, her paintings were based on "beauty by mistake," and New York was the secret but authentic homeland of her painting.

Franz said, "Perhaps New York's unintentional beauty is much richer and more varied than the excessively strict and composed beauty of human design. But it's not our European beauty. It's an alien world."

Didn't they then at last agree on something?

No. There is a difference. Sabina was very much attracted by the alien quality of New York's beauty. Franz found it intriguing but frightening; it made him feel homesick for Europe.

### SABINA'S COUNTRY

Sabina understood Franz's distaste for America. He was the embodiment of Europe: his mother was Viennese, his father French, and he himself was Swiss.

Franz greatly admired Sabina's country. Whenever she told him about herself and her friends from home, Franz heard the words "prison," "persecution," "enemy tanks," "emigration," "pamphlets," "banned books," "banned exhibitions," and he felt a curious mixture of envy and nostalgia.

He made a confession to Sabina. "A philosopher once wrote that everything in my work is unverifiable speculation and called me a 'pseudo-Socrates.' I felt terribly humiliated and made a furious response. And just think, that laughable episode was the greatest conflict I've ever experienced! The pinnacle of the dramatic possibilities available to my life! We live in two different dimensions, you and I. You came into my life like Gulliver entering the land of the Lilliputians."

Sabina protested. She said that conflict, drama, and tragedy didn't mean a thing; there was nothing inherently valuable in them, nothing deserving of respect or admiration. What was truly enviable was Franz's work and the fact that he had the peace and quiet to devote himself to it.

Franz shook his head. "When a society is rich, its people don't need to work with their hands; they can devote themselves to activities of the spirit. We have more and more universities and more and more students. If students are going to earn degrees, they've got to come up with dissertation topics. And since dissertations can be written about everything under the sun, the number of topics is infinite. Sheets of paper covered with words pile up in archives sadder than cemeteries, because no one ever visits them, not even on All Souls' Day. Culture is perishing in overproduction, in an avalanche of words, in the madness of quantity. That's why one banned book in your former country means infinitely more than the billions of words spewed out by our universities."

It is in this spirit that we may understand Franz's weakness for revolution. First he sympathized with Cuba, then with China, and when the cruelty of their regimes began to appall him, he resigned himself with a sigh to a sea of words with no weight and no resemblance to life. He became a professor in Geneva (where there are no demonstrations), and in a burst of abnegation (in womanless, paradeless solitude) he published several scholarly books, all of which received considerable acclaim. Then one day along came Sabina. She was a revelation. She came from a land where revolutionary illusion had long since faded but where the thing he admired most in revolution remained: life on a large scale; a life of risk, daring, and the danger of death. Sabina had renewed his faith in the grandeur of human endeavor. Superimposing the painful drama of her country on her person, he found her even more beautiful.

The trouble was that Sabina had no love for that drama. The words "prison," "persecution," "banned books," "occupation," "tanks" were ugly, without the slightest trace of romance. The only word that evoked in her a sweet, nostalgic memory of her homeland was the word "cemetery."

CEMETERY

Cemeteries in Bohemia are like gardens. The graves are covered with grass and colorful flowers. Modest tombstones are lost in the greenery. When the sun goes down, the cemetery sparkles with tiny candles. It looks as though the dead are dancing at a children's ball. Yes, a children's ball, because the dead are as innocent as children. No matter how brutal life becomes, peace always reigns in the cemetery. Even in wartime, in Hitler's time, in Stalin's time, through all occupations. When she felt low, she would get into the car, leave Prague far behind, and walk through one or another of the country cemeteries she loved so well. Against a backdrop of blue hills, they were as beautiful as a lullaby.

For Franz a cemetery was an ugly dump of stones and bones.

## 6

"I'd never drive. I'm scared stiff of accidents! Even if they don't kill you, they mark you for life!" And so saying, the sculptor made an instinctive grab for the finger he had nearly chopped off one day while whittling away at a wood statue. It was a miracle the finger had been saved.

"What do you mean?" said Marie-Claude in a raucous voice. She was in top form. "I was in a serious accident once, and I wouldn't have missed it for the world. And I've never had more fun than when I was in that hospital! I couldn't sleep a wink, so I just read and read, day and night."

They all looked at her in amazement. She basked in it. Franz reacted with a mixture of disgust (he knew that after the accident in question his wife had fallen into a deep depression and complained incessantly) and admiration (her ability to transform everything she experienced was a sign of true vitality).

"It was there I began to divide books into day books and night books," she went on. "Really, there are books meant for daytime reading and books that can be read only at night."

Now they all looked at her in amazement and admiration, all, that is, but the sculptor, who was still holding his finger and wrinkling his face at the memory of the accident.

Marie-Claude turned to him and asked, "Which category would you put Stendhal in?"

The sculptor had not heard the question and shrugged his shoulders uncomfortably. An art critic standing next to him said he thought of Stendhal as daytime reading.

Marie-Claude shook her head and said in her raucous voice, "No, no, you're wrong! You're wrong! Stendhal is a night author!"

Franz's participation in the debate on night art and day art was disturbed by the fact that he was expecting Sabina to show up at any minute. They had spent many days pondering whether or not she should accept the invitation to this cocktail party. It was a party Marie-Claude was giving for all painters and sculptors who had ever exhibited in her private gallery. Ever since Sabina had met Franz, she had avoided his wife. But because they feared being found out, they came to the conclusion that it would be more natural and therefore less suspicious for her to come.

While throwing unobtrusive looks in the direction of the

entrance hall, Franz heard his eighteen-year-old daughter, Marie-Anne, holding forth at the other end of the room. Excusing himself from the group presided over by his wife, he made his way to the group presided over by his daughter. Some were in chairs, others standing, but Marie-Anne was cross-legged on the floor. Franz was certain that Marie-Claude would soon switch to the carpet on her side of the room, too. Sitting on the floor when you had guests was at the time a gesture signifying simplicity, informality, liberal politics, hospitality, and a Parisian way of life. The passion with which Marie-Claude sat on all floors was such that Franz began to worry she would take to sitting on the floor of the shop where she bought her cigarettes.

"What are you working on now, Alain?" Marie-Anne asked the man at whose feet she was sitting.

Alain was so naive and sincere as to try to give the gallery owner's daughter an honest answer. He started explaining his new approach to her, a combination of photography and oil, but he had scarcely got through three sentences when Marie-Anne began whistling a tune. The painter was speaking slowly and with great concentration and did not hear the whistling.

"Will you tell me why you're whistling?" Franz whispered.

"Because I don't like to hear people talk about politics," she answered out loud.

And in fact, two men standing in the same circle were discussing the coming elections in France. Marie-Anne, who felt it her duty to direct the proceedings, asked the men whether they were planning to go to the Rossini opera an Italian company was putting on in Geneva the following week. Meanwhile, Alain the painter sank into greater and greater detail about his new approach to painting. Franz was ashamed for his daughter. To put her in her place, he announced that whenever she went to the opera she complained terribly of boredom.

"You're awful," said Marie-Anne, trying to punch him in the stomach from a sitting position. "The star tenor is so handsome. So handsome. I've seen him twice now, and I'm in love with him."

Franz could not get over how much like her mother his daughter was. Why couldn't she be like him? But there was nothing he could do about it. She was not like him. How many times had he heard Marie-Claude proclaim she was in love with this or that painter, singer, writer, politician, and once even with a racing cyclist? Of course, it was all mere cocktail party rhetoric, but he could not help recalling now and then that more than twenty years ago she had gone about saying the same thing about him and threatening him with suicide to boot.

At that point, Sabina entered the room. Marie-Claude walked up to her. While Marie-Anne went on about Rossini, Franz trained his attention on what the two women were saying. After a few friendly words of greeting, Marie-Claude lifted the ceramic pendant from Sabina's neck and said in a very loud voice, "What is that? How ugly!"

Those words made a deep impression on Franz. They were not meant to be combative; the raucous laughter immediately following them made it clear that by rejecting the pendant Marie-Claude did not wish to jeopardize her friendship with Sabina. But it was not the kind of thing she usually said.

"I made it myself," said Sabina.

"That pendant is ugly, really!" Marie-Claude repeated very loudly. "You shouldn't wear it."

Franz knew his wife didn't care whether the pendant was ugly or not. An object was ugly if she willed it ugly, beautiful if she willed it beautiful. Pendants worn by her friends were a priori beautiful. And even if she did find them ugly, she would never say so, because flattery had long since become second nature to her.

Why, then, did she decide that the pendant Sabina had made herself was ugly?

Franz suddenly saw the answer plainly: Marie-Claude proclaimed Sabina's pendant ugly because she could afford to do so.

Or to be more precise: Marie-Claude proclaimed Sabina's pendant ugly to make it clear that she could afford to tell Sabina her pendant was ugly.

Sabina's exhibition the year before had not been particularly successful, so Marie-Claude did not set great store by Sabina's favor. Sabina, however, had every reason to set store by Marie-Claude's. Yet that was not at all evident from her behavior.

Yes, Franz saw it plainly: Marie-Claude had taken advantage of the occasion to make clear to Sabina (and others) what the real balance of power was between the two of them.

## 7

### **A Short Dictionary of Misunderstood Words** (*concluded*)

#### THE OLD CHURCH IN AMSTERDAM

There are houses running along one side of the street, and behind the large ground-floor shop-front windows all the whores have little rooms and plushly pillowed armchairs in which they sit up close to the glass wearing bras and panties. They look like big bored cats.

On the other side of the street is a gigantic Gothic cathedral dating from the fourteenth century.

Between the whores' world and God's world, like a river

dividing two empires, stretches an intense smell of urine.

Inside the Old Church, all that is left of the Gothic style is the high, bare, white walls, the columns, the vaulting, and the windows. There is not a single image on the walls, not a single piece of statuary anywhere. The church is as empty as a gymnasium, except in the very center, where several rows of chairs have been arranged in a large square around a miniature podium for the minister. Behind the chairs are wooden booths, stalls for wealthy burghers.

The chairs and stalls seem to have been placed there without the slightest concern for the shape of the walls or position of the columns, as if wishing to express their indifference to or disdain for Gothic architecture. Centuries ago Calvinist faith turned the cathedral into a hangar, its only function being to keep the prayers of the faithful safe from rain and snow.

Franz was fascinated by it: the Grand March of History had passed through this gigantic hall!

Sabina recalled how after the Communist coup all the castles in Bohemia were nationalized and turned into manual training centers, retirement homes, and also cow sheds. She had visited one of the cow sheds: hooks for iron rings had been hammered into the stucco walls, and cows tied to the rings gazed dreamily out of the windows at the castle grounds, now overrun with chickens.

"It's the emptiness of it that fascinates me," said Franz. "People collect altars, statues, paintings, chairs, carpets, and books, and then comes a time of joyful relief and they throw it all out like so much refuse from yesterday's dinner table. Can't you just picture Hercules' broom sweeping out this cathedral?"

"The poor had to stand, while the rich had stalls," said Sabina, pointing to them. "But there was something that bound the bankers to beggars: a hatred of beauty."

"What is beauty?" said Franz, and he saw himself attending a recent gallery preview at his wife's side, and at her insistence. The endless vanity of speeches and words, the vanity of culture, the vanity of art.

When Sabina was working in the student brigade, her soul poisoned by the cheerful marches issuing incessantly from the loudspeakers, she borrowed a motorcycle one Sunday and headed for the hills. She stopped at a tiny remote village she had never seen before, leaned the motorcycle against the church, and went in. A mass happened to be in progress. Religion was persecuted by the regime, and most people gave the church a wide berth. The only people in the pews were old men and old women, because they did not fear the regime. They feared only death.

The priest intoned words in a singsong voice, and the people repeated them after him in unison. It was a litany. The same words kept coming back, like a wanderer who cannot tear his eyes away from the countryside or like a man who cannot take leave of life. She sat in one of the last pews, closing her eyes to hear the music of the words, opening them to stare up at the blue vault dotted with large gold stars. She was entranced.

What she had unexpectedly met there in the village church was not God; it was beauty. She knew perfectly well that neither the church nor the litany was beautiful in and of itself, but they were beautiful compared to the construction site, where she spent her days amid the racket of the songs. The mass was beautiful because it appeared to her in a sudden, mysterious revelation as a world betrayed.

From that time on she had known that beauty is a world betrayed. The only way we can encounter it is if its persecutors have overlooked it somewhere. Beauty hides behind the scenes of the May Day parade. If we want to find it, we must demolish the scenery.

"This is the first time I've ever been fascinated by a church," said Franz.

It was neither Protestantism nor asceticism that made him so enthusiastic; it was something else, something highly personal, something he did not dare discuss with Sabina. He thought he heard a voice telling him to seize Hercules' broom and sweep all of Marie-Claude's previews, all of Marie-Anne's singers, all lectures and symposia, all useless speeches and vain words—sweep them out of his life. The great empty space of Amsterdam's Old Church had appeared to him in a sudden and mysterious revelation as the image of his own liberation.

STRENGTH

Stroking Franz's arms in bed in one of the many hotels where they made love, Sabina said, "The muscles you have! They're unbelievable!"

Franz took pleasure in her praise. He climbed out of bed, got down on his haunches, grabbed a heavy oak chair by one leg, and lifted it slowly into the air. "You never have to be afraid," he said. "I can protect you no matter what. I used to be a judo champion."

When he raised the hand with the heavy chair above his head, Sabina said, "It's good to know you're so strong."

But deep down she said to herself, Franz may be strong, but his strength is directed outward; when it comes to the people he lives with, the people he loves, he's weak. Franz's weakness is called goodness. Franz would never give Sabina orders. He would never command her, as Tomas had, to lay the mirror on the floor and walk back and forth on it naked. Not that he lacks sensuality; he simply lacks the strength to give orders. There are things that can be accomplished only by violence. Physical love is unthinkable without violence.

Sabina watched Franz walk across the room with the chair

above his head; the scene struck her as grotesque and filled her with an odd sadness.

Franz set the chair down on the floor opposite Sabina and sat in it. "I enjoy being strong, of course," he said, "but what good do these muscles do me in Geneva? They're like an ornament, a peacock feather. I've never fought anyone in my life."

Sabina proceeded with her melancholy musings: What if she had a man who ordered her about? A man who wanted to master her? How long would she put up with him? Not five minutes! From which it follows that no man was right for her. Strong or weak.

"Why don't you ever use your strength on me?" she said.

"Because love means renouncing strength," said Franz softly.

Sabina realized two things: first, that Franz's words were noble and just; second, that they disqualified him from her love life.

LIVING IN TRUTH

Such is the formula set forth by Kafka somewhere in the diaries or letters. Franz couldn't quite remember where. But it captivated him. What does it mean to live in truth? Putting it negatively is easy enough: it means not lying, not hiding, and not dissimulating. From the time he met Sabina, however, Franz had been living in lies. He told his wife about nonexistent congresses in Amsterdam and lectures in Madrid; he was afraid to walk with Sabina through the streets of Geneva. And he enjoyed the lying and hiding: it was all so new to him. He was as excited as a teacher's pet who has plucked up the courage to play truant.

For Sabina, living in truth, lying neither to ourselves nor to others, was possible only away from the public: the moment someone keeps an eye on what we do, we involuntarily make allowances for that eye, and nothing we do is truthful. Having a public, keeping a public in mind, means living in lies. Sabina despised literature in which people give away all kinds of intimate secrets about themselves and their friends. A man who loses his privacy loses everything, Sabina thought. And a man who gives it up of his own free will is a monster. That was why Sabina did not suffer in the least from having to keep her love secret. On the contrary, only by doing so could she live in truth.

Franz, on the other hand, was certain that the division of life into private and public spheres is the source of all lies: a person is one thing in private and something quite different in public. For Franz, living in truth meant breaking down the barriers between the private and the public. He was fond of quoting André Breton on the desirability of living "in a glass house" into which everyone can look and there are no secrets.

When he heard his wife telling Sabina, "That pendant is ugly!" he knew he could no longer live in lies and had to stand up for Sabina. He had not done so only because he was afraid of betraying their secret love.

The day after the cocktail party, he was supposed to go to Rome with Sabina for the weekend. He could not get "That pendant is ugly!" out of his mind, and it made him see Marie-Claude in a completely new light. Her aggressiveness—invulnerable, noisy, and full of vitality—relieved him of the burden of goodness he had patiently borne all twenty-three years of their marriage. He recalled the enormous inner space of the Old Church in Amsterdam and felt the strange incomprehensible ecstasy that void had evoked in him.

He was packing his overnight bag when Marie-Claude came into the room, chatting about the guests at the party, energetically endorsing the views of some and laughing off the views of others.

Franz looked at her for a long time and said, "There isn't any conference in Rome."

She did not see the point. "Then why are you going?"

"I've had a mistress for nine months," he said. "I don't want to meet her in Geneva. That's why I've been traveling so much. I thought it was time you knew about it."

After the first few words he lost his nerve. He turned away so as not to see the despair on Marie-Claude's face, the despair he expected his words to produce.

After a short pause he heard her say, "Yes, I think it's time I knew about it."

Her voice was so firm that Franz turned in her direction. She did not look at all disturbed; in fact, she looked like the very same woman who had said the day before in a raucous voice, "That pendant is ugly!"

She continued: "Now that you've plucked up the courage to tell me you've been deceiving me for nine months, do you think you can tell me who she is?"

He had always told himself he had no right to hurt Marie-Claude and should respect the woman in her. But where had the woman in her gone? In other words, what had happened to the mother image he mentally linked with his wife? His mother, sad and wounded, his mother, wearing unmatched shoes, had departed from Marie-Claude—or perhaps not, perhaps she had never been inside Marie-Claude at all. The whole thing came to him in a flash of hatred.

"I have no reason to hide it from you," he said.

If he had not succeeded in wounding her with his infidelity, he was certain the revelation of her rival would do the trick. Looking her straight in the eye, he told her about Sabina.

A while later he met Sabina at the airport. As the plane gained altitude, he felt lighter and lighter. At last, he said to himself, after nine months he was living in truth.

# 8

Sabina felt as though Franz had pried open the door of their privacy. As though she were peering into the heads of Marie-Claude, of Marie-Anne, of Alain the painter, of the sculptor who held on to his finger—of all the people she knew in Geneva. Now she would willy-nilly become the rival of a woman who did not interest her in the least. Franz would ask for a divorce, and she would take Marie-Claude's place in his large conjugal bed. Everyone would follow the process from a greater or lesser distance, and she would be forced to playact before them all; instead of being Sabina, she would have to act the role of Sabina, decide how best to act the role. Once her love had been publicized, it would gain weight, become a burden. Sabina cringed at the very thought of it.

They had supper at a restaurant in Rome. She drank her wine in silence.

"You're not angry, are you?" Franz asked.

She assured him she was not. She was still confused and unsure whether to be happy or not. She recalled the time they met in the sleeping compartment of the Amsterdam express, the time she had wanted to go down on her knees before him and beg him to hold her, squeeze her, never let her go. She had longed to come to the end of the dangerous road of betrayals. She had longed to call a halt to it all.

Try as she might to intensify that longing, summon it to her aid, lean on it, the feeling of distaste only grew stronger.

They walked back to the hotel through the streets of Rome. Because the Italians around them were making a racket, shouting and gesticulating, they could walk along in silence without hearing their silence.

Sabina spent a long time washing in the bathroom; Franz

waited for her under the blanket. As always, the small lamp was lit.

When she came out, she turned it off. It was the first time she had done so. Franz should have paid better attention. He did not notice it, because light did not mean anything to him. As we know, he made love with his eyes shut.

In fact, it was his closed eyes that made Sabina turn out the light. She could not stand those lowered eyelids a moment longer. The eyes, as the saying goes, are windows to the soul. Franz's body, which thrashed about on top of hers with closed eyes, was therefore a body without a soul. It was like a newborn animal, still blind and whimpering for the dug. Muscular Franz in coitus was like a gigantic puppy suckling at her breasts. He actually had her nipple in his mouth as if he were sucking milk! The idea that he was a mature man below and a suckling infant above, that she was therefore having intercourse with a baby, bordered on the disgusting. No, she would never again see his body moving desperately over hers, would never again offer him her breast, bitch to whelp, today was the last time, irrevocably the last time!

She knew, of course, that she was being supremely unfair, that Franz was the best man she had ever had—he was intelligent, he understood her paintings, he was handsome and good—but the more she thought about it, the more she longed to ravish his intelligence, defile his kindheartedness, and violate his powerless strength.

That night, she made love to him with greater frenzy than ever before, aroused by the realization that this was the last time. Making love, she was far, far away. Once more she heard the golden horn of betrayal beckoning her in the distance, and she knew she would not hold out. She sensed an expanse of freedom before her, and the boundlessness of it excited her. She made mad, unrestrained love to Franz as she never had before.

Franz sobbed as he lay on top of her; he was certain he understood: Sabina had been quiet all through dinner and said not a word about his decision, but this was her answer. She had made a clear show of her joy, her passion, her consent, her desire to live with him forever.

He felt like a rider galloping off into a magnificent void, a void of no wife, no daughter, no household, the magnificent void swept clean by Hercules' broom, a magnificent void he would fill with his love.

Each was riding the other like a horse, and both were galloping off into the distance of their desires, drunk on the betrayals that freed them. Franz was riding Sabina and had betrayed his wife; Sabina was riding Franz and had betrayed Franz.

## 9

For twenty years he had seen his mother—a poor, weak creature who needed his protection—in his wife. This image was deeply rooted in him, and he could not rid himself of it in two days. On the way home his conscience began to bother him: he was afraid that Marie-Claude had fallen apart after he left and that he would find her terribly sick at heart. Stealthily he unlocked the door and went into his room. He stood there for a moment and listened: Yes, she was at home. After a moment's hesitation he went into her room, ready to greet her as usual.

"What?" she exclaimed, raising her eyebrows in mock surprise. "You? Here?"

"Where else can I go?" he wanted to say (genuinely surprised), but said nothing.

"Let's set the record straight, shall we? I have nothing against your moving in with her at once."

When he made his confession on the day he left for Rome, he had no precise plan of action. He expected to come home and talk it all out in a friendly atmosphere so as not to harm Marie-Claude any more than necessary. It never occurred to him that she would calmly and coolly urge him to leave.

Even though it facilitated things, he could not help feeling disappointed. He had been afraid of wounding her all his life and voluntarily stuck to a stultifying discipline of monogamy, and now, after twenty years, he suddenly learned that it had all been superfluous and he had given up scores of women because of a misunderstanding!

That afternoon, he gave his lecture, then went straight to Sabina's from the university. He had decided to ask her whether he could spend the night. He rang the doorbell, but no one answered. He went and sat at the café across the street and stared long and hard at the entrance to her building.

Evening came, and he did not know where to turn. All his life he had shared his bed with Marie-Claude. If he went home to Marie-Claude, where should he sleep? He could, of course, make up a bed on the sofa in the next room. But wouldn't that be merely an eccentric gesture? Wouldn't it look like a sign of ill will? He wanted to remain friends with her, after all! Yet getting into bed with her was out of the question. He could just hear her asking him ironically why he didn't prefer Sabina's bed. He took a room in a hotel.

The next day, he rang Sabina's doorbell morning, noon, and night.

The day after, he paid a visit to the concierge, who had no information and referred him to the owner of the flat. He phoned her and found out that Sabina had given notice two days before.

During the next few days, he returned at regular intervals,

still hoping to find her in, but one day he found the door open and three men in overalls loading the furniture and paintings into a van parked outside.

He asked them where they were taking the furniture.

They replied that they were under strict instructions not to reveal the address.

He was about to offer them a few francs for the secret address when suddenly he felt he lacked the strength to do it. His grief had broken him utterly. He understood nothing, had no idea what had happened; all he knew was that he had been waiting for it to happen ever since he met Sabina. What must be must be. Franz did not oppose it.

He found a small flat for himself in the old part of town. When he knew his wife and daughter were away, he went back to his former home to fetch his clothes and most essential books. He was careful to remove nothing that Marie-Claude might miss.

One day, he saw her through the window of a café. She was sitting with two women, and her face, long riddled with wrinkles from her unbridled gift for grimaces, was in a state of animation. The women were listening closely and laughing continually. Franz could not get over the feeling that she was telling them about him. Surely she knew that Sabina had disappeared from Geneva at the very time Franz decided to live with her. What a funny story it would make! He was not the least bit surprised at becoming a butt to his wife's friends.

When he got home to his new flat, where every hour he could hear the bells of Saint-Pierre, he found that the department store had delivered his new desk. He promptly forgot about Marie-Claude and her friends. He even forgot about Sabina for the time being. He sat down at the desk. He was glad to have picked it out himself. For twenty years he had lived among furniture not of his own choosing. Marie-Claude had taken care of everything. At last he had ceased to be a little boy;

for the first time in his life he was on his own. The next day he hired a carpenter to make a bookcase for him. He spent several days designing it and deciding where it should stand.

And at some point, he realized to his great surprise that he was not particularly unhappy. Sabina's physical presence was much less important than he had suspected. What was important was the golden footprint, the magic footprint she had left on his life and no one could ever remove. Just before disappearing from his horizon, she had slipped him Hercules' broom, and he had used it to sweep everything he despised out of his life. A sudden happiness, a feeling of bliss, the joy that came of freedom and a new life—these were the gifts she had left him.

Actually, he had always preferred the unreal to the real. Just as he felt better at demonstrations (which, as I have pointed out, are all playacting and dreams) than in a lecture hall full of students, so he was happier with Sabina the invisible goddess than the Sabina who had accompanied him throughout the world and whose love he constantly feared losing. By giving him the unexpected freedom of a man living on his own, she provided him with a halo of seductiveness. He became very attractive to women, and one of his students fell in love with him.

And so within an amazingly short period the backdrop of his life had changed completely. Until recently he had lived in a large upper-middle-class flat with a servant, a daughter, and a wife; now he lived in a tiny flat in the old part of town, where almost every night he was joined by his young student-mistress. He did not need to squire her through the world from hotel to hotel; he could make love to her in his own flat, in his own bed, with his own books and ashtray on the bedside table!

She was a modest girl and not particularly pretty, but she admired Franz in the way Franz had only recently admired Sabina. He did not find it unpleasant. And if he did perhaps feel that trading Sabina for a student with glasses was something of a comedown, his innate goodness saw to it that he cared for her and lavished on her the paternal love that had never had a true outlet before, given that Marie-Anne had always behaved less like his daughter than like a copy of Marie-Claude.

One day, he paid a visit to his wife. He told her he would like to remarry.

Marie-Claude shook her head.

"But a divorce won't make any difference to you! You won't lose a thing! I'll give you all the property!"

"I don't care about property," she said.

"Then what do you care about?"

"Love," she said with a smile.

"Love?" Franz asked in amazement.

"Love is a battle," said Marie-Claude, still smiling. "And I plan to go on fighting. To the end."

"Love is a battle?" said Franz. "Well, I don't feel at all like fighting." And he left.

## 10

After four years in Geneva, Sabina settled in Paris, but she could not escape her melancholy. If someone had asked her what had come over her, she would have been hard pressed to find words for it.

When we want to give expression to a dramatic situation in our lives, we tend to use metaphors of heaviness. We say that something has become a great burden to us. We either bear the burden or fail and go down with it, we struggle with it, win or lose. And Sabina—what *had* come over her? Nothing. She had left a man because she felt like leaving him. Had he persecuted her? Had he tried to take revenge on her? No. Her drama was a drama not of heaviness but of lightness. What fell to her lot was not the burden but the unbearable lightness of being.

Until that time, her betrayals had filled her with excitement and joy, because they opened up new paths to new adventures of betrayal. But what if the paths came to an end? One could betray one's parents, husband, country, love, but when parents, husband, country, and love were gone—what was left to betray?

Sabina felt emptiness all around her. What if that emptiness was the goal of all her betrayals?

Naturally she had not realized it until now. How could she have? The goals we pursue are always veiled. A girl who longs for marriage longs for something she knows nothing about. The boy who hankers after fame has no idea what fame is. The thing that gives our every move its meaning is always totally unknown to us. Sabina was unaware of the goal that lay behind her longing to betray. The unbearable lightness of being—was that the goal? Her departure from Geneva brought her considerably closer to it.

Three years after moving to Paris, she received a letter from Prague. It was from Tomas's son. Somehow or other he had found out about her and got hold of her address, and now he was writing to her as his father's "closest friend." He informed her of the deaths of Tomas and Tereza. For the past few years they had been living in a village, where Tomas was employed as a driver at a collective farm. From time to time they would drive over to the next town and spend the night in a cheap hotel. The road there wound through some hills, and their pickup had crashed and hurtled down a steep incline. Their bodies had been crushed to a pulp. The police determined later that the brakes were in disastrous condition.

She could not get over the news. The last link to her past had been broken.

According to her old habit, she decided to calm herself by taking a walk in a cemetery. The Montparnasse Cemetery was the closest. It was all tiny houses, miniature chapels over each grave. Sabina could not understand why the dead would want to have imitation palaces built over them. The cemetery was vanity transmogrified into stone. Instead of growing more sensible in death, the inhabitants of the cemetery were sillier than they had been in life. Their monuments were meant to display how important they were. There were no fathers, brothers, sons, or grandmothers buried there, only public figures, the bearers of titles, degrees, and honors; even the postal clerk celebrated his chosen profession, his social significance—his dignity.

Walking along a row of graves, she noticed people gathering for a burial. The funeral director had an armful of flowers and was giving one to each mourner. He handed one to Sabina as well. She joined the group. They made a detour past many monuments before they came to the grave, free for the moment of its heavy gravestone. She leaned over the hole. It was extremely deep. She dropped in the flower. It sailed down to the coffin in graceful somersaults. In Bohemia the graves were not so deep. In Paris the graves were deeper, just as the buildings were taller. Her eye fell on the stone, which lay next to the grave. It chilled her, and she hurried home.

She thought about that stone all day. Why had it horrified her so?

She answered herself: When graves are covered with stones, the dead can no longer get out.

But the dead can't get out anyway! What difference does it make whether they're covered with soil or stones?

The difference is that if a grave is covered with a stone it means we don't want the deceased to come back. The heavy stone tells the deceased, "Stay where you are!"

That made Sabina think about her father's grave. There was soil above his grave with flowers growing out of it and a maple tree reaching down to it, and the roots and flowers offered his corpse a path out of the grave. If her father had been covered with a stone, she would never have been able to communicate with him after he died, and hear his voice in the trees pardoning her.

What was it like in the cemetery where Tereza and Tomas were buried?

Once more she started thinking about them. From time to time they would drive over to the next town and spend the night in a cheap hotel. That passage in the letter had caught her eye. It meant they were happy. And again she pictured Tomas as if he were one of her paintings: Don Juan in the foreground, a specious stage-set by a naive painter, and through a crack in the set—Tristan. He died as Tristan, not as Don Juan. Sabina's parents had died in the same week. Tomas and Tereza in the same second. Suddenly she missed Franz terribly.

When she told him about her cemetery walks, he gave a shiver of disgust and called cemeteries bone and stone dumps. A gulf of misunderstanding had immediately opened between them. Not until that day at the Montparnasse Cemetery did she see what he meant. She was sorry to have been so impatient with him. Perhaps if they had stayed together longer, Sabina and Franz would have begun to understand the words they used. Gradually, timorously, their vocabularies would have come together, like bashful lovers, and the music of one would have begun to intersect with the music of the other. But it was too late now.

Yes, it was too late, and Sabina knew she would leave Paris, move on, and on again, because were she to die here they would cover her up with a stone, and in the mind of a woman for whom no place is home the thought of an end to all flight is unbearable.

## 11

All Franz's friends knew about Marie-Claude; they all knew about the girl with the oversized glasses. But no one knew about Sabina. Franz was wrong when he thought his wife had told her friends about her. Sabina was a beautiful woman, and Marie-Claude did not want people going about comparing their faces.

Because Franz was so afraid of being found out, he had never asked for any of Sabina's paintings or drawings or even a snapshot of her. As a result, she disappeared from his life without a trace. There was not a scrap of tangible evidence to show that he had spent the most wonderful year of his life with her.

Which only increased his desire to remain faithful to her.

Sometimes when they were alone in his flat together, the girl would lift her eyes from a book, throw him an inquiring glance, and say, "What are you thinking about?"

Sitting in his armchair, staring up at the ceiling, Franz always found some plausible response, but in fact he was thinking of Sabina.

Whenever he published an article in a scholarly journal, the girl was the first to read it and discuss it with him. But all he could think of was what Sabina would have said about it. Everything he did, he did for Sabina, the way Sabina would have liked to see it done.

It was a perfectly innocent form of infidelity and one eminently suited to Franz, who would never have done his bespectacled student-mistress any harm. He nourished the cult of Sabina more as religion than as love.

Indeed, according to the theology of that religion it was Sabina who had sent him the girl. Between his earthly love and his unearthly love, therefore, there was perfect peace. And if unearthly love must (for theological reasons) contain a strong dose of the inexplicable and incomprehensible (we have only to recall the dictionary of misunderstood words and the long lexicon of misunderstandings!), his earthly love rested on true understanding.

The student-mistress was much younger than Sabina, and the musical composition of her life had scarcely been outlined; she was grateful to Franz for the motifs he gave her to insert. Franz's Grand March was now her creed as well. Music was now her Dionysian intoxication. They often went dancing together. They lived in truth, and nothing they did was secret. They sought out the company of friends, colleagues, students, and strangers, and enjoyed sitting, drinking, and chatting with them. They took frequent excursions to the Alps. Franz would bend over, the girl hopped onto his back, and off he ran through the meadows, declaiming at the top of his voice a long German poem his mother had taught him as a child. The girl laughed with glee, admiring his legs, shoulders, and lungs as she clasped his neck.

The only thing she could not quite fathom was the curious sympathy he had for the countries occupied by the Russian empire. On the anniversary of the invasion, they attended a memorial meeting organized by a Czech group in Geneva.

The room was nearly empty. The speaker had artificially waved gray hair. He read out a long speech that bored even the few enthusiasts who had come to hear it. His French was grammatically correct but heavily accented. From time to time, to stress a point, he would raise his index finger, as if threatening the audience.

The girl with the glasses could barely suppress her yawns, while Franz smiled blissfully at her side. The longer he looked at the pleasing gray-haired man with the admirable index finger, the more he saw him as a secret messenger, an angelic intermediary between him and his goddess. He closed his eyes and dreamed. He closed his eyes as he had closed them on Sabina's body in fifteen European hotels and one in America.

# PART FOUR

# Soul and Body

# 1

When Tereza came home, it was almost half past one in the morning. She went into the bathroom, put on her pajamas, and lay down next to Tomas. He was asleep. She leaned over his face and, kissing it, detected a curious aroma coming from his hair. She took another whiff and yet another. She sniffed him up and down like a dog before realizing what it was: the aroma of a woman's sex organs.

At six the alarm went off. Karenin's great moment had arrived. He always woke up much earlier than they did, but did not dare to disturb them. He would wait impatiently for the alarm, because it gave him the right to jump up on their bed, trample their bodies, and butt them with his muzzle. For a time they had tried to curb him and pushed him off the bed, but he was more headstrong than they were and ended by defending his rights. Lately, Tereza realized, she positively enjoyed being welcomed into the day by Karenin. Waking up was sheer delight for him: he always showed a naive and simple amazement at the discovery that he was back on earth; he was sincerely pleased. She, on the other hand, awoke with great reluctance, with a desire to stave off the day by keeping her eyes closed.

Now he was standing in the entrance hall, gazing up at the hat stand, where his leash and collar hung ready. She slipped his head through the collar, and off they went together to do the shopping. She needed to pick up some milk, butter, and bread and, as usual, his morning roll. Later, he trotted back alongside her, roll in mouth, looking proudly from side to side, gratified by the attention he attracted from the passersby.

Once home, he would stretch out with his roll on the threshold of the bedroom and wait for Tomas to take notice of him, creep up to him, snarl at him, and make believe he was trying to snatch his roll away from him. That was how it went every day. Not until they had chased each other through the flat for at least five minutes would Karenin scramble under a table and gobble up the roll.

This time, however, he waited in vain for his morning ritual. Tomas had a small transistor radio on the table in front of him and was listening to it intently.

## 2

It was a program about the Czech emigration, a montage of private conversations recorded with the latest bugging devices by a Czech spy who had infiltrated the émigré community and then returned in great glory to Prague. It was insignificant prattle dotted with some harsh words about the occupation regime, but here and there one émigré would call another an imbecile or a fraud. These trivial remarks were the point of the broadcast. They were meant to prove not merely that émigrés had bad things to say about the Soviet Union (which neither surprised nor upset anyone in the country), but that they call one another names and make free use of dirty words. People use filthy language all day long, but when they turn on the radio and hear a well-known personality, someone they respect, saying "fuck" in every sentence, they feel somehow let down.

"It all started with Prochazka," said Tomas.

Jan Prochazka, a forty-year-old Czech novelist with the strength and vitality of an ox, began criticizing public affairs vociferously even before 1968. He then became one of the best-loved figures of the Prague Spring, that dizzying liberalization of Communism which ended with the Russian invasion. Shortly after the invasion the press initiated a smear campaign against him, but the more they smeared, the more people liked him. Then (in 1970, to be exact) the Czech radio broadcast a series of private talks between Prochazka and a professor friend of his which had taken place two years before (that is, in the spring of 1968). For a long time, neither of them had any idea that the professor's flat was bugged and their every step dogged. Prochazka loved to regale his friends with hyperbole and excess. Now his excesses had become a weekly radio series. The secret police, who produced and directed the show, took pains to emphasize the sequences in which Prochazka made fun of his friends—Dubcek, for instance. People slander their friends at the drop of a hat, but they were more shocked by the much-loved Prochazka than by the much-hated secret police.

Tomas turned off the radio and said, "Every country has its secret police. But a secret police that broadcasts its tapes over the radio—there's something that could happen only in Prague, something absolutely without precedent!"

"I know a precedent," said Tereza. "When I was fourteen, I kept a secret diary. I was terrified that someone might read it, so I kept it hidden in the attic. Mother sniffed it out. One day at dinner, while we were all hunched over our soup, she took it out of her pocket and said, 'Listen carefully now, everybody!' And after every sentence, she burst out laughing. They all laughed so hard they couldn't eat."

# 3

He always tried to get her to stay in bed and let him have breakfast alone. She never gave in. Tomas was at work from seven to four, Tereza from four to midnight. If she were to miss breakfast with him, the only time they could actually talk together was on Sundays. That was why she got up when he did and then went back to bed.

This morning, however, she was afraid of going back to sleep, because at ten she was due at the sauna on Zofin Island. The sauna, though coveted by the many, could accommodate only the few, and the only way to get in was by pull. Luckily, the cashier was the wife of a professor removed from the university after 1968 and the professor a friend of a former patient of Tomas's. Tomas told the patient, the patient told the professor, the professor told his wife, and Tereza had a ticket waiting for her once a week.

She walked there. She detested the trams constantly packed with people pushing into one another's hate-filled embraces, stepping on one another's feet, tearing off one another's coat buttons, and shouting insults.

It was drizzling. As people rushed along, they began opening umbrellas over their heads, and all at once the streets were crowded, too. Arched umbrella roofs collided with one another. The men were courteous, and when passing Tereza they held their umbrellas high over their heads and gave her room to go by. But the women would not yield; each looked straight ahead, waiting for the other woman to acknowledge her inferiority and step aside. The meeting of the umbrellas was a test of strength. At first Tereza gave way, but when she realized her courtesy was not being reciprocated, she started clutching her umbrella like the other women and ramming it forcefully against the oncoming umbrellas. No one ever said "Sorry." For the most part no one said anything, though once or twice she did hear a "Fat cow!" or "Fuck you!"

The women thus armed with umbrellas were both young and old, but the younger among them proved the more steeled warriors. Tereza recalled the days of the invasion and the girls in miniskirts carrying flags on long staffs. Theirs was a sexual vengeance: the Russian soldiers had been kept in enforced celibacy for several long years and must have felt they had landed on a planet invented by a science fiction writer, a planet of stunning women who paraded their scorn on beautiful long legs the likes of which had not been seen in Russia for the past five or six centuries.

She had taken many pictures of those young women against a backdrop of tanks. How she had admired them! And now these same women were bumping into her, meanly and spitefully. Instead of flags, they held umbrellas, but they held them with the same pride. They were ready to fight as obstinately against a foreign army as against an umbrella that refused to move out of their way.

# 4

She came out into Old Town Square—the stern spires of Tyn Church, the irregular rectangle of Gothic and baroque houses. Old Town Hall, which dated from the fourteenth century and had once stretched over a whole side of the square, was in ruins and had been so for twenty-seven years. Warsaw, Dresden, Berlin, Cologne, Budapest—all were horribly scarred in the last war. But their inhabitants had built them up again and painstakingly restored the old historical sections. The people of Prague had an inferiority complex with respect to these other cities. Old Town Hall was the only monument of note destroyed in the war, and they decided to leave it in ruins so that no Pole or German could accuse them of having suffered less than their share. In front of the glorious ruins, a reminder for now and eternity of the evils perpetrated by war, stood a steel-bar reviewing stand for some demonstration or other that the Communist Party had herded the people of Prague to the day before or would be herding them to the day after.

Gazing at the remains of Old Town Hall, Tereza was suddenly reminded of her mother: that perverse need one has to expose one's ruins, one's ugliness, to parade one's misery, to uncover the stump of one's amputated arm and force the whole world to look at it. Everything had begun reminding her of her mother lately. Her mother's world, which she had fled ten years before, seemed to be coming back to her, surrounding her on all sides. That was why she told Tomas that morning about how her mother had read her secret diary at the dinner table to an accompaniment of guffaws. When a private talk over a bottle of wine is broadcast on the radio, what can it mean but that the world is turning into a concentration camp?

Almost from childhood, Tereza had used the term to express how she felt about life with her family. A concentration camp is a world in which people live crammed together constantly, night and day. Brutality and violence are merely secondary (and not in the least indispensable) characteristics. A concentration camp is the complete obliteration of privacy. Prochazka, who was not allowed to chat with a friend over a bottle of wine in the shelter of privacy, lived (unknown to him—a fatal error on his part!) in a concentration camp. Tereza lived in the concentration camp when she lived with her mother. Almost from childhood, she knew that a concentration camp was nothing exceptional or startling but something very basic, a given into which we are born and from which we can escape only with the greatest of efforts.

## 5

The women sitting on the three terraced benches were packed in so tightly that they could not help touching. Sweating away next to Tereza was a woman of about thirty with a very pretty face. She had two unbelievably large, pendulous breasts hanging from her shoulders, bouncing at the slightest movement. When the woman got up, Tereza saw that her behind was also like two enormous sacks and that it had nothing in common with her fine face.

Perhaps the woman stood frequently in front of the mirror observing her body, trying to peer through it into her soul, as Tereza had done since childhood. Surely she, too, had harbored the blissful hope of using her body as a poster for her soul. But what a monstrous soul it would have to be if it reflected that body, that rack for four pouches.

Tereza got up and rinsed herself off under the shower. Then she went out into the open. It was still drizzling. Standing just above the Vltava on a slatted deck, and sheltered from the eyes of the city by a few square feet of tall wooden panel, she looked down to see the head of the woman she had just been thinking about. It was bobbing on the surface of the rushing river.

The woman smiled up at her. She had a delicate nose, large brown eyes, and a childish glance.

As she climbed the ladder, her tender features gave way to two sets of quivering pouches spraying tiny drops of cold water right and left.

## 6

Tereza went in to get dressed and stood in front of the large mirror.

No, there was nothing monstrous about her body. She had no pouches hanging from her shoulders; in fact, her breasts were quite small. Her mother used to ridicule her for having such small breasts, and she had had a complex about them until Tomas came along. But reconciled to their size as she was, she was still mortified by the very large, very dark circles around her nipples. Had she been able to design her own body, she would have chosen inconspicuous nipples, the kind that scarcely protrude from the arch of the breast and all but blend in color with the rest of the skin. She thought of her areolae as big crimson targets painted by a primitivist of pornography for the poor.

Looking at herself, she wondered what she would be like if her nose grew a millimeter a day. How long would it take before her face began to look like someone else's?

And if various parts of her body began to grow and shrink and Tereza no longer looked like herself, would she still be herself, would she still be Tereza?

Of course. Even if Tereza were completely unlike Tereza, her soul inside her would be the same and look on in amazement at what was happening to her body.

Then what was the relationship between Tereza and her body? Had her body the right to call itself Tereza? And if not, then what did the name refer to? Merely something incorporeal, intangible?

(These are questions that had been going through Tereza's head since she was a child. Indeed, the only truly serious questions are ones that even a child can formulate. Only the most naive of questions are truly serious. They are the questions with no answers. A question with no answer is a barrier that cannot be breached. In other words, it is questions with no answers that set the limits of human possibilities, describe the boundaries of human existence.)

Tereza stood bewitched before the mirror, staring at her body as if it were alien to her, alien and yet assigned to her and no one else. She felt disgusted by it. It lacked the power to become the only body in Tomas's life. It had disappointed and deceived her. All that night she had had to inhale the aroma of another woman's groin from his hair!

Suddenly she longed to dismiss her body as one dismisses a servant: to stay on with Tomas only as a soul and send her body into the world to behave as other female bodies behave with male bodies. If her body had failed to become the only body for

Tomas, and thereby lost her the biggest battle of her life, it could just as well go off on its own!

# 7

She went home and forced herself to eat a stand-up lunch in the kitchen. At half past three, she put Karenin on his leash and walked (walking again) to the outskirts of town where her hotel was. When they fired Tereza from her job at the magazine, she found work behind the bar of a hotel. It happened several months after she came back from Zurich: they could not forgive her, in the end, for the week she spent photographing Russian tanks. She got the job through friends, other people who had taken refuge there when thrown out of work by the Russians: a former professor of theology in the accounting office, an ambassador (who had protested against the invasion on foreign television) at the reception desk.

She was worried about her legs again. While working as a waitress in the small-town restaurant, she had been horrified at the sight of the older waitresses' varicose veins, a professional hazard that came of a life of walking, running, and standing with heavy loads. But the new job was less demanding: although she began each shift by dragging out heavy cases of beer and mineral water, all she had to do then was stand behind the bar, serve the customers their drinks, and wash out the glasses in the small sink on her side of the bar. And through it all she had Karenin lying docilely at her feet.

It was long past midnight before she had finished her accounts and delivered the cash receipts to the hotel director. She then went to say good-bye to the ambassador, who had night duty. The door behind the reception desk led to a tiny room with a narrow cot where he could take a nap. The wall above the cot was covered with framed photographs of himself and various people smiling at the camera or shaking his hand or sitting next to him at a table and signing something or other. Some of them were autographed. In the place of honor hung a picture showing, side by side with his own face, the smiling face of John F. Kennedy.

When Tereza entered the room that night, she found him talking not to Kennedy but to a man of about sixty whom she had never seen before and who fell silent as soon as he saw her.

"It's all right," said the ambassador. "She's a friend. You can speak freely in front of her." Then he turned to Tereza. "His son got five years today."

During the first days of the invasion, she learned, the man's son and some friends had stood watch over the entrance to a building housing the Russian army special staff. Since any Czechs they saw coming or going were clearly agents in the service of the Russians, he and his friends trailed them, traced the number plates of their cars, and passed on the information to the pro-Dubcek clandestine radio and television broadcasters, who then warned the public. In the process the boy and his friends had given one of the traitors a thorough going over.

The boy's father said, "This photograph was the only corpus delicti. He denied it all until they showed it to him."

He took a clipping out of his wallet. "It came out in the *Times* in the autumn of 1968."

It was a picture of a young man grabbing another man by the throat and a crowd looking on in the background. "Collaborator Punished" read the caption.

Tereza let out her breath. No, it wasn't one of hers.

Walking home with Karenin through nocturnal Prague, she thought of the days she had spent photographing tanks. How naive they had been, thinking they were risking their lives for their country when in fact they were helping the Russian police.

She got home at half past one. Tomas was asleep. His hair gave off the aroma of a woman's groin.

## 8

What is flirtation? One might say that it is behavior leading another to believe that sexual intimacy is possible, while preventing that possibility from becoming a certainty. In other words, flirting is a promise of sexual intercourse without a guarantee.

When Tereza stood behind the bar, the men whose drinks she poured flirted with her. Was she annoyed by the unending ebb and flow of flattery, double entendres, off-color stories, propositions, smiles, and glances? Not in the least. She had an irresistible desire to expose her body (that alien body she wanted to expel into the big wide world) to the undertow.

Tomas kept trying to convince her that love and lovemaking were two different things. She refused to understand. Now she was surrounded by men she did not care for in the slightest. What would making love with them be like? She yearned to try it, if only in the form of that no-guarantee promise called flirting.

Let there be no mistake: Tereza did not wish to take revenge on Tomas; she merely wished to find a way out of the maze. She knew that she had become a burden to him: she took things too seriously, turning everything into a tragedy, and failed to grasp the lightness and amusing insignificance of physical love. How she wished she could learn lightness! She yearned for someone to help her out of her anachronistic shell.

If for some women flirting is second nature, insignificant, routine, for Tereza it had developed into an important field of research with the goal of teaching her who she was and what she was capable of. But by making it important and serious, she deprived it of its lightness, and it became forced, labored, overdone. She disturbed the balance between promise and lack of guarantee (which, when maintained, is a sign of flirtistic virtuosity); she promised too ardently, and without making it clear that the promise involved no guarantee on her part. Which is another way of saying that she gave everyone the impression of being there for the taking. But when men responded by asking for what they felt they had been promised, they met with strong resistance, and their only explanation for it was that she was deceitful and malicious.

## 9

One day, a boy of about sixteen perched himself on a bar stool and dropped a few provocative phrases that stood out in the general conversation like a false line in a drawing, a line that can be neither continued nor erased.

"That's some pair of legs you've got there."

"So you can see through wood!" she fired back.

"I've watched you in the street," he responded, but by then she had turned away and was serving another customer. When she had finished, he ordered a cognac. She shook her head.

"But I'm eighteen!" he objected.

"May I see your identification card?" Tereza said.

"You may not," the boy answered.

"Then how about a soft drink?" said Tereza.

Without a word, the boy stood up from the bar stool and left. He was back about a half hour later. With exaggerated gestures, he took a seat at the bar. There was enough alcohol on his breath to cover a ten-foot radius. "Give me that soft drink," he commanded.

"Why, you're drunk!" said Tereza.

The boy pointed to a sign hanging on the wall behind Tereza's back: Sale of Alcoholic Beverages to Minors Is Strictly Prohibited. "You are prohibited from serving me alcohol," he said, sweeping his arm from the sign to Tereza, "but I am not prohibited from being drunk."

"Where did you get so drunk?" Tereza asked.

"In the bar across the street," he said, laughing, and asked again for a soft drink.

"Well, why didn't you stay there?"

"Because I wanted to look at you," he said. "I love you!"

His face contorted oddly as he said it, and Tereza had trouble deciding whether he was sneering, making advances, or joking. Or was he simply so drunk that he had no idea what he was saying?

She put the soft drink down in front of him and went back to her other customers. The "I love you!" seemed to have exhausted the boy's resources. He emptied his glass in silence, left money on the counter, and slipped out before Tereza had time to look up again.

A moment after he left, a short, bald-headed man, who was on his third vodka, said, "You ought to know that serving young people alcohol is against the law."

"I didn't serve him alcohol! That was a soft drink!"

"I saw what you slipped into it!"

"What are you talking about?"

"Give me another vodka," said the bald man, and added, "I've had my eye on you for some time now."

"Then why not be grateful for the view of a beautiful woman and keep your mouth shut?" interjected a tall man who had stepped up to the bar in time to observe the entire scene.

"You stay out of this!" shouted the bald man. "What business is it of yours?"

"And what business is it of yours, if I may ask?" the tall man retorted.

Tereza served the bald man his vodka. He downed it at one gulp, paid, and departed.

"Thank you," said Tereza to the tall man.

"Don't mention it," said the tall man, and went his way, too.

## 10

A few days later, he turned up at the bar again. When she saw him, she smiled at him like a friend. "Thanks again. That bald fellow comes in all the time. He's terribly unpleasant."

"Forget him."

"What makes him want to hurt me?"

"He's a petty little drunk. Forget him."

"If you say so."

The tall man looked in her eyes. "Promise?"

"I promise."

"I like hearing you make me promises," he said, still looking in her eyes.

The flirtation was on: the behavior leading another to believe that sexual intimacy is possible, even though the possibility itself remains in the realm of theory, in suspense.

"What's a beautiful girl like you doing in the ugliest part of Prague?"

"And you?" she countered. "What are you doing in the ugliest part of Prague?"

He told her he lived nearby. He was an engineer and had stopped off on his way home from work the other day by sheer chance.

## *11*

When Tereza looked at Tomas, her eyes went not to his eyes but to a point three or four inches higher, to his hair, which gave off the aroma of other women's groins.

"I can't take it anymore, Tomas. I know I shouldn't complain. Ever since you came back to Prague for me, I've forbidden myself to be jealous. I don't want to be jealous. I suppose I'm just not strong enough to stand up to it. Help me, please!"

He put his arm in hers and took her to the park where years before they had gone on frequent walks. The park had red, blue, and yellow benches. They sat down.

"I understand you. I know what you want," said Tomas. "I've taken care of everything. All you have to do is climb Petrin Hill."

"Petrin Hill?" She felt a surge of anxiety. "Why Petrin Hill?"

"You'll see when you get up there."

She was terribly upset about the idea of going. Her body was so weak that she could scarcely lift it off the bench. But she was constitutionally unable to disobey Tomas. She forced herself to stand.

She looked back. He was still sitting on the bench, smiling at her almost cheerfully. With a wave of the hand he signaled her to move on.

## 12

Coming out at the foot of Petrin Hill, that great green mound rising up in the middle of Prague, she was surprised to find it devoid of people. This was strange, because at other times half of Prague seemed to be milling about. It made her anxious. But the hill was so quiet and the quiet so comforting that she yielded fully to its embrace. On her way up, she paused several times to look back: below her she saw the towers and bridges; the saints were shaking their fists and lifting their stone eyes to the clouds. It was the most beautiful city in the world.

At last she reached the top. Beyond the ice-cream and souvenir stands (none of which happened to be open) stretched a broad lawn spotted here and there with trees. She noticed several men on the lawn. The closer she came to them, the slower she walked. There were six in all. They were standing or strolling along at a leisurely pace like golfers looking over the course and weighing various clubs in their hands, trying to get into the proper frame of mind for a match.

She finally came near them. Of the six men, three were there to play the same role as she: they were unsettled; they seemed eager to ask all sorts of questions, but feared making nuisances of themselves and so held their tongues and merely looked about inquisitively.

The other three radiated condescending benevolence. One of them had a rifle in his hand. Spotting Tereza, he waved at her and said with a smile, "Yes, this is the place."

She gave a nod in reply, but still felt extremely anxious.

The man added: "To avoid an error, this was *your* choice, wasn't it?"

It would have been easy to say, "No, no! It wasn't my choice at all!" but she could not imagine disappointing Tomas. What excuse, what apology could she find for going back home? And so she said, "Yes, of course. It was my choice."

The man with the rifle continued: "Let me explain why I wish to know. The only time we do this is when we are certain that the people who come to us have chosen to die of their own accord. We consider it a service."

He gave her so quizzical a glance that she had to assure him once more: "No, no, don't worry. It was my choice."

"Would you like to go first?" he asked.

Because she wanted to put off the execution as long as she could, she said, "No, please, no. If it's at all possible, I'd like to be last."

"As you please," he said, and went off to the others. Neither of his assistants was armed; their sole function was to attend to the people who were to die. They took them by the arms and walked them across the lawn. The grassy surface proved quite an expanse; it ran as far as the eye could see. The people to be executed were allowed to choose their own trees. They paused at each one and looked it over carefully, unable to make up their minds. Two of them eventually chose plane trees, but the third wandered on and on, no tree apparently striking him as worthy of his death. The assistant who held him by the arm guided him along gently and patiently until at last the man lost the courage to go on and stopped at a luxuriant maple.

Then the assistants blindfolded all three men.

And so three men, their eyes blindfolded, their heads turned to the sky, stood with their backs against three trees on the endless lawn.

The man with the rifle took aim and fired. There was nothing to be heard but the singing of birds: the rifle was equipped with a silencing device. There was nothing to be seen but the collapse of the man who had been leaning against the maple.

Without taking a step, the man with the rifle turned in a different direction, and one of the other men silently crumpled. And seconds later (again the man with the rifle merely turned in place), the third man sank to the lawn.

## 13

One of the assistants went up to Tereza; he was holding a dark-blue ribbon.

She realized he had come to blindfold her. "No," she said, shaking her head, "I want to watch."

But that was not the real reason why she refused to be blindfolded. She was not one of those heroic types who are determined to stare down the firing squad. She simply wanted to postpone death. Once her eyes were covered, she would be in death's antechamber, from which there was no return.

The man did not force her; he merely took her arm. But as they walked across the open lawn, Tereza was unable to choose a tree. No one forced her to hurry, but she knew that in the end she would not escape. Seeing a flowering chestnut ahead of her, she walked up and stopped in front of it. She leaned her back against its trunk and looked up. She saw the leaves resplendent in the sun; she heard the sounds of the city, faint and sweet, like thousands of distant violins.

The man raised his rifle.

Tereza felt her courage slipping away. Her weakness drove her to despair, but she could do nothing to counteract it. "But it wasn't my choice," she said.

He immediately lowered the barrel of his rifle and said in a gentle voice, "If it wasn't your choice, we can't do it. We haven't the right."

He said it kindly, as if apologizing to Tereza for not being able to shoot her if it was not her choice. His kindness tore at her heartstrings, and she turned her face to the bark of the tree and burst into tears.

# 14

Her whole body racked with sobs, she embraced the tree as if it were not a tree, as if it were her long-lost father, a grandfather she had never known, a great-grandfather, a great-great-grandfather, a hoary old man come to her from the depths of time to offer her his face in the form of rough tree bark.

Then she turned her head. The three men were far off in the distance by then, wandering across the greensward like golfers. The one with the rifle even held it like a golf club.

Walking down the paths of Petrin Hill, she could not wean her thoughts from the man who was supposed to shoot her but did not. Oh, how she longed for him! Someone had to help her, after all! Tomas wouldn't. Tomas was sending her to her death. Someone else would have to help her!

The closer she got to the city, the more she longed for the man with the rifle and the more she feared Tomas. He would never forgive her for failing to keep her word. He would never forgive her her cowardice, her betrayal. She had come to the street where they lived, and knew she would see him in a minute or two. She was so afraid of seeing him that her stomach was in knots and she thought she was going to be sick.

# 15

The engineer started trying to lure her up to his flat. She refused the first two invitations, but accepted the third.

After her usual stand-up lunch in the kitchen, she set off. It was just before two.

As she approached his house, she could feel her legs slowing down of their own accord.

But then it occurred to her that she was actually being sent to him by Tomas. Hadn't he told her time and again that love and sexuality had nothing in common? Well, she was merely testing his words, confirming them. She could almost hear him say, "I understand you. I know what you want. I've taken care of everything. You'll see when you get up there."

Yes, all she was doing was following Tomas's commands.

She wouldn't stay long; long enough for a cup of coffee; long enough to feel what it was like to reach the very border of infidelity. She would push her body up to the border, let it stand there for a moment as at the stake, and then, when the engineer tried to put his arms around her, she would say, as she said to the man with the rifle on Petrin Hill, "It wasn't my choice."

Whereupon the man would lower the barrel of his rifle and say in a gentle voice, "If it wasn't your choice, I can't do it. I haven't the right."

And she would turn her face to the bark of the tree and burst into tears.

# 16

The building had been constructed at the turn of the century in a workers' district of Prague. She entered a hall with dirty whitewashed walls, climbed a flight of worn stone stairs with iron banisters, and turned to the left. It was the second door, no name, no bell. She knocked.

He opened the door.

The entire flat consisted of a single room with a curtain setting off the first five or six feet from the rest and therefore forming a kind of makeshift anteroom. It had a table, a hot plate, and a refrigerator. Stepping beyond the curtain, she saw the oblong of a window at the end of a long, narrow space, with books along one side and a daybed and armchair against the other.

"It's a very simple place I have here," said the engineer. "I hope you don't find it depressing."

"No, not at all," said Tereza, looking at the wall covered with bookshelves. He had no desk, but hundreds of books. She liked seeing them, and the anxiety that had plagued her died down somewhat. From childhood, she had regarded books as the emblems of a secret brotherhood. A man with this sort of library couldn't possibly hurt her.

He asked her what she'd like to drink. Wine?

No, no, no wine. Coffee, if anything.

He disappeared behind the curtain, and she went over to the bookshelves. One of the books caught her eye at once. It was a translation of Sophocles' *Oedipus.* How odd to find it here! Years ago, Tomas had given it to her, and after she had read it he went on and on about it. Then he sent his reflections to a newspaper, and the article turned their life upside down. But now, just looking at the spine of the book seemed to calm her. It made her feel as though Tomas had purposely left a trace, a message that her presence here was his doing. She took the book off the shelf and opened it. When the tall engineer came back into the room, she would ask him why he had it, whether he had read it, and what he thought of it. That would be her ruse to turn the conversation away from the hazardous terrain of a stranger's flat to the intimate world of Tomas's thoughts.

Then she felt his hand on her shoulder. The man took the book out of her hand, put it back on the shelf without a word, and led her over to the daybed.

Again she recalled the words she had used with the Petrin executioner, and said them aloud: "But it wasn't my choice!"

She believed them to be a miraculous formula that would instantly change the situation, but in that room the words lost their magic power. I have a feeling they even strengthened the man in his resolve: he pressed her to himself and put his hand on her breast.

Oddly enough, the touch of his hand immediately erased what remained of her anxiety. For the engineer's hand referred to her body, and she realized that she (her soul) was not at all involved, only her body, her body alone. The body that had betrayed her and that she had sent out into the world among other bodies.

## 17

He undid the first button on her blouse and indicated she was to continue. She did not comply. She had sent her body out into the world, and refused to take any responsibility for it. She neither resisted nor assisted him, her soul thereby announcing that it did not condone what was happening but had decided to remain neutral.

She was nearly immobile while he undressed her. When he kissed her, her lips failed to react. But suddenly she felt her groin becoming moist, and she was afraid.

The excitement she felt was all the greater because she was excited against her will. In other words, her soul did condone the proceedings, albeit covertly. But she also knew that if the feeling of excitement was to continue, her soul's approval would have to keep mute. The moment it said its yes aloud, the moment it tried to take an active part in the love scene, the excitement would subside. For what made the soul so excited was that the body was acting against its will; the body was betraying it, and the soul was looking on.

Then he pulled off her panties and she was completely naked. When her soul saw her naked body in the arms of a stranger, it was so incredulous that it might as well have been watching the planet Mars at close range. In the light of the incredible, the soul for the first time saw the body as something other than banal; for the first time it looked on the body with fascination: all the body's matchless, inimitable, unique qualities had suddenly come to the fore. This was not the most ordinary of bodies (as the soul had regarded it until then); this was the most extraordinary body. The soul could not tear its eyes away from the body's birthmark, the round brown blemish above its hairy triangle. It looked upon that mark as its seal, a holy seal it had imprinted on the body, and now a stranger's penis was moving blasphemously close to it.

Peering into the engineer's face, she realized that she would never allow her body, on which her soul had left its mark, to take pleasure in the embrace of someone she neither knew nor wished to know. She was filled with an intoxicating hatred. She collected a gob of saliva to spit in the stranger's face. He was observing her with as much eagerness as she him, and noting her rage, he quickened the pace of his movements on her body. Tereza could feel orgasm advancing from afar, and shouted "No, no, no!" to resist it, but resisted, constrained, deprived of an outlet, the ecstasy lingered all the longer in her body, flowing through her veins like a shot of morphine. She thrashed in his arms, swung her fists in the air, and spat in his face.

## *18*

Toilets in modern water closets rise up from the floor like white water lilies. The architect does all he can to make the body forget how paltry it is, and to make man ignore what happens to his intestinal wastes after the water from the tank flushes them down the drain. Even though the sewer pipelines reach far into our houses with their tentacles, they are carefully hidden from view, and we are happily ignorant of the invisible Venice of shit underlying our bathrooms, bedrooms, dance halls, and parliaments.

The bathroom in the old working-class flat on the outskirts of Prague was less hypocritical: the floor was covered with gray tile and the toilet rising up from it was broad, squat, and pitiful. It did not look like a white water lily; it looked like what it was: the enlarged end of a sewer pipe. And since it lacked even a wooden seat, Tereza had to perch on the cold enamel rim.

She was sitting there on the toilet, and her sudden desire to void her bowels was in fact a desire to go to the extreme of humiliation, to become only and utterly a body, the body her mother used to say was good for nothing but digesting and excreting. And as she voided her bowels, Tereza was overcome by a feeling of infinite grief and loneliness. Nothing could be more miserable than her naked body perched on the enlarged end of a sewer pipe.

Her soul had lost its onlooker's curiosity, its malice and pride; it had retreated deep into the body again, to the farthest gut, waiting desperately for someone to call it out.

## 19

She stood up from the toilet, flushed it, and went into the anteroom. The soul trembled in her body, her naked, spurned body. She still felt on her anus the touch of the paper she had used to wipe herself.

And suddenly something unforgettable occurred: suddenly she felt a desire to go in to him and hear his voice, his words. If he spoke to her in a soft, deep voice, her soul would take courage and rise to the surface of her body, and she would burst out crying. She would put her arms around him the way she had put her arms around the chestnut tree's thick trunk in her dream.

Standing there in the anteroom, she tried to withstand the strong desire to burst out crying in his presence. She knew that her failure to withstand it would have ruinous consequences. She would fall in love with him.

Just then, his voice called to her from the inner room. Now

that she heard that voice by itself (divorced from the engineer's tall stature), it amazed her: it was high-pitched and thin. How could she have ignored it all this time?

Perhaps the surprise of that unpleasant voice was what saved her from temptation. She went inside, picked up her clothes from the floor, threw them on, and left.

## 20

She had done her shopping and was on her way home. Karenin had the usual roll in his mouth. It was a cold morning; there was a slight frost. They were passing a housing development, where in the spaces between buildings the tenants maintained small flower and vegetable gardens, when Karenin suddenly stood stock still and riveted his eyes on something. She looked over, but could see nothing out of the ordinary. Karenin gave a tug, and she followed along behind. Only then did she notice the black head and large beak of a crow lying on the cold dirt of a barren plot. The bodiless head bobbed slowly up and down, and the beak gave out an occasional hoarse and mournful croak.

Karenin was so excited he dropped his roll. Tereza tied him to a tree to prevent him from hurting the crow. Then she knelt down and tried to dig up the soil that had been stamped down around the bird to bury it alive. It was not easy. She broke a nail. The blood began to flow.

All at once a rock landed nearby. She turned and caught sight of two nine- or ten-year-old boys peeking out from behind a wall. She stood up. They saw her move, saw the dog by the tree, and ran off.

Once more she knelt down and scratched away at the dirt. At last she succeeded in pulling the crow out of its grave. But the crow was lame and could neither walk nor fly. She wrapped it up in the red scarf she had been wearing around her neck, and pressed it to her body with her left hand. With her right hand she untied Karenin from the tree. It took all the strength she could muster to quiet him down and make him heel.

She rang the doorbell, not having a free hand for the key. Tomas opened the door. She handed him the leash, and with the words "Hold him!" took the crow into the bathroom. She laid it on the floor under the washbasin. It flapped its wings a little, but could move no more than that. There was a thick yellow liquid oozing from it. She made a bed of old rags to protect it from the cold tiles. From time to time the bird would give a hopeless flap of its lame wing and raise its beak as a reproach.

## 21

She sat transfixed on the edge of the bath, unable to take her eyes off the dying crow. In its solitude and desolation she saw a reflection of her own fate, and she repeated several times to herself, I have no one left in the world but Tomas.

Did her adventure with the engineer teach her that casual sex has nothing to do with love? That it is light, weightless? Was she calmer now?

Not in the least.

She kept picturing the following scene: She had come out of the toilet and her body was standing in the anteroom naked and spurned. Her soul was trembling, terrified, buried in the depths of her bowels. If at that moment the man in the inner room had addressed her soul, she would have burst out crying and fallen into his arms.

She imagined what it would have been like if the woman standing in the anteroom had been one of Tomas's mistresses and if the man inside had been Tomas. All he would have had to do was say one word, a single word, and the girl would have thrown her arms around him and wept.

Tereza knew what happens during the moment love is born: the woman cannot resist the voice calling forth her terrified soul; the man cannot resist the woman whose soul thus responds to his voice. Tomas had no defense against the lure of love, and Tereza feared for him every minute of every hour.

What weapons did she have at her disposal? None but her fidelity. And she offered him that at the very outset, the very first day, as if aware she had nothing more to give. Their love was an oddly asymmetrical construction: it was supported by the absolute certainty of her fidelity like a gigantic edifice supported by a single column.

Before long, the crow stopped flapping its wings, and gave no more than the twitch of a broken, mangled leg. Tereza refused to be separated from it. She could have been keeping vigil over a dying sister. In the end, however, she did step into the kitchen for a bite to eat.

When she returned, the crow was dead.

# 22

In the first year of her love, Tereza would cry out during intercourse. Screaming, as I have pointed out, was meant to blind and deafen the senses. With time she screamed less, but her soul was still blinded by love, and saw nothing. Making love with the engineer in the absence of love was what finally restored her soul's sight.

During her next visit to the sauna, she stood before the mirror again and, looking at herself, reviewed the scene of physical love that had taken place in the engineer's flat. It was not her lover she remembered. In fact, she would have been hard put to describe him. She may not even have noticed what he looked like naked. What she did remember (and what she now observed, aroused, in the mirror) was her own body: her pubic triangle and the circular blotch located just above it. The blotch, which until then she had regarded as the most prosaic of skin blemishes, had become an obsession. She longed to see it again and again in that implausible proximity to an alien penis.

Here I must stress again: She had no desire to see another man's organs. She wished to see her own private parts in close proximity to an alien penis. She did not desire her lover's body. She desired her own body, newly discovered, intimate and alien beyond all others, incomparably exciting.

Looking at her body speckled with droplets of shower water, she imagined the engineer dropping in at the bar. Oh, how she longed for him to come, longed for him to invite her back! Oh, how she yearned for it!

# 23

Every day she feared that the engineer would make his appearance and she would be unable to say no. But the days passed, and the fear that he would come merged gradually into the dread that he would not.

A month had gone by, and still the engineer stayed away. Tereza found it inexplicable. Her frustrated desire receded and turned into a troublesome question: *Why* did he fail to come?

Waiting on customers one day, she came upon the bald-headed man who had attacked her for serving alcohol to a minor. He was telling a dirty joke in a loud voice. It was a joke she had heard a hundred times before from the drunks in the small town where she had once served beer. Once more, she had the feeling that her mother's world was intruding on her. She curtly interrupted the bald man.

"I don't take orders from you," the man responded in a huff. "You ought to thank your lucky stars we let you stay here in the bar."

"*We?* Who do you mean by *we?*"

"Us," said the man, holding up his glass for another vodka. "I won't have any more insults out of you, is that clear? Oh, and by the way," he added, pointing to Tereza's neck, which was wound round with a strand of cheap pearls, "where did you get those from? You can't tell me your husband gave them to you. A window washer! He can't afford gifts like that. It's your customers, isn't it? I wonder what you give them in exchange?"

"You shut your mouth this instant!" she hissed.

"Just remember that prostitution is a criminal offense," he went on, trying to grab hold of the necklace.

Suddenly Karenin jumped up, leaned his front paws on the bar, and began to snarl.

# 24

The ambassador said: "He's with the secret police."

"Then why is he so open about it? What good is a secret police that can't keep its secrets?"

The ambassador positioned himself on the cot by folding his legs under his body, as he had learned to do in yoga class. Kennedy, beaming down on him from the frame on the wall, gave his words a special consecration.

"The secret police have several functions, my dear," he began in an avuncular tone. "The first is the classical one. They keep an ear out for what people are saying and report it to their superiors.

"The second function is intimidatory. They want to make it seem as if they have us in their power; they want us to be afraid. That is what your bald-headed friend was after.

"The third function consists of staging situations that will compromise us. Gone are the days when they tried to accuse us of plotting the downfall of the state. That would only increase our popularity. Now they slip hashish in our pockets or claim we've raped a twelve-year-old girl. They can always dig up some girl to back them."

The engineer immediately popped back into Tereza's mind. Why had he never come?

"They need to trap people," the ambassador went on, "to force them to collaborate and set other traps for other people, so that gradually they can turn the whole nation into a single organization of informers."

Tereza could think of nothing but the possibility that the engineer had been sent by the police. And who was that strange boy who drank himself silly and told her he loved her? It was because of him that the bald police spy had launched into her and the engineer stood up for her. So all three had been playing parts in a prearranged scenario meant to soften her up for the seduction!

How could she have missed it? The flat was so odd, and he didn't belong there at all! Why would an elegantly dressed engineer live in a miserable place like that? *Was* he an engineer? And if so, how could he leave work at two in the afternoon? Besides, how many engineers read Sophocles? No, that was no engineer's library! The whole place had more the flavor of a flat confiscated from a poor imprisoned intellectual. Her father was put in prison when she was ten, and the state had confiscated their flat and all her father's books. Who knows to what use the flat had then been put?

Now she saw clearly why the engineer had never returned: he had accomplished his mission. What mission? The drunken undercover agent had inadvertently given it away when he said, "Just remember that prostitution is a criminal offense." Now that self-styled engineer would testify that she had slept with him and demanded to be paid! They would threaten to blow it up into a scandal unless she agreed to report on the people who got drunk in her bar.

"Don't worry," the ambassador comforted her. "Your story doesn't sound the least bit dangerous."

"I suppose it doesn't," she said in a tight voice, as she walked out into the Prague night with Karenin.

# 25

People usually escape from their troubles into the future; they draw an imaginary line across the path of time, a line beyond which their current troubles will cease to exist. But Tereza saw no such line in her future. Only looking back could bring her consolation. It was Sunday again. They got into the car and drove far beyond the limits of Prague.

Tomas was at the wheel, Tereza next to him, and Karenin in the back, occasionally leaning over to lick their ears. After two hours, they came to a small town known for its spa where they had been for several days six years earlier. They wanted to spend the night there.

They pulled into the square and got out of the car. Nothing had changed. They stood facing the hotel they had stayed at. The same old linden trees rose up before it. Off to the left ran an old wooden colonnade culminating in a stream spouting its medicinal water into a marble bowl. People were bending over it, the same small glasses in hand.

When Tomas looked back at the hotel, he noticed that something had in fact changed. What had once been the Grand now bore the name Baikal. He looked at the street sign on the corner of the building: Moscow Square. Then they took a walk (Karenin tagged along on his own, without a leash) through all the streets they had known, and examined all their names: Stalingrad Street, Leningrad Street, Rostov Street, Novosibirsk Street, Kiev Street, Odessa Street. There was a Tchaikovsky Sanatorium, a Tolstoy Sanatorium, a Rimsky-Korsakov Sanatorium; there was a Hotel Suvorov, a Gorky Cinema, and a Café Pushkin. All the names were taken from Russian geography, from Russian history.

Tereza suddenly recalled the first days of the invasion. People in every city and town had pulled down the street signs; sign posts had disappeared. Overnight, the country had become nameless. For seven days, Russian troops wandered the countryside, not knowing where they were. The officers searched for newspaper offices, for television and radio stations to occupy, but could not find them. Whenever they asked, they would get either a shrug of the shoulders or false names and directions.

Hindsight now made that anonymity seem quite dangerous to the country. The streets and buildings could no longer return to their original names. As a result, a Czech spa had suddenly metamorphosed into a miniature imaginary Russia, and the past that Tereza had gone there to find had turned out to be confiscated. It would be impossible for them to spend the night.

## 26

They started back to the car in silence. She was thinking about how all things and people seemed to go about in disguise. An old Czech town was covered with Russian names. Czechs taking pictures of the invasion had unconsciously worked for the secret police. The man who sent her to die had worn a mask of Tomas's face over his own. The spy played the part of an engineer, and the engineer tried to play the part of the man from Petrin. The emblem of the book in his flat proved a sham designed to lead her astray.

Recalling the book she had held in her hand there, she had

a sudden flash of insight that made her cheeks burn red. What had been the sequence of events? The engineer announced he would bring in some coffee. She walked over to the bookshelves and took down Sophocles' *Oedipus.* Then the engineer came back. But without the coffee!

Again and again she returned to that situation: How long was he away when he went for the coffee? Surely a minute at the least. Maybe two or even three. And what had he been up to for so long in that miniature anteroom? Or had he gone to the toilet? She tried to remember hearing the door shut or the water flush. No, she was positive she'd heard no water; she would have remembered that. And she was almost certain the door hadn't closed. What *had* he been up to in that anteroom?

It was only too clear. If they meant to trap her, they would need more than the engineer's testimony. They would need incontrovertible evidence. In the course of his suspiciously long absence, the engineer could only have been setting up a movie camera in the anteroom. Or, more likely, he had let in someone with a still camera, who then had photographed them from behind the curtain.

Only a few weeks earlier, she had scoffed at Prochazka for failing to see that he lived in a concentration camp, where privacy ceased to exist. But what about her? By getting out from under her mother's roof, she thought in all innocence that she had once and for all become master of her privacy. But no, her mother's roof stretched out over the whole world and would never let her be. Tereza would never escape her.

As they walked down the garden-lined steps leading back to the square, Tomas asked her, "What's wrong?"

Before she could respond, someone called out a greeting to Tomas.

# 27

He was a man of about fifty with a weather-beaten face, a farm worker whom Tomas had once operated on and who was sent to the spa once a year for treatment. He invited Tomas and Tereza to have a glass of wine with him. Since the law prohibited dogs from entering public places, Tereza took Karenin back to the car while the men found a table at a nearby café. When she came up to them, the man was saying, "We live a quiet life. Two years ago they even elected me chairman of the collective."

"Congratulations," said Tomas.

"You know how it is. People are dying to move to the city. The big shots, they're happy when somebody wants to stay put. They can't fire us from our jobs."

"It would be ideal for us," said Tereza.

"You'd be bored to tears, ma'am. There's nothing to do there. Nothing at all."

Tereza looked into the farm worker's weather-beaten face. She found him very kind. For the first time in ages, she had found someone kind! An image of life in the country arose before her eyes: a village with a belfry, fields, woods, a rabbit scampering along a furrow, a hunter with a green cap. She had never lived in the country. Her image of it came entirely from what she had heard. Or read. Or received unconsciously from distant ancestors. And yet it lived within her, as plain and clear as the daguerreotype of her great-grandmother in the family album.

"Does it give you any trouble?" Tomas asked.

The farmer pointed to the area at the back of the neck where the brain is connected to the spinal cord. "I still have pains here from time to time."

Without getting out of his seat, Tomas palpated the spot

and put his former patient through a brief examination. "I no longer have the right to prescribe drugs," he said after he had finished, "but tell the doctor taking care of you now that you talked to me and I recommended you use this." And tearing a sheet of paper from the pad in his wallet, he wrote out the name of a medicine in large letters.

## 28

They started back to Prague.

All the way Tereza brooded about the photograph showing her naked body embracing the engineer. She tried to console herself with the thought that even if the picture did exist, Tomas would never see it. The only value it had for them was as a blackmailing device. It would lose that value the moment they sent it to Tomas.

But what if the police decided somewhere along the way that they couldn't use her? Then the picture would become a mere plaything in their hands, and nothing would prevent them from slipping it in an envelope and sending it off to Tomas. Just for the fun of it.

What would happen if Tomas were to receive such a picture? Would he throw her out? Perhaps not. Probably not. But the fragile edifice of their love would certainly come tumbling down. For that edifice rested on the single column of her fidelity, and loves are like empires: when the idea they are founded on crumbles, they, too, fade away.

And now she had an image before her eyes: a rabbit scampering along a furrow, a hunter with a green cap, and the belfry of a village church rising up over the woods.

She wanted to tell Tomas that they should leave Prague. Leave the children who bury crows alive in the ground, leave the police spies, leave the young women armed with umbrellas. She wanted to tell him that they should move to the country. That it was their only path to salvation.

She turned to him. But Tomas did not respond. He kept his eyes on the road ahead. Having thus failed to scale the fence of silence between them, she lost all courage to speak. She felt as she had felt when walking down Petrin Hill. Her stomach was in knots, and she thought she was going to be sick. She was afraid of Tomas. He was too strong for her; she was too weak. He gave her commands that she could not understand; she tried to carry them out, but did not know how.

She wanted to go back to Petrin Hill and ask the man with the rifle to wind the blindfold around her eyes and let her lean against the trunk of the chestnut tree. She wanted to die.

## 29

Waking up, she realized she was at home alone.

She went outside and set off in the direction of the embankment. She wanted to see the Vltava. She wanted to stand on its banks and look long and hard into its waters, because the sight of the flow was soothing and healing. The river flowed from century to century, and human affairs play themselves out on its banks. Play themselves out to be forgotten the next day, while the river flows on.

Leaning against the balustrade, she peered into the water. She was on the outskirts of Prague, and the Vltava had already flowed through the city, leaving behind the glory of the Castle and churches; like an actress after a performance, it was tired and contemplative; it flowed on between its dirty banks, bounded by walls and fences that themselves bounded factories and abandoned playgrounds.

She was staring at the water—it seemed sadder and darker here—when suddenly she spied a strange object in the middle of the river, something red—yes, it was a bench. A wooden bench on iron legs, the kind Prague's parks abound in. It was floating down the Vltava. Followed by another. And another and another, and only then did Tereza realize that all the park benches of Prague were floating downstream, away from the city, many, many benches, more and more, drifting by like the autumn leaves that the water carries off from the woods—red, yellow, blue.

She turned and looked behind her as if to ask the passersby what it meant. Why are Prague's park benches floating downstream? But everyone passed her by, indifferent, for little did they care that a river flowed from century to century through their ephemeral city.

Again she looked down at the river. She was grief-stricken. She understood that what she saw was a farewell.

When most of the benches had vanished from sight, a few latecomers appeared: one more yellow one, and then another, blue, the last.

# PART FIVE

# Lightness and Weight

# 1

When Tereza unexpectedly came to visit Tomas in Prague, he made love to her, as I pointed out in Part One, that very day, or rather, that very hour, but suddenly thereafter she became feverish. As she lay in his bed and he stood over her, he had the irrepressible feeling that she was a child who had been put in a bulrush basket and sent downstream to him.

The image of the abandoned child had consequently become dear to him, and he often reflected on the ancient myths in which it occurred. It was apparently with this in mind that he picked up a translation of Sophocles' *Oedipus*.

The story of Oedipus is well known: Abandoned as an infant, he was taken to King Polybus, who raised him. One day, when he had grown into a youth, he came upon a dignitary riding along a mountain path. A quarrel arose, and Oedipus killed the dignitary. Later he became the husband of Queen Jocasta and ruler of Thebes. Little did he know that the man he had killed in the mountains was his father and the woman with whom he slept his mother. In the meantime, fate visited a plague on his subjects and tortured them with great pestilences. When Oedipus realized that he himself was the cause of their suffering, he put out his own eyes and wandered blind away from Thebes.

## 2

Anyone who thinks that the Communist regimes of Central Europe are exclusively the work of criminals is overlooking a basic truth: the criminal regimes were made not by criminals but by enthusiasts convinced they had discovered the only road to paradise. They defended that road so valiantly that they were forced to execute many people. Later it became clear that there was no paradise, that the enthusiasts were therefore murderers.

Then everyone took to shouting at the Communists: You're the ones responsible for our country's misfortunes (it had grown poor and desolate), for its loss of independence (it had fallen into the hands of the Russians), for its judicial murders!

And the accused responded: We didn't know! We were deceived! We were true believers! Deep in our hearts we are innocent!

In the end, the dispute narrowed down to a single question: Did they really not know or were they merely making believe?

Tomas followed the dispute closely (as did his ten million fellow Czechs) and was of the opinion that while there had definitely been Communists who were not completely unaware of the atrocities (they could not have been ignorant of the horrors that had been perpetrated and were still being perpetrated in postrevolutionary Russia), it was probable that the majority of the Communists had not in fact known of them.

But, he said to himself, whether they knew or didn't know is not the main issue; the main issue is whether a man is innocent because he didn't know. Is a fool on the throne relieved of all responsibility merely because he is a fool?

Let us concede that a Czech public prosecutor in the early fifties who called for the death of an innocent man was deceived by the Russian secret police and the government of his own country. But now that we all know the accusations to have been absurd and the executed to have been innocent, how can that selfsame public prosecutor defend his purity of heart by beating himself on the chest and proclaiming, My conscience is clear! I didn't know! I was a believer! Isn't his "I didn't know! I was a believer!" at the very root of his irreparable guilt?

It was in this connection that Tomas recalled the tale of Oedipus: Oedipus did not know he was sleeping with his own mother, yet when he realized what had happened, he did not feel innocent. Unable to stand the sight of the misfortunes he had wrought by "not knowing," he put out his eyes and wandered blind away from Thebes.

When Tomas heard Communists shouting in defense of their inner purity, he said to himself, As a result of your "not knowing," this country has lost its freedom, lost it for centuries, perhaps, and you shout that you feel no guilt? How can you stand the sight of what you've done? How is it you aren't horrified? Have you no eyes to see? If you had eyes, you would have to put them out and wander away from Thebes!

The analogy so pleased him that he often used it in conversation with friends, and his formulation grew increasingly precise and elegant.

Like all intellectuals at the time, he read a weekly newspaper published in three hundred thousand copies by the Union of Czech Writers. It was a paper that had achieved considerable autonomy within the regime and dealt with issues forbidden to others. Consequently, it was the writers' paper that raised the issue of who bore the burden of guilt for the judicial murders resulting from the political trials that marked the early years of Communist power.

Even the writers' paper merely repeated the same question: Did they know or did they not? Because Tomas found this question second-rate, he sat down one day, wrote down his reflections on Oedipus, and sent them to the weekly. A month later he received an answer: an invitation to the editorial offices. The editor who greeted him was short but as straight as a ruler. He suggested that Tomas change the word order in one of the sentences. And soon the text made its appearance—on the next to the last page, in the Letters to the Editor section.

Tomas was far from overjoyed. They had considered it necessary to ask him to the editorial offices to approve a change in word order, but then, without asking him, shortened his text by so much that it was reduced to its basic thesis (making it too schematic and aggressive). He didn't like it anymore.

All this happened in the spring of 1968. Alexander Dubcek was in power, along with those Communists who felt guilty and were willing to do something about their guilt. But the other Communists, the ones who kept shouting how innocent they were, were afraid that the enraged nation would bring them to justice. They complained daily to the Russian ambassador, trying to drum up support. When Tomas's letter appeared, they shouted: See what things have come to! Now they're telling us publicly to put our eyes out!

Two or three months later the Russians decided that free

speech was inadmissible in their *gubernia,* and in a single night they occupied Tomas's country with their army.

# 3

When Tomas came back to Prague from Zurich, he took up in his hospital where he had left off. Then one day the chief surgeon called him in.

"You know as well as I do," he said, "that you're no writer or journalist or savior of the nation. You're a doctor and a scientist. I'd be very sad to lose you, and I'll do everything I can to keep you here. But you've got to retract that article you wrote about Oedipus. Is it terribly important to you?"

"To tell you the truth," said Tomas, recalling how they had amputated a good third of the text, "it couldn't be any less important."

"You know what's at stake," said the chief surgeon.

He knew, all right. There were two things in the balance: his honor (which consisted in his refusing to retract what he had said) and what he had come to call the meaning of his life (his work in medicine and research).

The chief surgeon went on: "The pressure to make public retractions of past statements—there's something medieval about it. What does it mean, anyway, to 'retract' what you've said? How can anyone state categorically that a thought he once had is no longer valid? In modern times an idea can be *refuted,* yes, but not *retracted.* And since to retract an idea is impossible, merely verbal, formal sorcery, I see no reason why you shouldn't do as they wish. In a society run by terror, no statements whatsoever can be taken seriously. They are all forced, and it is the duty of every honest man to ignore them. Let me conclude by saying that it is in my interest and in your patients' interest that you stay on here with us."

"You're right, I'm sure," said Tomas, looking very unhappy.

"But?" The chief surgeon was trying to guess his train of thought.

"I'm afraid I'd be ashamed."

"Ashamed! You mean to say you hold your colleagues in such high esteem that you care what they think?"

"No, I don't hold them in high esteem," said Tomas.

"Oh, by the way," the chief surgeon added, "you won't have to make a public statement. I have their assurance. They're bureaucrats. All they need is a note in their files to the effect that you've nothing against the regime. Then if someone comes and attacks them for letting you work at the hospital, they're covered. They've given me their word that anything you say will remain between you and them. They have no intention of publishing a word of it."

"Give me a week to think it over," said Tomas, and there the matter rested.

## 4

Tomas was considered the best surgeon in the hospital. Rumor had it that the chief surgeon, who was getting on towards retirement age, would soon ask him to take over. When that rumor was supplemented by the rumor that the authorities had requested a statement of self-criticism from him, no one doubted he would comply.

That was the first thing that struck him: although he had never given people cause to doubt his integrity, they were ready to bet on his dishonesty rather than on his virtue.

The second thing that struck him was their reaction to the position they attributed to him. I might divide it into two basic types:

The first type of reaction came from people who themselves (they or their intimates) had retracted something, who had themselves been forced to make public peace with the occupation regime or were prepared to do so (unwillingly, of course—no one wanted to do it).

These people began to smile a curious smile at him, a smile he had never seen before: the sheepish smile of secret conspiratorial consent. It was the smile of two men meeting accidentally in a brothel: both slightly abashed, they are at the same time glad that the feeling is mutual, and a bond of something akin to brotherhood develops between them.

Their smiles were all the more complacent because he had never had the reputation of being a conformist. His supposed acceptance of the chief surgeon's proposal was therefore further proof that cowardice was slowly but surely becoming the norm of behavior and would soon cease being taken for what it actually was. He had never been friends with these people, and he realized with dismay that if he did in fact make the statement the chief surgeon had requested of him, they would start inviting him to parties and he would have to make friends with them.

The second type of reaction came from people who themselves (they or their intimates) had been persecuted, who had refused to compromise with the occupation powers or were convinced they would refuse to compromise (to sign a statement) even though no one had requested it of them (for instance, because they were too young to be seriously involved).

One of the latter, Doctor S., a talented young physician, asked Tomas one day, "Well, have you written it up for them?"

"What in the world are you talking about?" Tomas asked in return.

"Why, your retraction," he said. There was no malice in his voice. He even smiled. One more smile from that thick herbal of smiles: the smile of smug moral superiority.

"Tell me, what do you know about my retraction?" said Tomas. "Have you read it?"

"No," said S.

"Then what are you babbling about?"

Still smug, still smiling, S. replied, "Look, we know how it goes. You incorporate it into a letter to the chief surgeon or to some minister or somebody, and he promises it won't leak out and humiliate the author. Isn't that right?"

Tomas shrugged his shoulders and let S. go on.

"But even after the statement is safely filed away, the author knows that it can be made public at any moment. So from then on he doesn't open his mouth, never criticizes a thing, never makes the slightest protest. The first peep out of him and into print it goes, sullying his good name far and wide. On the whole, it's rather a nice method. One could imagine worse."

"Yes, it's a very nice method," said Tomas, "but would you mind telling me who gave you the idea I'd agreed to go along with it?"

S. shrugged his shoulders, but the smile did not disappear from his face.

And suddenly Tomas grasped a strange fact: *everyone* was smiling at him, *everyone* wanted him to write the retraction; it would make *everyone* happy! The people with the first type of reaction would be happy because by inflating cowardice, he would make their actions seem commonplace and thereby give them back their lost honor. The people with the second type of reaction, who had come to consider their honor a special privilege never to be yielded, nurtured a secret love for the cowards, for without them their courage would soon erode into a trivial, monotonous grind admired by no one.

Tomas could not bear the smiles. He thought he saw them everywhere, even on the faces of strangers in the street. He began losing sleep. Could it be? Did he really hold those people in such high esteem? No. He had nothing good to say about them and was angry with himself for letting their glances upset him so. It was completely illogical. How could someone who had so little respect for people be so dependent on what they thought of him?

Perhaps his deep-seated mistrust of people (his doubts as to their right to decide his destiny and to judge him) had played its part in his choice of profession, a profession that excluded him from public display. A man who chooses to be a politician, say, voluntarily makes the public his judge, with the naive assurance that he will gain its favor. And if the crowd does express its disapproval, it merely goads him on to bigger and better things, much in the way Tomas was spurred on by the difficulty of a diagnosis.

A doctor (unlike a politician or an actor) is judged only by his patients and immediate colleagues, that is, behind closed doors, man to man. Confronted by the looks of those who judge him, he can respond at once with his own look, to explain or defend himself. Now (for the first time in his life) Tomas found himself in a situation where the looks fixed on him were so numerous that he was unable to register them. He could answer them neither with his own look nor with words. He was at everyone's mercy. People talked about him inside and outside the hospital (it was a time when news about who betrayed, who denounced, and who collaborated spread through nervous Prague with the uncanny speed of a bush telegraph); although he knew about it, he could do nothing to stop it. He was surprised at how unbearable he found it, how panic-stricken it made him feel. The interest they showed in him was as unpleasant as an elbowing crowd or the pawings of the people who tear our clothes off in nightmares.

He went to the chief surgeon and told him he would not write a word.

The chief surgeon shook his hand with greater energy than usual and said that he had anticipated Tomas's decision.

"Perhaps you can find a way to keep me on even without a statement," said Tomas, trying to hint that a threat by all his colleagues to resign upon his dismissal would suffice.

But his colleagues never dreamed of threatening to resign, and so before long (the chief surgeon shook his hand even more energetically than the previous time—it was black and blue for days), he was forced to leave the hospital.

## 5

First he went to work in a country clinic about fifty miles from Prague. He commuted daily by train and came home exhausted. A year later, he managed to find a more advantageous but much inferior position at a clinic on the outskirts of Prague. There, he could no longer practice surgery, and became a general practitioner. The waiting room was jammed, and he had scarcely five minutes for each patient; he told them how much aspirin to take, signed their sick-leave documents, and referred them to specialists. He considered himself more civil servant than doctor.

One day, at the end of office hours, he was visited by a man of about fifty whose portliness added to his dignity. He introduced himself as representing the Ministry of the Interior, and invited Tomas to join him for a drink across the street.

He ordered a bottle of wine. "I have to drive home," said Tomas by way of refusal. "I'll lose my license if they find I've been drinking." The man from the Ministry of the Interior smiled. "If anything happens, just show them this." And he handed Tomas a card engraved with his name (though clearly not his real name) and the telephone number of the Ministry.

He then went into a long speech about how much he admired Tomas and how the whole Ministry was distressed at the thought of so respected a surgeon dispensing aspirin at an outlying clinic. He gave Tomas to understand that although he couldn't come out and say it, the police did not agree with drastic tactics like removing specialists from their posts.

Since no one had thought to praise Tomas in quite some time, he listened to the plump official very carefully, and he was surprised by the precision and detail of the man's knowledge of his professional career. How defenseless we are in the face of flattery! Tomas was unable to prevent himself from taking seriously what the Ministry official said.

But it was not out of mere vanity. More important was Tomas's lack of experience. When you sit face to face with someone who is pleasant, respectful, and polite, you have a hard time reminding yourself that *nothing* he says is true, that *nothing* is sincere. Maintaining nonbelief (constantly, systematically, without the slightest vacillation) requires a tremendous effort and the proper training—in other words, frequent police interrogations. Tomas lacked that training.

The man from the Ministry went on: "We know you had an excellent position in Zurich, and we very much appreciate your having returned. It was a noble deed. You realized your place was here." And then he added, as if scolding Tomas for something, "But your place is at the operating table, too!"

"I couldn't agree more," said Tomas.

There was a short pause, after which the man from the Ministry said in mournful tones, "Then tell me, Doctor, do you really think that Communists should put out their eyes? You, who have given so many people the gift of health?"

"But that's preposterous!" Tomas cried in self-defense. "Why don't you read what I wrote?"

"I have read it," said the man from the Ministry in a voice that was meant to sound very sad.

"Well, did I write that Communists ought to put out their eyes?"

"That's how everyone understood it," said the man from the Ministry, his voice growing sadder and sadder.

"If you'd read the complete version, the way I wrote it originally, you wouldn't have read that into it. The published version was slightly cut."

"What was that?" asked the man from the Ministry, pricking up his ears. "You mean they didn't publish it the way you wrote it?"

"They cut it."

"A lot?"

"By about a third."

The man from the Ministry appeared sincerely shocked. "That was very improper of them."

Tomas shrugged his shoulders.

"You should have protested! Demanded they set the record straight immediately!"

"The Russians came before I had time to think about it. We all had other things to think about then."

"But you don't want people to think that you, a doctor, wanted to deprive human beings of their right to see!"

"Try to understand, will you? It was a letter to the editor, buried in the back pages. No one even noticed it. No one but the Russian embassy staff, because it's what they look for."

"Don't say that! Don't think that! I myself have talked to many people who read your article and were amazed you could have written it. But now that you tell me it didn't come out the way you wrote it, a lot of things fall into place. Did they put you up to it?"

"To writing it? No. I submitted it on my own."

"Do you know the people there?"

"What people?"

"The people who published your article."

"No."

"You mean you never spoke to them?"

"They asked me to come in once in person."

"Why?"

"About the article."

"And who was it you talked to?"

"One of the editors."

"What was his name?"

Not until that point did Tomas realize that he was under interrogation. All at once he saw that his every word could put someone in danger. Although he obviously knew the name of the editor in question, he denied it: "I'm not sure."

"Now, now," said the man in a voice dripping with indignation over Tomas's insincerity, "you can't tell me he didn't introduce himself!"

It is a tragicomic fact that our proper upbringing has become an ally of the secret police. We do not know how to lie. The "Tell the truth!" imperative drummed into us by our ma-

mas and papas functions so automatically that we feel ashamed of lying even to a secret policeman during an interrogation. It is simpler for us to argue with him or insult him (which makes no sense whatever) than to lie to his face (which is the only thing to do).

When the man from the Ministry accused him of insincerity, Tomas nearly felt guilty; he had to surmount a moral barrier to be able to persevere in his lie: "I suppose he did introduce himself," he said, "but because his name didn't ring a bell, I immediately forgot it."

"What did he look like?"

The editor who had dealt with him was a short man with a light brown crew cut. Tomas tried to choose diametrically opposed characteristics: "He was tall," he said, "and had long black hair."

"Aha," said the man from the Ministry, "and a big chin!"

"That's right," said Tomas.

"A little stooped."

"That's right," said Tomas again, realizing that now the man from the Ministry had pinpointed an individual. Not only had Tomas informed on some poor editor but, more important, the information he had given was false.

"And what did he want to see you about? What did you talk about?"

"It had something to do with word order."

It sounded like a ridiculous attempt at evasion. And again the man from the Ministry waxed indignant at Tomas's refusal to tell the truth: "First you tell me they cut your text by a third, then you tell me they talked to you about word order! Is that logical?"

This time Tomas had no trouble responding, because he had told the absolute truth. "It's not logical, but that's how it was." He laughed. "They asked me to let them change the word order in one sentence and then cut a third of what I had written."

The man from the Ministry shook his head, as if unable to grasp so immoral an act. "That was highly irregular on their part."

He finished his wine and concluded: "You have been manipulated, Doctor, used. It would be a pity for you and your patients to suffer as a result. We are very much aware of your positive qualities. We'll see what can be done."

He gave Tomas his hand and pumped it cordially. Then each went off to his own car.

## 6

After the talk with the man from the Ministry, Tomas fell into a deep depression. How could he have gone along with the jovial tone of the conversation? If he hadn't refused to have anything at all to do with the man (he was not prepared for what happened and did not know what was condoned by law and what was not), he could at least have refused to drink wine with him as if they were friends! Supposing someone had seen him, someone who knew the man. He could only have inferred that Tomas was working with the police! And why did he even tell him that the article had been cut? Why did he throw in that piece of information? He was extremely displeased with himself.

Two weeks later, the man from the Ministry paid him another visit. Once more he invited him out for a drink, but this time Tomas requested that they stay in his office.

"I understand perfectly, Doctor," said the man, with a smile.

Tomas was intrigued by his words. He said them like a chess player who is letting his opponent know he made an error in the previous move.

They sat opposite each other, Tomas at his desk. After about ten minutes, during which they talked about the flu epidemic raging at the time, the man said, "We've given your case a lot of thought. If we were the only ones involved, there would be nothing to it. But we have public opinion to take into account. Whether you meant to or not, you fanned the flames of anti-Communist hysteria with your article. I must tell you there was even a proposal to take you to court for that article. There's a law against public incitement to violence."

The man from the Ministry of the Interior paused to look Tomas in the eye. Tomas shrugged his shoulders. The man assumed his comforting tone again. "We voted down the proposal. No matter what your responsibility in the affair, society has an interest in seeing you use your abilities to the utmost. The chief surgeon of your hospital speaks very highly of you. We have reports from your patients as well. You are a fine specialist. Nobody requires a doctor to understand politics. You let yourself be carried away. It's high time we settled this thing once and for all. That's why we've put together a sample statement for you. All you have to do is make it available to the press, and we'll make sure it comes out at the proper time." He handed Tomas a piece of paper.

Tomas read what was in it and panicked. It was much worse than what the chief surgeon had asked him to sign two years before. It did not stop at a retraction of the Oedipus article. It contained words of love for the Soviet Union, vows of fidelity to the Communist Party; it condemned the intelligentsia, which wanted to push the country into civil war; and, above all, it denounced the editors of the writers' weekly (with special emphasis on the tall, stooped editor; Tomas had never met him, though he knew his name and had seen pictures of him), who had consciously distorted his article and used it for their own devices, turning it into a call for counterrevolution: too cowardly to write such an article themselves, they had hid behind a naive doctor.

The man from the Ministry saw the panic in Tomas's eyes. He leaned over and gave his knee a friendly pat under the table. "Remember now, Doctor, it's only a sample! Think it over, and if there's something you want to change, I'm sure we can come to an agreement. After all, it's *your* statement!"

Tomas held the paper out to the secret policeman as if he were afraid to keep it in his hands another second, as if he were worried someone would find his fingerprints on it.

But instead of taking the paper, the man from the Ministry spread his arms in feigned amazement (the same gesture the Pope uses to bless the crowds from his balcony). "Now why do a thing like that, Doctor? Keep it. Think it over calmly at home."

Tomas shook his head and patiently held the paper in his outstretched hand. In the end, the man from the Ministry was forced to abandon his papal gesture and take the paper back.

Tomas was on the point of telling him emphatically that he would neither write nor sign any text whatever, but at the last moment he changed his tone and said mildly, "I'm no illiterate, am I? Why should I sign something I didn't write myself?"

"Very well, then, Doctor. Let's do it your way. You write it up yourself, and we'll go over it together. You can use what you've just read as a model."

Why didn't Tomas give the secret policeman an immediate and unconditional no?

This is what probably went through his head: Besides using

a statement like that to demoralize the nation in general (which is clearly the Russian strategy), the police could have a concrete goal in his case: they might be gathering evidence for a trial against the editors of the weekly that had published Tomas's article. If that was so, they would need his statement for the hearing and for the smear campaign the press would conduct against them. Were he to refuse flatly, on principle, there was always the danger that the police would print the prepared statement over his signature, whether he gave his consent or not. No newspaper would dare publish his denial. No one in the world would believe that he hadn't written or signed it. People derived too much pleasure from seeing their fellow man morally humiliated to spoil that pleasure by hearing out an explanation.

By giving the police the hope that he would write a text of his own, he gained a bit of time. The very next day he resigned from the clinic, assuming (correctly) that after he had descended voluntarily to the lowest rung of the social ladder (a descent being made by thousands of intellectuals in other fields at the time), the police would have no more hold over him and he would cease to interest them. Once he had reached the lowest rung on the ladder, they would no longer be able to publish a statement in his name, for the simple reason that no one would accept it as genuine. Humiliating public statements are associated exclusively with the signatories' rise, not fall.

But in Tomas's country, doctors are state employees, and the state may or may not release them from its service. The official with whom Tomas negotiated his resignation knew him by name and reputation and tried to talk him into staying on. Tomas suddenly realized that he was not at all sure he had made the proper choice, but he felt bound to it by then by an unspoken vow of fidelity, so he stood fast. And that is how he became a window washer.

# 7

Leaving Zurich for Prague a few years earlier, Tomas had quietly said to himself, *"Es muss sein!"* He was thinking of his love for Tereza. No sooner had he crossed the border, however, than he began to doubt whether it actually did have to be. Later, lying next to Tereza, he recalled that he had been led to her by a chain of laughable coincidences that took place seven years earlier (when the chief surgeon's sciatica was in its early stages) and were about to return him to a cage from which he would be unable to escape.

Does that mean his life lacked any *"Es muss sein!,"* any overriding necessity? In my opinion, it did have one. But it was not love, it was his profession. He had come to medicine not by coincidence or calculation but by a deep inner desire.

Insofar as it is possible to divide people into categories, the surest criterion is the deep-seated desires that orient them to one or another lifelong activity. Every Frenchman is different. But all actors the world over are similar—in Paris, Prague, or the back of beyond. An actor is someone who in early childhood consents to exhibit himself for the rest of his life to an anonymous public. Without that basic consent, which has nothing to do with talent, which goes deeper than talent, no one can become an actor. Similarly, a doctor is someone who consents to spend his life involved with human bodies and all that they entail. That basic consent (and not talent or skill) enables him to enter the dissecting room during the first year of medical school and persevere for the requisite number of years.

Surgery takes the basic imperative of the medical profession to its outermost border, where the human makes contact with the divine. When a person is clubbed violently on the head, he collapses and stops breathing. Some day, he will stop breathing anyway. Murder simply hastens a bit what God will eventually see to on His own. God, it may be assumed, took murder into account; He did not take surgery into account. He never suspected that someone would dare to stick his hand into the mechanism He had invented, wrapped carefully in skin, and sealed away from human eyes. When Tomas first positioned his scalpel on the skin of a man asleep under an anesthetic, then breached the skin with a decisive incision, and finally cut it open with a precise and even stroke (as if it were a piece of fabric—a coat, a skirt, a curtain), he experienced a brief but intense feeling of blasphemy. Then again, that was what attracted him to it! That was the *"Es muss sein!"* rooted deep inside him, and it was planted there not by chance, not by the chief's sciatica, or by anything external.

But how could he take something so much a part of him and cast it off so fast, so forcefully, and so lightly?

He would respond that he did it so as not to let the police misuse him. But to be quite frank, even if it was theoretically possible (and even if a number of cases have actually occurred), it was not too likely that the police would make public a false statement over his signature.

Granted, a man has a right to fear dangers that are less than likely to occur. Granted, he was annoyed with himself and at his clumsiness, and desired to avoid further contact with the police and the concomitant feeling of helplessness. And granted, he had lost his profession anyway, because the mechanical aspirin-medicine he practiced at the clinic had nothing in common with his concept of medicine. Even so, the way he rushed into his decision seems rather odd to me. Could it perhaps conceal something else, something deeper that escaped his reasoning?

# 8

Even though he came to love Beethoven through Tereza, Tomas was not particularly knowledgeable about music, and I doubt that he knew the true story behind Beethoven's famous "*Muss es sein? Es muss sein!*" motif.

This is how it goes: A certain Dembscher owed Beethoven fifty florins, and when the composer, who was chronically short of funds, reminded him of the debt, Dembscher heaved a mournful sigh and said, "*Muss es sein?*" To which Beethoven replied, with a hearty laugh, "*Es muss sein!*" and immediately jotted down these words and their melody. On this realistic motif he then composed a canon for four voices: three voices sing "*Es muss sein, es muss sein, ja, ja, ja, ja!*" (It must be, it must be, yes, yes, yes, yes!), and the fourth voice chimes in with "*Heraus mit dem Beutel!*" (Out with the purse!).

A year later, the same motif showed up as the basis for the fourth movement of the last quartet, Opus 135. By that time, Beethoven had forgotten about Dembscher's purse. The words "*Es muss sein!*" had acquired a much more solemn ring; they seemed to issue directly from the lips of Fate. In Kant's language, even "Good morning," suitably pronounced, can take the shape of a metaphysical thesis. German is a language of *heavy* words. "*Es muss sein!*" was no longer a joke; it had become "*der schwer gefasste Entschluss*" (the difficult or weighty resolution).

So Beethoven turned a frivolous inspiration into a serious quartet, a joke into metaphysical truth. It is an interesting tale of light going to heavy or, as Parmenides would have it, positive going to negative. Yet oddly enough, the transformation fails to surprise us. We would have been shocked, on the other hand, if Beethoven had transformed the seriousness of his quartet into the trifling joke of a four-voice canon about Dembscher's purse. Had he done so, however, he would have been in the spirit of Parmenides and made heavy go to light, that is, negative to positive! First (as an unfinished sketch) would have come the great metaphysical truth and last (as a finished masterpiece)—the most frivolous of jokes! But we no longer know how to think as Parmenides thought.

It is my feeling that Tomas had long been secretly irritated by the stern, aggressive, solemn "*Es muss sein!*" and that he harbored a deep desire to follow the spirit of Parmenides and make heavy go to light. Remember that at one point in his life he broke completely with his first wife and his son and that he was relieved when both his parents broke with him. What could be at the bottom of it all but a rash and not quite rational move to reject what proclaimed itself to be his weighty duty, his "*Es muss sein!*"?

That, of course, was an external "*Es muss sein!*" reserved for him by social convention, whereas the "*Es muss sein!*" of his love for medicine was internal. So much the worse for him. Internal imperatives are all the more powerful and therefore all the more of an inducement to revolt.

Being a surgeon means slitting open the surface of things and looking at what lies hidden inside. Perhaps Tomas was led to surgery by a desire to know what lies hidden on the other side of "*Es muss sein!*"; in other words, what remains of life when a person rejects what he previously considered his mission.

The day he reported to the good-natured woman responsible for the cleanliness of all shop windows and display cases in Prague, and was confronted with the result of his decision in all its concrete and inescapable reality, he went into a state of shock, a state that kept him in its thrall during the first few days of his new job. But once he got over the astounding strangeness of his new life (it took him about a week), he suddenly realized he was simply on a long holiday.

Here he was, doing things he didn't care a damn about, and enjoying it. Now he understood what made people (people he always pitied) happy when they took a job without feeling the compulsion of an internal "*Es muss sein!*" and forgot it the moment they left for home every evening. This was the first time he had felt that blissful indifference. Whenever anything went wrong on the operating table, he would be despondent and unable to sleep. He would even lose his taste for women. The "*Es muss sein!*" of his profession had been like a vampire sucking his blood.

Now he roamed the streets of Prague with brush and pole, feeling ten years younger. The salesgirls all called him "doctor" (the Prague bush telegraph was working better than ever) and asked his advice about their colds, aching backs, and irregular periods. They seemed almost embarrassed to watch him douse the glass with water, fit the brush on the end of the pole, and start washing. If they could have left their customers alone in the shops, they would surely have grabbed the pole from his hands and washed the windows for him.

Most of Tomas's orders came from large shops, but his boss sent him out to private customers, too. People were still reacting to the mass persecution of Czech intellectuals with the euphoria of solidarity, and when his former patients found out that Tomas was washing windows for a living, they would phone in and order him by name. Then they would greet him with a bottle of champagne or slivovitz, sign for thirteen windows on the order slip, and chat with him for two hours, drinking his health all the while. Tomas would move on to his next flat or shop in a capital mood. While the families of Russian officers settled in throughout the land and radios intoned ominous reports of police functionaries who had replaced cashiered broadcasters, Tomas reeled through the streets of Prague from one glass of wine to the next like someone going from party to party. It was his grand holiday.

He had reverted to his bachelor existence. Tereza was suddenly out of his life. The only times he saw her were when she came back from the bar late at night and he woke befuddled from a half-sleep, and in the morning, when she was the befuddled one and he was hurrying off to work. Each workday, he had sixteen hours to himself, an unexpected field of freedom. And from Tomas's early youth that had meant women.

## 9

When his friends asked him how many women he had had in his life, he would try to evade the question, and when they pressed him further he would say, "Well, two hundred, give or take a few." The envious among them accused him of stretching the truth. "That's not so many," he said by way of self-defense. "I've been involved with women for about twenty-five years now. Divide two hundred by twenty-five and you'll see it comes to only eight or so new women a year. That's not so many, is it?"

But setting up house with Tereza cramped his style. Because of the organizational difficulties it entailed, he had been forced to relegate his erotic activities to a narrow strip of time (between the operating room and home) which, though he had used it intensively (as a mountain farmer tills his narrow plot for all it is worth), was nothing like the sixteen hours that now had suddenly been bestowed on him. (I say sixteen hours because the eight hours he spent washing windows were filled with new salesgirls, housewives, and female functionaries, each of whom represented a potential erotic engagement.)

What did he look for in them? What attracted him to them? Isn't making love merely an eternal repetition of the same?

Not at all. There is always the small part that is unimaginable. When he saw a woman in her clothes, he could naturally imagine more or less what she would look like naked (his experience as a doctor supplementing his experience as a lover), but between the approximation of the idea and the precision of reality there was a small gap of the unimaginable, and it was this hiatus that gave him no rest. And then, the pursuit of the unimaginable does not stop with the revelations of nudity; it goes much further: How would she behave while undressing? What would she say when he made love to her? How would her sighs sound? How would her face distort at the moment of orgasm?

What is unique about the "I" hides itself exactly in what is unimaginable about a person. All we are able to imagine is what makes everyone like everyone else, what people have in common. The individual "I" is what differs from the common stock, that is, what cannot be guessed at or calculated, what must be unveiled, uncovered, conquered.

Tomas, who had spent the last ten years of his medical practice working exclusively with the human brain, knew that there was nothing more difficult to capture than the human "I." There are many more resemblances between Hitler and Einstein or Brezhnev and Solzhenitsyn than there are differences. Using numbers, we might say that there is one-millionth part dissimilarity to nine hundred ninety-nine thousand nine hundred ninety-nine millionths parts similarity.

Tomas was obsessed by the desire to discover and appropriate that one-millionth part; he saw it as the core of his obsession. He was not obsessed with women; he was obsessed with what in each of them is unimaginable, obsessed, in other words, with the one-millionth part that makes a woman dissimilar to others of her sex.

(Here too, perhaps, his passion for surgery and his passion for women came together. Even with his mistresses, he could never quite put down the imaginary scalpel. Since he longed to take possession of something deep inside them, he needed to slit them open.)

We may ask, of course, why he sought that millionth part dissimilarity in sex and nowhere else. Why couldn't he find it, say, in a woman's gait or culinary caprices or artistic taste?

To be sure, the millionth part dissimilarity is present in all areas of human existence, but in all areas other than sex it is exposed and needs no one to discover it, needs no scalpel. One woman prefers cheese at the end of the meal, another loathes cauliflower, and although each may demonstrate her originality thereby, it is an originality that demonstrates its own irrelevance and warns us to pay it no heed, to expect nothing of value to come of it.

Only in sexuality does the millionth part dissimilarity become precious, because, not accessible in public, it must be conquered. As recently as fifty years ago, this form of conquest took considerable time (weeks, even months!), and the worth of the conquered object was proportional to the time the conquest took. Even today, when conquest time has been drastically cut, sexuality seems still to be a strongbox hiding the mystery of a woman's "I."

So it was a desire not for pleasure (the pleasure came as an extra, a bonus) but for possession of the world (slitting open the outstretched body of the world with his scalpel) that sent him in pursuit of women.

# 10

Men who pursue a multitude of women fit neatly into two categories. Some seek their own subjective and unchanging dream of a woman in all women. Others are prompted by a desire to possess the endless variety of the objective female world.

The obsession of the former is *lyrical:* what they seek in women is themselves, their ideal, and since an ideal is by definition something that can never be found, they are disappointed again and again. The disappointment that propels them from woman to woman gives their inconstancy a kind of romantic excuse, so that many sentimental women are touched by their unbridled philandering.

The obsession of the latter is *epic,* and women see nothing the least bit touching in it: the man projects no subjective ideal on women, and since everything interests him, nothing can disappoint him. This inability to be disappointed has something scandalous about it. The obsession of the epic womanizer strikes people as lacking in redemption (redemption by disappointment).

Because the lyrical womanizer always runs after the same type of woman, we even fail to notice when he exchanges one mistress for another. His friends perpetually cause misunderstandings by mixing up his lovers and calling them by the same name.

In pursuit of knowledge, epic womanizers (and of course Tomas belonged in their ranks) turn away from conventional feminine beauty, of which they quickly tire, and inevitably end up as curiosity collectors. They are aware of this and a little ashamed of it, and to avoid causing their friends embarrassment, they refrain from appearing in public with their mistresses.

Tomas had been a window washer for nearly two years

when he was sent to a new customer whose bizarre appearance struck him the moment he saw her. Though bizarre, it was also discreet, understated, within the bounds of the agreeably ordinary (Tomas's fascination with curiosities had nothing in common with Fellini's fascination with monsters): she was very tall, quite a bit taller than he was, and she had a delicate and very long nose in a face so unusual that it was impossible to call it attractive (everyone would have protested!), yet (in Tomas's eyes, at least) it could not be called unattractive. She was wearing slacks and a white blouse, and looked like an odd combination of giraffe, stork, and sensitive young boy.

She fixed him with a long, careful, searching stare that was not devoid of irony's intelligent sparkle. "Come in, Doctor," she said.

Although he realized that she knew who he was, he did not want to show it, and asked, "Where can I get some water?"

She opened the door to the bathroom. He saw a washbasin, bathtub, and toilet bowl; in front of bath, basin, and bowl lay miniature pink rugs.

When the woman who looked like a giraffe and a stork smiled, her eyes screwed up, and everything she said seemed full of irony or secret messages.

"The bathroom is all yours," she said. "You can do whatever your heart desires in it."

"May I have a bath?" Tomas asked.

"Do you like baths?" she asked.

He filled his pail with warm water and went into the living room. "Where would you like me to start?"

"It's up to you," she said with a shrug of the shoulders.

"May I see the windows in the other rooms?"

"So you want to have a look around?" Her smile seemed to indicate that window washing was only a caprice that did not interest her.

He went into the adjoining room. It was a bedroom with one large window, two beds pushed next to each other, and, on the wall, an autumn landscape with birches and a setting sun.

When he came back, he found an open bottle of wine and two glasses on the table. "How about a little something to keep your strength up during the big job ahead?"

"I wouldn't mind a little something, actually," said Tomas, and sat down at the table.

"You must find it interesting, seeing how people live," she said.

"I can't complain," said Tomas.

"All those wives at home alone, waiting for you."

"You mean grandmothers and mothers-in-law."

"Don't you ever miss your original profession?"

"Tell me, how did you find out about my original profession?"

"Your boss likes to boast about you," said the stork-woman.

"After all this time!" said Tomas in amazement.

"When I spoke to her on the phone about having the windows washed, she asked whether I didn't want you. She said you were a famous surgeon who'd been kicked out of the hospital. Well, naturally she piqued my curiosity."

"You have a fine sense of curiosity," he said.

"Is it so obvious?"

"Yes, in the way you use your eyes."

"And how do I use my eyes?"

"You squint. And then, the questions you ask."

"You mean you don't like to respond?"

Thanks to her, the conversation had been delightfully flirtatious from the outset. Nothing she said had any bearing on the outside world; it was all directed inward, towards themselves. And because it dealt so palpably with him and her, there was nothing simpler than to complement words with touch. Thus, when Tomas mentioned her squinting eyes, he stroked them, and she did the same to his. It was not a spontaneous reaction; she seemed to be consciously setting up a "do as I do" kind of game. And so they sat there face to face, their hands moving in stages along each other's bodies.

Not until Tomas reached her groin did she start resisting. He could not quite guess how seriously she meant it. Since much time had now passed and he was due at his next customer's in ten minutes, he stood up and told her he had to go.

Her face was red. "I have to sign the order slip," she said.

"But I haven't done a thing," he objected.

"That's my fault." And then in a soft, innocent voice she drawled, "I suppose I'll just have to order you back and have you finish what I kept you from starting."

When Tomas refused to hand her the slip to sign, she said to him sweetly, as if asking him for a favor, "Give it to me. Please?" Then she squinted again and added, "After all, I'm not paying for it, my husband is. And you're not being paid for it, the state is. The transaction has nothing whatever to do with the two of us."

## 11

The odd asymmetry of the woman who looked like a giraffe and a stork continued to excite his memory: the combination of the flirtatious and the gawky; the very real sexual desire offset by the ironic smile; the vulgar conventionality of the flat and the originality of its owner. What would she be like when they made love? Try as he might, he could not picture it. He thought of nothing else for several days.

The next time he answered her summons, the wine and two glasses stood waiting on the table. And this time everything went like clockwork. Before long, they were standing face to face in the bedroom (where the sun was setting on the birches in the painting) and kissing. But when he gave her his standard "Strip!" command, she not only failed to comply but countercommanded, "No, you first!"

Unaccustomed to such a response, he was somewhat taken aback. She started to open his fly. After ordering "Strip!" several more times (with comic failure), he was forced to accept a compromise. According to the rules of the game she had set up during his last visit ("do as I do"), she took off his trousers, he took off her skirt, then she took off his shirt, he her blouse, until at last they stood there naked. He placed his hand on her moist genitals, then moved his fingers along to the anus, the spot he loved most in all women's bodies. Hers was unusually prominent, evoking the long digestive tract that ended there with a slight protrusion. Fingering her strong, healthy orb, that most splendid of rings called by doctors the sphincter, he suddenly felt her fingers on the corresponding part of his own anatomy. She was mimicking his moves with the precision of a mirror.

Even though, as I have pointed out, he had known approximately two hundred women (plus the considerable lot that had accrued during his days as a window washer), he had yet to be faced with a woman who was taller than he was, squinted at him, and fingered his anus. To overcome his embarrassment, he forced her down on the bed.

So precipitous was his move that he caught her off guard. As her towering frame fell on its back, he caught among the red blotches on her face the frightened expression of equilibrium lost. Now that he was standing over her, he grabbed her under the knees and lifted her slightly parted legs in the air, so that they suddenly looked like the raised arms of a soldier surrendering to a gun pointed at him.

Clumsiness combined with ardor, ardor with clumsiness—they excited Tomas utterly. He made love to her for a very long time, constantly scanning her red-blotched face for that frightened expression of a woman whom someone has tripped and who is falling, the inimitable expression that moments earlier had conveyed excitement to his brain.

Then he went to wash in the bathroom. She followed him in and gave him long-drawn-out explanations of where the soap was and where the sponge was and how to turn on the hot water. He was surprised that she went into such detail over such simple matters. At last he had to tell her that he understood everything perfectly, and motioned to her to leave him alone in the bathroom.

"Won't you let me stay and watch?" she begged.

At last he managed to get her out. As he washed and urinated into the washbasin (standard procedure among Czech doctors), he had the feeling she was running back and forth outside the bathroom, looking for a way to break in. When he turned off the water and the flat was suddenly silent, he felt he was being watched. He was nearly certain that there was a peephole somewhere in the bathroom door and that her beautiful eye was squinting through it.

He went off in the best of moods, trying to fix her essence in his memory, to reduce that memory to a chemical formula capable of defining her uniqueness (her millionth part dissimilarity). The result was a formula consisting of three givens:

1) clumsiness with ardor,

2) the frightened face of one who has lost her equilibrium and is falling, and

3) legs raised in the air like the arms of a soldier surrendering to a pointed gun.

Going over them, he felt the joy of having acquired yet another piece of the world, of having taken his imaginary scalpel and snipped yet another strip off the infinite canvas of the universe.

## 12

At about the same time, he had the following experience: He had been meeting a young woman in a room that an old friend put at his disposal every day until midnight. After a month or two, she reminded him of one of their early encounters: they had made love on a rug under the window while it was thundering and lightning outside; they had made love for the length of the storm; it had been unforgettably beautiful!

Tomas was appalled. Yes, he remembered making love to her on the rug (his friend slept on a narrow couch that Tomas found uncomfortable), but he had completely forgotten the storm! It was odd. He could recall each of their times together; he had even kept close track of the ways they made love (she refused to be entered from behind); he remembered several of the things she had said during intercourse (she would ask him to squeeze her hips and to stop looking at her all the time); he even remembered the cut of her lingerie; but the storm had left no trace.

Of each erotic experience his memory recorded only the steep and narrow path of sexual conquest: the first piece of verbal aggression, the first touch, the first obscenity he said to her and she to him, the minor perversions he could make her acquiesce in and the ones she held out against. All else he excluded (almost pedantically) from his memory. He even forgot where he had first seen one or another woman, if that event occurred before his sexual offensive began.

The young woman smiled dreamily as she went on about the storm, and he looked at her in amazement and something akin to shame: she had experienced something beautiful, and he had failed to experience it with her. The two ways in which their memories reacted to the evening storm sharply delimit love and nonlove.

By the word "nonlove" I do not wish to imply that he took a cynical attitude to the young woman, that, as present-day parlance has it, he looked upon her as a sex object; on the contrary, he was quite fond of her, valued her character and intelligence, and was willing to come to her aid if ever she needed him. He was not the one who behaved shamefully towards her; it was his memory, for it was his memory that, unbeknown to him, had excluded her from the sphere of love.

The brain appears to possess a special area which we might call *poetic memory* and which records everything that charms or touches us, that makes our lives beautiful. From the time he met Tereza, no woman had the right to leave the slightest impression on that part of his brain.

Tereza occupied his poetic memory like a despot and exterminated all trace of other women. That was unfair, because the young woman he made love to on the rug during the storm was not a bit less worthy of poetry than Tereza. She shouted, "Close your eyes! Squeeze my hips! Hold me tight!"; she could not stand it that when Tomas made love he kept his eyes open, focused and observant, his body ever so slightly arched above her, never pressing against her skin. She did not want him to study her. She wanted to draw him into the magic stream that may be entered only with closed eyes. The reason she refused to get down on all fours was that in that position their bodies did not touch at all and he could observe her from a distance of several feet. She hated that distance. She wanted to merge with him. That is why, looking him straight in the eye, she insisted she had not had an orgasm even though the rug was fairly dripping with it. "It's not sensual pleasure I'm after," she would say, "it's happiness. And pleasure without happiness is not pleasure." In other words, she was pounding on the gate of his poetic memory. But the gate was shut. There was no room for her in his poetic memory. There was room for her only on the rug.

His adventure with Tereza began at the exact point where his adventures with other women left off. It took place on the other side of the imperative that pushed him into conquest after conquest. He had no desire to uncover anything in Tereza. She had come to him uncovered. He had made love to her before he could grab for the imaginary scalpel he used to open the prostrate body of the world. Before he could start wondering what she would be like when they made love, he loved her.

Their love story did not begin until afterward: she fell ill and he was unable to send her home as he had the others. Kneeling by her as she lay sleeping in his bed, he realized that someone had sent her downstream in a bulrush basket. I have said before that metaphors are dangerous. Love begins with a metaphor. Which is to say, love begins at the point when a woman enters her first word into our poetic memory.

## 13

Recently she had made another entry into his mind. Returning home with the milk one morning as usual, she stood in the doorway with a crow wrapped in her red scarf and pressed against her breast. It was the way gypsies held their babies. He would never forget it: the crow's enormous plaintive beak up next to her face.

She had found it half-buried, the way Cossacks used to dig their prisoners into the ground. "It was children," she said, and her words did more than state a fact; they revealed an unexpected repugnance for people in general. It reminded him of something she had said to him not long before: "I'm beginning to be grateful to you for not wanting to have children."

And then she had complained to him about a man who had been bothering her at work. He had grabbed at a cheap necklace of hers and suggested that the only way she could have afforded it was by doing some prostitution on the side. She was very upset about it. More than necessary, thought Tomas. He suddenly felt dismayed at how little he had seen of her the last two years; he had so few opportunities to press her hands in his to stop them from trembling.

The next morning he had gone to work with Tereza on his mind. The woman who gave the window washers their assignments told him that a private customer had insisted on him personally. Tomas was not looking forward to it; he was afraid it was still another woman. Fully occupied with Tereza, he was in no mood for adventure.

When the door opened, he gave a sigh of relief. He saw a tall, slightly stooped man before him. The man had a big chin and seemed vaguely familiar.

"Come in," said the man with a smile, taking him inside.

There was also a young man standing there. His face was bright red. He was looking at Tomas and trying to smile.

"I assume there's no need for me to introduce you two," said the man.

"No," said Tomas, and without returning the smile he held out his hand to the young man. It was his son.

Only then did the man with the big chin introduce himself.

"I knew you looked familiar!" said Tomas. "Of course! Now I place you. It was the name that did it."

They sat down at what was like a small conference table. Tomas realized that both men opposite him were his own involuntary creations. He had been forced to produce the younger one by his first wife, and the features of the older one had taken shape when he was under interrogation by the police.

To clear his mind of these thoughts, he said, "Well, which window do you want me to start with?"

Both men burst out laughing.

Clearly windows had nothing to do with the case. He had not been called in to do the windows; he had been lured into a trap. He had never before talked to his son. This was the first time he had shaken hands with him. He knew him only by sight and had no desire to know him any other way. As far as he was concerned, the less he knew about his son the better, and he hoped the feeling was mutual.

"Nice poster, isn't it?" said the editor, pointing at a large framed drawing on the wall opposite Tomas.

Tomas now glanced around the room. The walls were hung with interesting pictures, mostly photographs and posters. The drawing the editor had singled out came from one of the last issues of his paper before the Russians closed it down in 1969. It was an imitation of a famous recruitment poster from the Russian Civil War of 1918 showing a soldier, red star on his cap and extraordinarily stern look in his eyes, staring straight at you and aiming his index finger at you. The original Russian caption read: "Citizen, have you joined the Red Army?" It was replaced by a Czech text that read: "Citizen, have you signed the Two Thousand Words?"

That was an excellent joke! The "Two Thousand Words" was the first glorious manifesto of the 1968 Prague Spring. It called for the radical democratization of the Communist regime. First it was signed by a number of intellectuals, and then other people came forward and asked to sign, and finally there were so many signatures that no one could quite count them up. When the Red Army invaded their country and launched a series of political purges, one of the questions asked of each citizen was "Have you signed the Two Thousand Words?" Anyone who admitted to having done so was summarily dismissed from his job.

"A fine poster," said Tomas. "I remember it well."

"Let's hope the Red Army man isn't listening in on us," said the editor with a smile.

Then he went on, without the smile: "Seriously though, this isn't my flat. It belongs to a friend. We can't be absolutely certain the police can hear us; it's only a possibility. If I'd invited you to my place, it would have been a certainty."

Then he switched back to a playful tone. "But the way I look at it, we've got nothing to hide. And think of what a boon it will be to Czech historians of the future. The complete recorded lives of the Czech intelligentsia on file in the police archives! Do you know what effort literary historians have put into reconstructing in detail the sex lives of, say, Voltaire or Balzac or Tolstoy? No such problems with Czech writers. It's all on tape. Every last sigh."

And turning to the imaginary microphones in the wall, he said in a stentorian voice, "Gentlemen, as always in such circumstances, I wish to take this opportunity to encourage you in your work and to thank you on my behalf and on behalf of all future historians."

After the three of them had had a good laugh, the editor told the story of how his paper had been banned, what the artist who designed the poster was doing, and what had become of other Czech painters, philosophers, and writers. After the Russian invasion they had been relieved of their positions and become window washers, parking attendants, night watchmen, boilermen in public buildings, or at best—and usually with pull—taxi drivers.

Although what the editor said was interesting enough, Tomas was unable to concentrate on it. He was thinking about his son. He remembered passing him in the street during the past two months. Apparently these encounters had not been fortuitous. He had certainly never expected to find him in the company of a persecuted editor. Tomas's first wife was an orthodox Communist, and Tomas automatically assumed that his son was under her influence. He knew nothing about him. Of course he could have come out and asked him what kind of relationship he had with his mother, but he felt that it would have been tactless in the presence of a third party.

At last the editor came to the point. He said that more and more people were going to prison for no offense other than upholding their own opinions, and concluded with the words "And so we've decided to do something."

"What is it you want to do?" asked Tomas.

Here his son took over. It was the first time he had ever heard him speak. He was surprised to note that he stuttered.

"According to our sources," he said, "political prisoners are being subjected to very rough treatment. Several are in a bad way. And so we've decided to draft a petition and have it signed by the most important Czech intellectuals, the ones who still mean something."

No, it wasn't actually a stutter; it was more of a stammer, slowing down the flow of speech, stressing or highlighting every word he uttered whether he wanted to or not. He obviously felt himself doing it, and his cheeks, which had barely regained their natural pallor, turned scarlet again.

"And you've called me in for advice on likely candidates in my field?" Tomas asked.

"No," the editor said, laughing. "We don't want your advice. We want your signature!"

And again he felt flattered! Again he enjoyed the feeling that he had not been forgotten as a surgeon! He protested, but only out of modesty, "Wait a minute. Just because they kicked me out doesn't mean I'm a famous doctor!"

"We haven't forgotten what you wrote for our paper," said the editor, smiling at Tomas.

"Yes," sighed Tomas's son with an alacrity Tomas may have missed.

"I don't see how my name on a petition can help your political prisoners. Wouldn't it be better to have it signed by people who haven't fallen afoul of the regime, people who have at least some influence on the powers that be?"

The editor smiled. "Of course it would."

Tomas's son smiled, too; he smiled the smile of one who understands many things. "The only trouble is, they'd never sign!"

"Which doesn't mean we don't go after them," the editor continued, "or that we're too nice to spare them the embarrassment." He laughed. "You should hear the excuses they give. They're fantastic!"

Tomas's son laughed in agreement.

"Of course they all begin by claiming they agree with us right down the line," the editor went on. "We just need a different approach, they say. Something more prudent, more reasonable, more discreet. They're scared to sign and worried that if they don't they'll sink in our estimation."

Again Tomas's son and the editor laughed together.

Then the editor gave Tomas a sheet of paper with a short text calling upon the president of the republic, in a relatively respectful manner, to grant amnesty to all political prisoners.

Tomas ran the idea quickly through his mind. Amnesty to political prisoners? Would amnesty be granted because people jettisoned by the regime (and therefore themselves potential political prisoners) request it of the president? The only thing such a petition would accomplish was to keep political prisoners from being amnestied if there happened to be a plan afoot to do so!

His son interrupted his thoughts. "The main thing is to make the point that there still are a handful of people in this country who are not afraid. And to show who stands where. Separate the wheat from the chaff."

True, true, thought Tomas, but what had that to do with political prisoners? Either you called for an amnesty or you separated the wheat from the chaff. The two were not identical.

"On the fence?" the editor asked.

Yes. He *was* on the fence. But he was afraid to say so. There was a picture on the wall, a picture of a soldier pointing a threatening finger at him and saying, "Are you hesitating about joining the Red Army?" or "Haven't you signed the Two Thousand Words yet?" or "Have you too signed the Two Thousand Words?" or "You mean you don't want to sign the amnesty petition?!" But no matter what the soldier said, it was a threat.

The editor had barely finished saying what he thought about people who agree that the political prisoners should be granted amnesty but come up with thousands of reasons against signing the petition. In his opinion, their reasons were just so many excuses and their excuses a smoke screen for cowardice. What could Tomas say?

At last he broke the silence with a laugh, and pointing to the poster on the wall, he said, "With that soldier threatening me, asking whether I'm going to sign or not, I can't possibly think straight."

Then all three laughed for a while.

"All right," said Tomas after the laughter had died down. "I'll think it over. Can we get together again in the next few days?"

"Any time at all," said the editor, "but unfortunately the

petition can't wait. We plan to get it off to the president tomorrow."

"Tomorrow?" And suddenly Tomas recalled the portly policeman handing him the denunciation of none other than this tall editor with the big chin. Everyone was trying to make him sign statements he had not written himself.

"There's nothing to think over anyway," said his son. Although his words were aggressive, his intonation bordered on the supplicatory. Now that they were looking each other in the eye, Tomas noticed that when concentrating the boy slightly raised the left side of his upper lip. It was an expression he saw on his own face whenever he peered into the mirror to determine whether it was clean-shaven. Discovering it on the face of another made him uneasy.

When parents live with their children through childhood, they grow accustomed to that kind of similarity; it seems trivial to them or, if they stop and think about it, amusing. But Tomas was talking to his son for the first time in his life! He was not used to sitting face to face with his own asymmetrical mouth!

Imagine having an arm amputated and implanted on someone else. Imagine that person sitting opposite you and gesticulating with it in your face. You would stare at that arm as at a ghost. Even though it was your own personal, beloved arm, you would be horrified at the possibility of its touching you!

"Aren't you on the side of the persecuted?" his son added, and Tomas suddenly saw that what was really at stake in this scene they were playing was not the amnesty of political prisoners; it was his relationship with his son. If he signed, their fates would be united and Tomas would be more or less obliged to befriend him; if he failed to sign, their relations would remain null as before, though now not so much by his own will as by the will of his son, who would renounce his father for his cowardice.

He was in the situation of a chess player who cannot avoid checkmate and is forced to resign. Whether he signed the petition or not made not the slightest difference. It would alter nothing in his own life or in the lives of the political prisoners.

"Hand it over," he said, and took the sheet of paper.

# 14

As if rewarding him for his decision, the editor said, "That was a fine piece you wrote about Oedipus."

Handing him a pen, his son added, "Some ideas have the force of a bomb exploding."

Although the editor's words of praise pleased him, his son's metaphor struck him as forced and out of place. "Unfortunately, I was the only casualty," he said. "Thanks to those ideas, I can no longer operate on my patients."

It sounded cold, almost hostile.

Apparently hoping to counteract the discordant note, the editor said, by way of apology, "But think of all the people your article helped!"

From childhood, Tomas had associated the words "helping people" with one thing and one thing only: medicine. How could an article help people? What were these two trying to make him swallow, reducing his whole life to a single small idea about Oedipus or even less: to a single primitive "no!" in the face of the regime.

"Maybe it helped people, maybe it didn't," he said (in a voice still cold, though he probably did not realize it), "but as a surgeon I *know* I saved a few lives."

Another silence set in. Tomas's son broke it. "Ideas can save lives, too."

Watching his own mouth in the boy's face, Tomas thought, How strange to see one's own lips stammer.

"You know the best thing about what you wrote?" the boy went on, and Tomas could see the effort it cost him to speak. "Your refusal to compromise. Your clear-cut sense of what's good and what's evil, something we're beginning to lose. We have no idea anymore what it means to feel guilty. The Communists have the excuse that Stalin misled them. Murderers have the excuse that their mothers didn't love them. And suddenly you come out and say: there is no excuse. No one could be more innocent, in his soul and conscience, than Oedipus. And yet he punished himself when he saw what he had done."

Tomas tore his eyes away from his son's mouth and tried to focus on the editor. He was irritated and felt like arguing with them. "But it's all a misunderstanding! The border between good and evil is terribly fuzzy. I wasn't out to punish anyone, either. Punishing people who don't know what they've done is barbaric. The myth of Oedipus is a beautiful one, but treating it like this . . ." He had more to say, but suddenly he remembered that the place might be bugged. He had not the slightest ambition to be quoted by historians of centuries to come. He was simply afraid of being quoted by the police. Wasn't that what they wanted from him, after all? A condemnation of the article? He did not like the idea of feeding it to them from his own lips. Besides, he knew that anything anyone in the country said could be broadcast over the radio at any time. He held his tongue.

"I wonder what's made you change your mind," said the editor.

"What I wonder is what made me write the thing in the first place," said Tomas, and just then he remembered: She had landed at his bedside like a child sent downstream in a bulrush basket. Yes, that was why he had picked up the book and gone back to the stories of Romulus, Moses, and Oedipus. And now she was with him again. He saw her pressing the crow wrapped in red to her breast. The image of her brought him peace. It seemed to tell him that Tereza was alive, that she was with him in the same city, and that nothing else counted.

This time, the editor broke the silence. "I understand. I don't like the idea of punishment, either. After all," he added, smiling, "we don't call for punishment to be inflicted; we call for it to cease."

"I know," said Tomas. In the next few moments he would do something possibly noble but certainly, and totally, useless (because it would not help the political prisoners) and unpleasant to himself (because it took place under conditions the two of them had imposed on him).

"It's your duty to sign," his son added, almost pleading.

Duty? His son reminding him of his duty? That was the worst word anyone could have used on him! Once more, the image of Tereza appeared before his eyes, Tereza holding the crow in her arms. Then he remembered that she had been accosted by an undercover agent the day before. Her hands had started trembling again. She had aged. She was all that mattered to him. She, born of six fortuities, she, the blossom sprung from the chief surgeon's sciatica, she, the reverse side of all his "*Es muss sein!*"—she was the only thing he cared about.

Why even think about whether to sign or not? There was only one criterion for all his decisions: he must do nothing that could harm her. Tomas could not save political prisoners, but he could make Tereza happy. He could not really succeed in doing even that. But if he signed the petition, he could be fairly certain that she would have more frequent visits from undercover agents, and that her hands would tremble more and more.

"It is much more important to dig a half-buried crow out of

the ground," he said, "than to send petitions to a president."

He knew that his words were incomprehensible, but enjoyed them all the more for it. He felt a sudden, unexpected intoxication come over him. It was the same black intoxication he had felt when he solemnly announced to his wife that he no longer wished to see her or his son. It was the same black intoxication he had felt when he sent off the letter that meant the end of his career in medicine. He was not at all sure he was doing the right thing, but he was sure he was doing what he wanted to do.

"I'm sorry," he said, "but I'm not going to sign."

## 15

Several days later he read about the petition in the papers.

There was not a word, of course, about its being a politely worded plea for the release of political prisoners. None of the papers cited a single sentence from the short text. Instead, they went on at great length and in vague, menacing terms about an anti-state proclamation meant to lay the foundation for a new campaign against socialism. They also listed all the signatories, accompanying each of their names with slanderous attacks that gave Tomas gooseflesh.

Not that it was unexpected. The fact that any public undertaking (meeting, petition, street gathering) not organized by the Communist Party was automatically considered illegal and endangered all the participants was common knowledge. But it may have made him sorrier he had not signed the petition.

Why hadn't he signed? He could no longer quite remember what had prompted his decision.

And once more I see him the way he appeared to me at the very beginning of the novel: standing at the window and staring across the courtyard at the walls opposite.

This is the image from which he was born. As I have pointed out before, characters are not born like people, of woman; they are born of a situation, a sentence, a metaphor containing in a nutshell a basic human possibility that the author thinks no one else has discovered or said something essential about.

But isn't it true that an author can write only about himself?

Staring impotently across a courtyard, at a loss for what to do; hearing the pertinacious rumbling of one's own stomach during a moment of love; betraying, yet lacking the will to abandon the glamorous path of betrayal; raising one's fist with the crowds in the Grand March; displaying one's wit before hidden microphones—I have known all these situations, I have experienced them myself, yet none of them has given rise to the person my curriculum vitae and I represent. The characters in my novels are my own unrealized possibilities. That is why I am equally fond of them all and equally horrified by them. Each one has crossed a border that I myself have circumvented. It is that crossed border (the border beyond which my own "I" ends) which attracts me most. For beyond that border begins the secret the novel asks about. The novel is not the author's confession; it is an investigation of human life in the trap the world has become. But enough. Let us return to Tomas.

Alone in his flat, he stared across the courtyard at the dirty walls of the building opposite. He missed the tall, stooped man with the big chin and the man's friends, whom he did not know, who were not even members of his circle. He felt as though he had just met a beautiful woman on a railway platform, and before he could say anything to her, she had stepped into a sleeping car on its way to Istanbul or Lisbon.

Then he tried again to think through what he should have done. Even though he did his best to put aside everything belonging to the realm of the emotions (the admiration he had for the editor and the irritation his son caused him), he was still not sure whether he ought to have signed the text they gave him.

Is it right to raise one's voice when others are being silenced? Yes.

On the other hand, why did the papers devote so much space to the petition? After all, the press (totally manipulated by the state) could have kept it quiet and no one would have been the wiser. If they publicized the petition, then the petition played into the rulers' hands! It was manna from heaven, the perfect start and justification for a new wave of persecution.

What then should he have done? Sign or not?

Another way of formulating the question is, Is it better to shout and thereby hasten the end, or to keep silent and gain thereby a slower death?

Is there any answer to these questions?

And again he thought the thought we already know: Human life occurs only once, and the reason we cannot determine which of our decisions are good and which bad is that in a given situation we can make only one decision; we are not granted a second, third, or fourth life in which to compare various decisions.

History is similar to individual lives in this respect. There is only one history of the Czechs. One day it will come to an end as surely as Tomas's life, never to be repeated.

In 1618, the Czech estates took courage and vented their ire on the emperor reigning in Vienna by pitching two of his high officials out of a window in the Prague Castle. Their defiance led to the Thirty Years War, which in turn led to the almost complete destruction of the Czech nation. Should the Czechs have shown more caution than courage? The answer may seem simple; it is not.

Three hundred and twenty years later, after the Munich Conference of 1938, the entire world decided to sacrifice the Czechs' country to Hitler. Should the Czechs have tried to stand up to a power eight times their size? In contrast to 1618, they opted for caution. Their capitulation led to the Second World War, which in turn led to the forfeit of their nation's freedom for many decades or even centuries. Should they have shown more courage than caution? What should they have done?

If Czech history could be repeated, we should of course find it desirable to test the other possibility each time and compare the results. Without such an experiment, all considerations of this kind remain a game of hypotheses.

*Einmal ist keinmal.* What happens but once might as well not have happened at all. The history of the Czechs will not be repeated, nor will the history of Europe. The history of the Czechs and of Europe is a pair of sketches from the pen of mankind's fateful inexperience. History is as light as individual human life, unbearably light, light as a feather, as dust swirling into the air, as whatever will no longer exist tomorrow.

Once more, and with a nostalgia akin to love, Tomas thought of the tall, stooped editor. That man acted as though history were a finished picture rather than a sketch. He acted as though everything he did were to be repeated endlessly, to return eternally, without the slightest doubt about his actions. He was convinced he was right, and for him that was a sign not of narrowmindedness but of virtue. Yes, that man lived in a history different from Tomas's: a history that was not (or did not realize it was) a sketch.

## 16

Several days later, he was struck by another thought, which I record here as an addendum to the preceding chapter: Somewhere out in space there was a planet where all people would be born again. They would be fully aware of the life they had spent on earth and of all the experience they had amassed here.

And perhaps there was still another planet, where we would all be born a third time with the experience of our first two lives.

And perhaps there were yet more and more planets, where mankind would be born one degree (one life) more mature.

That was Tomas's version of eternal return.

Of course we here on earth (planet number one, the planet of inexperience) can only fabricate vague fantasies of what will happen to man on those other planets. Will he be wiser? Is maturity within man's power? Can he attain it through repetition?

Only from the perspective of such a utopia is it possible to use the concepts of pessimism and optimism with full justification: an optimist is someone who thinks that on planet number five the history of mankind will be less bloody. A pessimist is one who thinks otherwise.

## 17

One of Jules Verne's famous novels, a favorite of Tomas's in his childhood, is called *Two Years on Holiday,* and indeed two years is the maximum. Tomas was in his third year as a window washer.

In the last few weeks, he had come to realize (half sadly, half laughing to himself) that he had grown physically tired (he had one, sometimes two erotic engagements a day), and that although he had not lost his zest for women, he found himself straining his forces to the utmost. (Let me add that the strain was on his physical, not his sexual powers; his problem was with his breath, not with his penis, a state of affairs that had its comical side.)

One day he was having trouble reaching a prospect for his afternoon time slot, and it looked as though he was going to have one of his rare off days. He was desperate. He had phoned a certain young woman about ten times. A charming acting student whose body had been tanned on Yugoslavia's nudist beaches with an evenness that called to mind slow rotation on a mechanized spit.

After making one last call from his final job of the day and starting back to the office at four to hand in his signed order slips, he was stopped in the center of Prague by a woman he failed to recognize. "Wherever have you disappeared to? I haven't seen you in ages!"

Tomas racked his brains to place her. Had she been one of his patients? She was behaving like an intimate friend. He tried to answer in a manner that would conceal the fact that he did not recognize her. He was already thinking about how to lure her to his friend's flat (he had the key in his pocket) when he realized from a chance remark who the woman was: the budding actress with the perfect tan, the one he had been trying to reach all day.

This episode both amused and horrified him: it proved that he was as tired mentally as physically. Two years of holiday could not be extended indefinitely.

# 18

The holiday from the operating table was also a holiday from Tereza. After hardly seeing each other for six days, they would finally be together on Sundays, full of desire; but, as on the evening when Tomas came back from Zurich, they were estranged and had a long way to go before they could touch and kiss. Physical love gave them pleasure but no consolation. She no longer cried out as she had in the past, and, at the moment of orgasm, her grimace seemed to him to express suffering and a strange absence. Only at night, in sleep, were they tenderly united. Holding his hand, she would forget the chasm (the chasm of daylight) that divided them. But the nights gave him neither the time nor the means to protect and take care of her. In the mornings, it was heartrending to see her, and he feared for her: she looked sad and infirm.

One Sunday, she asked him to take her for a ride outside Prague. They drove to a spa, where they found all the streets relabeled with Russian names and happened to meet an old patient of Tomas's. Tomas was devastated by the meeting. Suddenly here was someone talking to him again as to a doctor, and he could feel his former life bridging the divide, coming back to him with its pleasant regularity of seeing patients and feeling their trusting eyes on him, those eyes he had pretended to ignore but in fact savored and now greatly missed.

Driving home, Tomas pondered the catastrophic mistake he had made by returning to Prague from Zurich. He kept his eyes trained on the road so as to avoid looking at Tereza. He was furious with her. Her presence at his side felt more unbearably fortuitous than ever. What was she doing here next to him? Who put her in the basket and sent her downstream? Why was *his* bed chosen as her shore? And why *she* and not some other woman?

Neither of them said a word the whole way.

When they got home, they had dinner in silence.

Silence lay between them like an agony. It grew heavier by the minute. To escape it they went straight to bed. He woke her in the middle of the night. She was crying.

"I was buried," she told him. "I'd been buried for a long time. You came to see me every week. Each time you knocked at the grave, and I came out. My eyes were full of dirt.

"You'd say, 'How can you see?' and try to wipe the dirt from my eyes.

"And I'd say, 'I can't see anyway. I have holes instead of eyes.'

"And then one day you went off on a long journey, and I knew you were with another woman. Weeks passed, and there was no sign of you. I was afraid of missing you, and stopped sleeping. At last you knocked at the grave again, but I was so worn down by a month of sleepless nights that I didn't think I could make it out of there. When I finally did come out, you seemed disappointed. You said I didn't look well. I could feel how awful I looked to you with my sunken cheeks and nervous gestures.

"'I'm sorry,' I apologized. 'I haven't slept a wink since you left.'

"'You see?' you said in a voice full of false cheer. 'What you need is a good rest. A month's holiday!'

"As if I didn't know what you had in mind! A month's holiday meant you didn't want to see me for a month, you had another woman. Then you left and I slipped down into my grave, knowing full well that I'd have another month of sleepless nights waiting for you and that when you came back and I was uglier you'd be even more disappointed."

He had never heard anything more harrowing. Holding her tightly in his arms and feeling her body tremble, he thought he could not endure his love.

Let the planet be convulsed with exploding bombs, the country ravished daily by new hordes, all his neighbors taken out and shot—he could accept it all more easily than he dared admit. But the grief implicit in Tereza's dream was something he could not endure.

He tried to reenter the dream she had told him. He pictured himself stroking her face and delicately—she mustn't be aware of it—brushing the dirt out of her eye sockets. Then he heard her say the unbelievably harrowing "I can't see anyway. I have holes instead of eyes."

His heart was about to break; he felt he was on the verge of a heart attack.

Tereza had gone back to sleep; he could not. He pictured her death. She was dead and having terrible nightmares; but because she was dead, he was unable to wake her from them. Yes, that is death: Tereza asleep, having terrible nightmares, and he unable to wake her.

## *19*

During the five years that had passed since the Russian army invaded Tomas's country, Prague had undergone considerable changes. The people Tomas met in the streets were different. Half of his friends had emigrated, and half of the half that remained had died. For it is a fact which will go unrecorded by historians that the years following the Russian invasion were a period of funerals: the death rate soared. I do not speak only of the cases (rather rare, of course) of people hounded to death, like Jan Prochazka, the novelist. Two weeks after his private conversations were broadcast daily over the radio, he entered the hospital. The cancer that had most likely lain dormant in his body until then suddenly blossomed like a rose. He was operated on in the presence of the police, who, when they realized he was doomed anyway, lost interest in him and let him die in the arms of his wife. But many also died without being directly subjected to persecution; the hopelessness pervading the entire country penetrated the soul to the body, shattering the latter. Some ran desperately from the favor of a regime that wanted to endow them with the honor of displaying them side by side with its new leaders. That is how the poet Frantisek Hrubin died—fleeing from the love of the Party. The Minister of Culture, from whom the poet did everything possible to hide, did not catch up with Hrubin until his funeral, when he made a speech over the grave about the poet's love for the Soviet Union. Perhaps he hoped his words would ring so outrageously false that they would wake Hrubin from the dead. But the world was too ugly, and no one decided to rise up out of the grave.

One day, Tomas went to the crematorium to attend the funeral of a famous biologist who had been thrown out of the university and the Academy of Sciences. The authorities had forbidden mention of the hour of the funeral in the death announcement, fearing that the services would turn into a demonstration. The mourners themselves did not learn until the last moment that the body would be cremated at half past six in the morning.

Entering the crematorium, Tomas did not understand what was happening: the hall was lit up like a film studio. Looking around in bewilderment, he noticed cameras set up in three places. No, it was not television; it was the police. They were filming the funeral to study who had attended it. An old colleague of the dead scientist, still a member of the Academy of Sciences, had been brave enough to make the funeral oration. He had never counted on becoming a film star.

When the services were over and everyone had paid his respects to the family of the deceased, Tomas noticed a group of men in one corner of the hall and spotted the tall, stooped editor among them. The sight of him made Tomas feel how much he missed these people who feared nothing and seemed bound by a deep friendship. He started off in the editor's direction with a smile and a greeting on his lips, but when the editor saw him he said, "Careful! Don't come any closer."

It was a strange thing to say. Tomas was not sure whether to interpret it as a sincere, friendly warning ("Watch out, we're being filmed; if you talk to us, you may be hauled in for another interrogation") or as irony ("If you weren't brave enough to sign the petition, be consistent and don't try the old-pals act on us"). Whatever the message meant, Tomas heeded it and moved off. He had the feeling that the beautiful woman on the railway platform had not only stepped into the sleeping car but, just as he was about to tell her how much he admired her, had put her finger over his lips and forbidden him to speak.

## 20

That afternoon, he had another interesting encounter. He was washing the display window of a large shoe shop when a young man came to a halt right next to him, leaned up close to the window, and began scrutinizing the prices.

"Prices are up," said Tomas without interrupting his pursuit of the rivulets trickling down the glass.

The man looked over at him. He was a hospital colleague of Tomas's, the one I have designated S., the very one who had sneered at Tomas while under the impression that Tomas had written a statement of self-criticism. Tomas was delighted to see him (naively so, as we delight in unexpected events), but what he saw in his former colleague's eyes (before S. had a chance to pull himself together) was a look of none-too-pleasant surprise.

"How are you?" S. asked.

Before Tomas could respond, he realized that S. was ashamed of having asked. It was patently ridiculous for a doctor practicing his profession to ask a doctor washing windows how he was.

To clear the air Tomas came out with as sprightly a "Fine, just fine!" as he could muster, but he immediately felt that no matter how hard he tried (in fact, *because* he tried so hard), his "fine" sounded bitterly ironic. And so he quickly added, "What's new at the hospital?"

"Nothing," S. answered. "Same as always."

His response, too, though meant to be as neutral as possible, was completely inappropriate, and they both knew it. And they knew they both knew it. How can things be the "same as always" when one of them is washing windows?

"How's the chief?" asked Tomas.

"You mean you don't see him?" asked S.

"No," said Tomas.

It was true. From the day he left, he had not seen the chief surgeon even once. And they had worked so well together; they had even tended to think of themselves as friends. So no matter how he said it, his "no" had a sad ring, and Tomas suspected that S. was angry with him for bringing up the subject: like the chief surgeon, S. had never dropped by to ask Tomas how he was doing or whether he needed anything.

All conversation between the two former colleagues had become impossible, even though they both regretted it, Tomas especially. He was not angry with his colleagues for having forgotten him. If only he could make that clear to the young man beside him. What he really wanted to say was "There's nothing to be ashamed of! It's perfectly normal for our paths not to cross. There's nothing to get upset about! I'm glad to see you!" But he was afraid to say it, because everything he had said so far failed to come out as intended, and these sincere words, too, would sound sarcastic to his colleague.

"I'm sorry," said S. after a long pause, "I'm in a real hurry." He held out his hand. "I'll give you a buzz."

During the period when his colleagues turned their noses up at him for his supposed cowardice, they all smiled at him. Now that they could no longer scorn him, now that they were constrained to respect him, they gave him a wide berth.

Then again, even his old patients had stopped sending for him, to say nothing of greeting him with champagne. The situation of the déclassé intellectual was no longer exceptional; it had turned into something permanent and unpleasant to confront.

## *21*

He went home, lay down, and fell asleep earlier than usual. An hour later he woke up with stomach pains. They were an old malady that appeared whenever he was depressed. He opened the medicine chest and let out a curse: it was completely empty;

he had forgotten to keep it stocked. He tried to keep the pain under control by force of will and was, in fact, fairly successful, but he could not fall asleep again. When Tereza came home at half past one, he felt like chatting with her. He told her about the funeral, about the editor's refusal to talk to him, and about his encounter with S.

"Prague has grown so ugly lately," said Tereza.

"I know," said Tomas.

Tereza paused and said softly, "The best thing to do would be to move away."

"I agree," said Tomas, "but there's nowhere to go."

He was sitting on the bed in his pajamas, and she came and sat down next to him, putting her arms around his body from the side.

"What about the country?" she said.

"The country?" he asked, surprised.

"We'd be alone there. You wouldn't meet that editor or your old colleagues. The people there are different. And we'd be getting back to nature. Nature is the same as it always was."

Just then Tomas felt another stab in his stomach. It made him feel old, feel that what he longed for more than anything else was peace and quiet.

"Maybe you're right," he said with difficulty. The pain made it hard for him to breathe.

"We'd have a little house and a little garden, but big enough to give Karenin room for a decent run."

"Yes," said Tomas.

He was trying to picture what it would be like if they did move to the country. He would have difficulty finding a new woman every week. It would mean an end to his erotic adventures.

"The only thing is, you'd be bored with me in the country," said Tereza as if reading his mind.

The pain grew more intense. He could not speak. It occurred to him that his womanizing was also something of an *"Es muss sein!"*—an imperative enslaving him. He longed for a holiday. But for an absolute holiday, a rest from *all* imperatives, from all "*Es muss sein!*" If he could take a rest (a permanent rest) from the hospital operating table, then why not from the *world* operating table, the one where his imaginary scalpel opened the strongbox women use to hide their illusory one-millionth part dissimilarity?

"Your stomach is acting up again!" Tereza exclaimed, only then realizing that something was wrong.

He nodded.

"Have you had your injection?"

He shook his head. "I forgot to lay in a supply of medication."

Though annoyed at his carelessness, she stroked his forehead, which was beaded with sweat from the pain.

"I feel a little better now."

"Lie down," she said, and covered him with a blanket. She went off to the bathroom and in a minute was back and lying next to him.

Without lifting his head from the pillow, he turned to her and nearly gasped: the grief burning in her eyes was unbearable.

"Tell me, Tereza, what's wrong? Something's been going on inside you lately. I can feel it. I know it."

"No." She shook her head. "There's nothing wrong."

"There's no point in denying it."

"It's still the same things," she said.

"The same things" meant her jealousy and his infidelities.

But Tomas would not let up. "No, Tereza. This time it's something different. It's never been this bad before."

"Well then, I'll tell you," she said. "Go and wash your hair."

He did not understand.

The tone of her explanation was sad, unantagonistic, almost gentle. "For months now your hair has had a strong odor to it. It smells of female genitals. I didn't want to tell you, but night after night I've had to breathe in the groin of some mistress of yours."

The moment she finished, his stomach began hurting again. He was desperate. The scrubbings he'd put himself through! Body, hands, face, to make sure not the slightest trace of their odors remained behind. He'd even avoided their fragrant soaps, carrying his own harsh variety with him at all times. But he'd forgotten about his hair! It had never occurred to him!

Then he remembered the woman who had straddled his face and wanted him to make love to her with it and with the crown of his head. He hated her now. What stupid ideas! He saw there was no use denying it. All he could do was laugh a silly laugh and head for the bathroom to wash his hair.

But she stroked his forehead again and said, "Stay here in bed. Don't bother washing it out. I'm used to it by now."

His stomach was killing him, and he longed for peace and quiet. "I'll write to that patient of mine, the one we met at the spa. Do you know the district where his village is?"

"No."

Tomas was having great trouble talking. All he could say was, "Woods . . . rolling hills . . ."

"That's right. That's what we'll do. We'll go away from here. But no talking now . . ." And she kept stroking his forehead. They lay there side by side, neither saying a word. Slowly the pain began to recede. Soon they were both asleep.

# 22

In the middle of the night, he woke up and realized to his surprise that he had been having one erotic dream after the other. The only one he could recall with any clarity was the last: an enormous naked woman, at least five times his size, floating on her back in a pool, her belly from crotch to navel covered with thick hair. Looking at her from the side of the pool, he was greatly excited.

How could he have been excited when his body was debilitated by a gastric disorder? And how could he be excited by the sight of a woman who would have repelled him had he seen her while conscious?

He thought: In the clockwork of the head, two cogwheels turn opposite each other. On the one, images; on the other, the body's reactions. The cog carrying the image of a naked woman meshes with the corresponding erection-command cog. But when, for one reason or another, the wheels go out of phase and the excitement cog meshes with a cog bearing the image of a swallow in flight, the penis rises at the sight of a swallow.

Moreover, a study by one of Tomas's colleagues, a specialist in human sleep, claimed that during *any* kind of dream men have erections, which means that the link between erections and naked women is only one of a thousand ways the Creator can set the clockwork moving in a man's head.

And what has love in common with all this? Nothing. If a cogwheel in Tomas's head goes out of phase and he is excited by seeing a swallow, it has absolutely no effect on his love for Tereza.

If excitement is a mechanism our Creator uses for His own amusement, love is something that belongs to us alone and enables us to flee the Creator. Love is our freedom. Love lies beyond "*Es muss sein!*"

Though that is not entirely true. Even if love is something other than a clockwork of sex that the Creator uses for His own amusement, it is still attached to it. It is attached to it like a tender naked woman to the pendulum of an enormous clock.

Thomas thought: Attaching love to sex is one of the most bizarre ideas the Creator ever had.

He also thought: One way of saving love from the stupidity of sex would be to set the clockwork in our head in such a way as to excite us at the sight of a swallow.

And with that sweet thought he started dozing off. But on the very threshold of sleep, in the no-man's-land of muddled concepts, he was suddenly certain he had just discovered the solution to all riddles, the key to all mysteries, a new utopia, a paradise: a world where man is excited by seeing a swallow and Tomas can love Tereza without being disturbed by the aggressive stupidity of sex.

Then he fell asleep.

## 23

Several half-naked women were trying to wind themselves around him, but he was tired, and to extricate himself from them he opened the door leading to the next room. There, just opposite him, he saw a young woman lying on her side on a couch. She, too, was half-naked: she wore nothing but panties. Leaning on her elbow, she looked up at him with a smile that said she had known he would come.

He went up to her. He was filled with a feeling of unutterable bliss at the thought that he had found her at last and could be there with her. He sat down at her side, said something to her, and she said something back. She radiated calm. Her hand made slow, supple movements. All his life he had longed for the calm of her movements. Feminine calm had eluded him all his life.

But just then the dream began its slide back to reality. He found himself back in that no-man's-land where we are neither asleep nor awake. He was horrified by the prospect of seeing the young woman vanish before his eyes and said to himself, God, how I'd hate to lose her! He tried desperately to remember who she was, where he'd met her, what they'd experienced together. How could he possibly forget when she knew him so well? He promised himself to phone her first thing in the morning. But no sooner had he made the promise than he realized he couldn't keep it: he didn't know her name. How could he forget the name of someone he knew so well? By that time he was almost completely awake, his eyes were open, and he was asking himself, Where am I? Yes, I'm in Prague, but that woman, does she live here too? Didn't I meet her somewhere else? Could she be from Switzerland? It took him quite some time to get it into his head that he didn't know the woman, that she wasn't from Prague or Switzerland, that she inhabited his dream and nowhere else.

He was so upset he sat straight up in bed. Tereza was breathing deeply beside him. The woman in the dream, he thought, was unlike any he had ever met. The woman he felt he knew most intimately of all had turned out to be a woman he did not even know. And yet she was the one he had always longed for. If a personal paradise were ever to exist for him, then in that paradise he would have to live by her side. The woman from his dream was the "*Es muss sein!*" of his love.

He suddenly recalled the famous myth from Plato's *Symposium:* People were hermaphrodites until God split them in two, and now all the halves wander the world over seeking one another. Love is the longing for the half of ourselves we have lost.

Let us suppose that such is the case, that somewhere in the world each of us has a partner who once formed part of our body. Tomas's other part is the young woman he dreamed about. The trouble is, man does not find the other part of himself. Instead, he is sent a Tereza in a bulrush basket. But what happens if he nevertheless later meets the one who was meant for him, the other part of himself? Whom is he to prefer? The woman from the bulrush basket or the woman from Plato's myth?

He tried to picture himself living in an ideal world with the young woman from the dream. He sees Tereza walking past the open windows of their ideal house. She is alone and stops to look in at him with an infinitely sad expression in her eyes. He cannot withstand her glance. Again, he feels her pain in his own heart. Again, he falls prey to compassion and sinks deep into her soul. He leaps out of the window, but she tells him bitterly to stay where he feels happy, making those abrupt, angular movements that so annoyed and displeased him. He grabs her nervous hands and presses them between his own to calm them. And he knows that time and again he will abandon the house of his happiness, time and again abandon his paradise and the woman from his dream and betray the "*Es muss sein!*" of his love to go off with Tereza, the woman born of six laughable fortuities.

All this time he was sitting up in bed and looking at the woman who was lying beside him and holding his hand in her sleep. He felt an ineffable love for her. Her sleep must have been very light at the moment because she opened her eyes and gazed up at him questioningly.

"What are you looking at?" she asked.

He knew that instead of waking her he should lull her back to sleep, so he tried to come up with an answer that would plant the image of a new dream in her mind.

"I'm looking at the stars," he said.

"Don't say you're looking at the stars. That's a lie. You're looking down."

"That's because we're in an airplane. The stars are below us."

"Oh, in an airplane," said Tereza, squeezing his hand even tighter and falling asleep again. And Tomas knew that Tereza was looking out of the round window of an airplane flying high above the stars.

# PART SIX

# The Grand March

# 1

Not until 1980 were we able to read in the *Sunday Times* how Stalin's son, Yakov, died. Captured by the Germans during the Second World War, he was placed in a camp together with a group of British officers. They shared a latrine. Stalin's son habitually left a foul mess. The British officers resented having their latrine smeared with shit, even if it was the shit of the son of the most powerful man in the world. They brought the matter to his attention. He took offense. They brought it to his attention again and again, and tried to make him clean the latrine. He raged, argued, and fought. Finally, he demanded a hearing with the camp commander. He wanted the commander to act as arbiter. But the arrogant German refused to talk about shit. Stalin's son could not stand the humiliation. Crying out to heaven in the most terrifying of Russian curses, he took a running jump into the electrified barbed-wire fence that surrounded the camp. He hit the target. His body, which would never again make a mess of the Britishers' latrine, was pinned to the wire.

# 2

Stalin's son had a hard time of it. All evidence points to the conclusion that his father killed the woman by whom he had the boy. Young Stalin was therefore both the Son of God (because his father was revered like God) and His cast-off. People feared him twofold: he could injure them by both his wrath (he was, after all, Stalin's son) and his favor (his father might punish his cast-off son's friends in order to punish him).

Rejection and privilege, happiness and woe—no one felt more concretely than Yakov how interchangeable opposites are, how short the step from one pole of human existence to the other.

Then, at the very outset of the war, he fell prisoner to the Germans, and other prisoners, belonging to an incomprehensible, standoffish nation that had always been intrinsically repulsive to him, accused him of being dirty. Was he, who bore on his shoulders a drama of the highest order (as fallen angel *and* Son of God), to undergo judgment not for something sublime (in the realm of God and the angels) but for shit? Were the very highest of drama and the very lowest so vertiginously close?

Vertiginously close? Can proximity cause vertigo?

It can. When the north pole comes so close as to touch the south pole, the earth disappears and man finds himself in a void that makes his head spin and beckons him to fall.

If rejection and privilege are one and the same, if there is no difference between the sublime and the paltry, if the Son of God can undergo judgment for shit, then human existence loses its dimensions and becomes unbearably light. When Stalin's son ran up to the electrified wire and hurled his body at it, the fence was like the pan of a scales sticking pitifully up in the air, lifted by the infinite lightness of a world that has lost its dimensions.

Stalin's son laid down his life for shit. But a death for shit is not a senseless death. The Germans who sacrificed their lives to expand their country's territory to the east, the Russians who died to extend their country's power to the west—yes, they died for something idiotic, and their deaths have no meaning or general validity. Amid the general idiocy of the war, the death of Stalin's son stands out as the sole metaphysical death.

## 3

When I was small and would leaf through the Old Testament retold for children and illustrated in engravings by Gustave Doré, I saw the Lord God standing on a cloud. He was an old man with eyes, nose, and a long beard, and I would say to myself that if He had a mouth, He had to eat. And if He ate, He had intestines. But that thought always gave me a fright, because even though I come from a family that was not particularly religious, I felt the idea of a divine intestine to be sacrilegious.

Spontaneously, without any theological training, I, a child, grasped the incompatibility of God and shit and thus came to question the basic thesis of Christian anthropology, namely, that man was created in God's image. Either/or: either man was created in God's image—and God has intestines!—or God lacks intestines and man is not like Him.

The ancient Gnostics felt as I did at the age of five. In the second century, the great Gnostic master Valentinus resolved the damnable dilemma by claiming that Jesus "ate and drank, but did not defecate."

Shit is a more onerous theological problem than is evil. Since God gave man freedom, we can, if need be, accept the idea that He is not responsible for man's crimes. The responsibility for shit, however, rests entirely with Him, the Creator of man.

## 4

In the fourth century, Saint Jerome completely rejected the notion that Adam and Eve had sexual intercourse in Paradise. On the other hand, Johannes Scotus Erigena, the great ninth-century theologian, accepted the idea. He believed, moreover, that Adam's virile member could be made to rise like an arm or a leg, when and as its owner wished. We must not dismiss this fancy as the recurrent dream of a man obsessed with the threat of impotence. Erigena's idea has a different meaning. If it were possible to raise the penis by means of a simple command, then sexual excitement would have no place in the world. The penis would rise not because we are excited but because we order it to do so. What the great theologian found incompatible with Paradise was not sexual intercourse and the attendant pleasure; what he found incompatible with Paradise was excitement. Bear in mind: There was pleasure in Paradise, but no excitement.

Erigena's argument holds the key to a theological justification (in other words, a theodicy) of shit. As long as man was allowed to remain in Paradise, either (like Valentinus' Jesus) he did not defecate at all, or (as would seem more likely) he did not look upon shit as something repellent. Not until after God expelled man from Paradise did He make him feel disgust. Man began to hide what shamed him, and by the time he removed the veil, he was blinded by a great light. Thus, immediately after his introduction to disgust, he was introduced to excitement. Without shit (in both the literal and figurative senses of the word), there would be no sexual love as we know it, accompanied by pounding heart and blinded senses.

In Part Three of this novel I told the tale of Sabina standing half-naked with a bowler hat on her head and the fully dressed Tomas at her side. There is something I failed to mention at the time. While she was looking at herself in the mirror, excited by her self-denigration, she had a fantasy of Tomas seating her on the toilet in her bowler hat and watching her void her bowels. Suddenly her heart began to pound and, on the verge of fainting, she pulled Tomas down to the rug and immediately let out an orgasmic shout.

## 5

The dispute between those who believe that the world was created by God and those who think it came into being of its own accord deals with phenomena that go beyond our reason and experience. Much more real is the line separating those who doubt being as it is granted to man (no matter how or by whom) from those who accept it without reservation.

Behind all the European faiths, religious and political, we find the first chapter of Genesis, which tells us that the world was created properly, that human existence is good, and that we are therefore entitled to multiply. Let us call this basic faith a *categorical agreement with being.*

The fact that until recently the word "shit" appeared in print as s--- has nothing to do with moral considerations. You can't claim that shit is immoral, after all! The objection to shit is a metaphysical one. The daily defecation session is daily proof of the unacceptability of Creation. Either/or: either shit is acceptable (in which case don't lock yourself in the bathroom!) or we are created in an unacceptable manner.

It follows, then, that the aesthetic ideal of the categorical agreement with being is a world in which shit is denied and everyone acts as though it did not exist. This aesthetic ideal is called *kitsch.*

"Kitsch" is a German word born in the middle of the sentimental nineteenth century, and from German it entered all Western languages. Repeated use, however, has obliterated its original metaphysical meaning: kitsch is the absolute denial of shit, in both the literal and the figurative senses of the word; kitsch excludes everything from its purview which is essentially unacceptable in human existence.

## 6

Sabina's initial inner revolt against Communism was aesthetic rather than ethical in character. What repelled her was not nearly so much the ugliness of the Communist world (ruined castles transformed into cow sheds) as the mask of beauty it tried to wear—in other words, Communist kitsch. The model of Communist kitsch is the ceremony called May Day.

She had seen May Day parades during the time when people were still enthusiastic or still did their best to feign enthusiasm. The women all wore red, white, and blue blouses, and the public, looking on from balconies and windows, could make out various five-pointed stars, hearts, and letters when the marchers went into formation. Small brass bands accompanied the individual groups, keeping everyone in step. As a group approached the reviewing stand, even the most blasé faces would beam with dazzling smiles, as if trying to prove they were properly joyful or, to be more precise, in proper *agreement.* Nor were they merely expressing political agreement with Communism; no, theirs was an agreement with being as such. The May Day ceremony drew its inspiration from the deep well of the categorical agreement with being. The unwritten, unsung motto of the parade was not "Long live Communism!" but "Long live life!" The power and cunning of Communist politics lay in the fact that it appropriated this slogan. For it was this idiotic tautology ("Long live life!") which attracted people indifferent to the theses of Communism to the Communist parade.

## 7

Ten years later (by which time she was living in America), a friend of some friends, an American senator, took Sabina for a drive in his gigantic car, his four children bouncing up and down in the back. The senator stopped the car in front of a stadium with an artificial skating rink, and the children jumped out and started running along the large expanse of grass surrounding it. Sitting behind the wheel and gazing dreamily after the four little bounding figures, he said to Sabina, "Just look at them." And describing a circle with his arm, a circle that was meant to take in stadium, grass, and children, he added, "Now, that's what I call happiness."

Behind his words there was more than joy at seeing children run and grass grow; there was a deep understanding of the plight of a refugee from a Communist country where, the senator was convinced, no grass grew or children ran.

At that moment an image of the senator standing on a reviewing stand in a Prague square flashed through Sabina's mind. The smile on his face was the smile Communist statesmen beamed from the height of their reviewing stand to the identically smiling citizens in the parade below.

## *8*

How did the senator know that children meant happiness? Could he see into their souls? What if, the moment they were out of sight, three of them jumped the fourth and began beating him up?

The senator had only one argument in his favor: his feeling. When the heart speaks, the mind finds it indecent to object. In the realm of kitsch, the dictatorship of the heart reigns supreme.

The feeling induced by kitsch must be a kind the multitudes can share. Kitsch may not, therefore, depend on an unusual situation; it must derive from the basic images people have engraved in their memories: the ungrateful daughter, the neglected father, children running on the grass, the motherland betrayed, first love.

Kitsch causes two tears to flow in quick succession. The first tear says: How nice to see children running on the grass!

The second tear says: How nice to be moved, together with all mankind, by children running on the grass!

It is the second tear that makes kitsch kitsch.

The brotherhood of man on earth will be possible only on a base of kitsch.

## 9

And no one knows this better than politicians. Whenever a camera is in the offing, they immediately run to the nearest child, lift it in the air, kiss it on the cheek. Kitsch is the aesthetic ideal of all politicians and all political parties and movements.

Those of us who live in a society where various political tendencies exist side by side and competing influences cancel or limit one another can manage more or less to escape the kitsch inquisition: the individual can preserve his individuality; the artist can create unusual works. But whenever a single political movement corners power, we find ourselves in the realm of *totalitarian kitsch.*

When I say "totalitarian," what I mean is that everything

that infringes on kitsch must be banished for life: every display of individualism (because a deviation from the collective is a spit in the eye of the smiling brotherhood); every doubt (because anyone who starts doubting details will end by doubting life itself); all irony (because in the realm of kitsch everything must be taken quite seriously); and the mother who abandons her family or the man who prefers men to women, thereby calling into question the holy decree "Be fruitful and multiply."

In this light, we can regard the gulag as a septic tank used by totalitarian kitsch to dispose of its refuse.

## 10

The decade immediately following the Second World War was a time of the most horrible Stalinist terror. It was the time when Tereza's father was arrested on some piddling charge and ten-year-old Tereza was thrown out of their flat. It was also the time when twenty-year-old Sabina was studying at the Academy of Fine Arts. There, her professor of Marxism expounded on the following theory of socialist art: Soviet society had made such progress that the basic conflict was no longer between good and evil but between good and better. So shit (that is, whatever is essentially unacceptable) could exist only "on the other side" (in America, for instance), and only from there, from the outside, as something alien (a spy, for instance), could it penetrate the world of "good and better."

And in fact, Soviet films, which flooded the cinemas of all Communist countries in that cruelest of times, were saturated with incredible innocence and chastity. The greatest conflict that could occur between two Russians was a lovers' misunderstanding: he thought she no longer loved him; she thought he no longer loved her. But in the final scene they would fall into each other's arms, tears of happiness trickling down their cheeks.

The current conventional interpretation of these films is this: that they showed the Communist ideal, whereas Communist reality was worse.

Sabina always rebelled against that interpretation. Whenever she imagined the world of Soviet kitsch becoming a reality, she felt a shiver run down her back. She would unhesitatingly prefer life in a real Communist regime with all its persecution and meat queues. Life in the real Communist world was still livable. In the world of the Communist ideal made real, in that world of grinning idiots, she would have nothing to say, she would die of horror within a week.

The feeling Soviet kitsch evoked in Sabina strikes me as very much like the horror Tereza experienced in her dream of being marched around a swimming pool with a group of naked women and forced to sing cheerful songs with them while corpses floated just below the surface of the pool. Tereza could not address a single question, a single word, to any of the women; the only response she would have got was the next stanza of the current song. She could not even give any of them a secret wink; they would immediately have pointed her out to the man standing in the basket above the pool, and he would have shot her dead.

Tereza's dream reveals the true function of kitsch: kitsch is a folding screen set up to curtain off death.

# 11

In the realm of totalitarian kitsch, all answers are given in advance and preclude any questions. It follows, then, that the true opponent of totalitarian kitsch is the person who asks questions. A question is like a knife that slices through the stage backdrop and gives us a look at what lies hidden behind it. In fact, that was exactly how Sabina had explained the meaning of her paintings to Tereza: on the surface, an intelligible lie; underneath, the unintelligible truth showing through.

But the people who struggle against what we call totalitarian regimes cannot function with queries and doubts. They, too, need certainties and simple truths to make the multitudes understand, to provoke collective tears.

Sabina had once had an exhibit that was organized by a political organization in Germany. When she picked up the catalogue, the first thing she saw was a picture of herself with a drawing of barbed wire superimposed on it. Inside she found a biography that read like the life of a saint or martyr: she had suffered, struggled against injustice, been forced to abandon her bleeding homeland, yet was carrying on the struggle. "Her paintings are a struggle for happiness" was the final sentence.

She protested, but they did not understand her.

Do you mean that modern art isn't persecuted under Communism?

"My enemy is kitsch, not Communism!" she replied, infuriated.

From that time on, she began to insert mystifications in her biography, and by the time she got to America she even managed to hide the fact that she was Czech. It was all merely a desperate attempt to escape the kitsch that people wanted to make of her life.

# 12

She stood in front of her easel with a half-finished canvas on it, the old man in the armchair behind her observing every stroke of her brush.

"It's time we went home," he said at last with a glance at his watch.

She laid down her palette and went into the bathroom to wash. The old man raised himself out of the armchair and reached for his cane, which was leaning against a table. The door of the studio led directly out to the lawn. It was growing dark. Fifty feet away was a white clapboard house. The ground-floor windows were lit. Sabina was moved by the two windows shining out into the dying day.

All her life she had proclaimed kitsch her enemy. But hadn't she in fact been carrying it with her? Her kitsch was her image of home, all peace, quiet, and harmony, and ruled by a loving mother and wise father. It was an image that took shape within her after the death of her parents. The less her life resembled that sweetest of dreams, the more sensitive she was to its magic, and more than once she shed tears when the ungrateful daughter in a sentimental film embraced the neglected father as the windows of the happy family's house shone out into the dying day.

She had met the old man in New York. He was rich and liked paintings. He lived alone with his wife, also aging, in a house in the country. Facing the house, but still on his land, stood an old stable. He had had it remodeled into a studio for Sabina and would follow the movements of her brush for days on end.

Now all three of them were having supper together. The old woman called Sabina "my daughter," but all indications would lead one to believe the opposite, namely, that Sabina was the mother and that her two children doted on her, worshipped her, would do anything she asked.

Had she then, herself on the threshold of old age, found the parents who had been snatched from her as a girl? Had she at last found the children she had never had herself?

She was well aware it was an illusion. Her days with the aging couple were merely a brief interval. The old man was seriously ill, and when his wife was left on her own, she would go and live with their son in Canada. Sabina's path of betrayals would then continue elsewhere, and from the depths of her being, a silly mawkish song about two shining windows and the happy family living behind them would occasionally make its way into the unbearable lightness of being.

Though touched by the song, Sabina did not take her feeling seriously. She knew only too well that the song was a beautiful lie. As soon as kitsch is recognized for the lie it is, it moves into the context of non-kitsch, thus losing its authoritarian power and becoming as touching as any other human weakness. For none among us is superman enough to escape kitsch completely. No matter how we scorn it, kitsch is an integral part of the human condition.

## *13*

Kitsch has its source in the categorical agreement with being.

But what is the basis of being? God? Mankind? Struggle? Love? Man? Woman?

Since opinions vary, there are various kitsches: Catholic, Protestant, Jewish, Communist, Fascist, democratic, feminist, European, American, national, international.

Since the days of the French Revolution, one half of Europe has been referred to as the left, the other half as the right. Yet to define one or the other by means of the theoretical principles it professes is all but impossible. And no wonder: political movements rest not so much on rational attitudes as on the fantasies, images, words, and archetypes that come together to make up this or that *political kitsch.*

The fantasy of the Grand March that Franz was so intoxicated by is the political kitsch joining leftists of all times and tendencies. The Grand March is the splendid march on the road to brotherhood, equality, justice, happiness; it goes on and on, obstacles notwithstanding, for obstacles there must be if the march is to be the Grand March.

The dictatorship of the proletariat or democracy? Rejection of the consumer society or demands for increased productivity? The guillotine or an end to the death penalty? It is all beside the point. What makes a leftist a leftist is not this or that theory but his ability to integrate any theory into the kitsch called the Grand March.

## 14

Franz was obviously not a devotee of kitsch. The fantasy of the Grand March played more or less the same role in his life as the mawkish song about the two brightly lit windows in Sabina's. What political party did Franz vote for? I am afraid he did not vote at all; he preferred to spend Election Day hiking in the mountains. Which does not, of course, imply that he was no longer touched by the Grand March. It is always nice to dream that we are part of a jubilant throng marching through the centuries, and Franz never quite forgot the dream.

One day, some friends phoned him from Paris. They were planning a march on Cambodia and invited him to join them.

Cambodia had recently been through American bombardment, a civil war, a paroxysm of carnage by local Communists that reduced the small nation by a fifth, and finally occupation by neighboring Vietnam, which by then was a mere vassal of Russia. Cambodia was racked by famine, and people were dying for want of medical care. An international medical committee had repeatedly requested permission to enter the country, but the Vietnamese had turned them down. The idea was for a group of important Western intellectuals to march to the Cambodian border and by means of this great spectacle performed before the eyes of the world to force the occupied country to allow the doctors in.

The friend who spoke to Franz was one he had marched with through the streets of Paris. At first Franz was thrilled by the invitation, but then his eye fell on his student-mistress sitting across the room in an armchair. She was looking up at him, her eyes magnified by the big round lenses in her glasses. Franz had the feeling those eyes were begging him not to go. And so he apologetically declined.

No sooner had he hung up than he regretted his decision. True, he had taken care of his earthly mistress, but he had neglected his unearthly love. Wasn't Cambodia the same as Sabina's country? A country occupied by its neighbor's Communist army! A country that had felt the brunt of Russia's fist! All at once, Franz felt that his half-forgotten friend had contacted him at Sabina's secret bidding.

Heavenly bodies know all and see all. If he went on the march, Sabina would gaze down on him enraptured; she would understand that he had remained faithful to her.

"Would you be terribly upset if I went on the march?" he asked the girl with the glasses, who counted every day away from him a loss, yet could not deny him a thing.

Several days later he was in a large jet taking off from Paris with twenty doctors and about fifty intellectuals (professors, writers, diplomats, singers, actors, and mayors) as well as four hundred reporters and photographers.

# 15

The plane landed in Bangkok. Four hundred and seventy doctors, intellectuals, and reporters made their way to the large ballroom of an international hotel, where more doctors, actors, singers, and professors of linguistics had gathered with several hundred journalists bearing notebooks, tape recorders, and cameras, still and video. On the podium, a group of twenty or so Americans sitting at a long table were presiding over the proceedings.

The French intellectuals with whom Franz had entered the ballroom felt slighted and humiliated. The march on Cambodia had been their idea, and here the Americans, supremely unabashed as usual, had not only taken over, but had taken over in English without a thought that a Dane or a Frenchman might not understand them. And because the Danes had long since forgotten that they once formed a nation of their own, the French were the only Europeans capable of protest. So high were their principles that they refused to protest in English, and made their case to the Americans on the podium in their mother tongue. The Americans, not understanding a word, reacted with friendly, agreeing smiles. In the end, the French had no choice but to frame their objection in English: "Why is this meeting in English when there are Frenchmen present?"

Though amazed at so curious an objection, the Americans, still smiling, acquiesced: the meeting would be run bilingually. Before it could resume, however, a suitable interpreter had to be found. Then, every sentence had to resound in both English and French, which made the discussion take twice as long, or rather more than twice as long, since all the French had some English and kept interrupting the interpreter to correct him, disputing every word.

The meeting reached its peak when a famous American actress rose to speak. Because of her, even more photographers and cameramen streamed into the auditorium, and every syllable she pronounced was accompanied by the click of another camera. The actress spoke about suffering children, about the barbarity of Communist dictatorship, the human right to security, the current threat to the traditional values of civilized society, the inalienable freedom of the human individual, and President Carter, who was deeply sorrowed by the events in Cambodia. By the time she had pronounced her closing words, she was in tears.

Then up jumped a young French doctor with a red mustache and shouted, "We're here to cure dying people, not to pay homage to President Carter! Let's not turn this into an American propaganda circus! We're not here to protest against Communism! We're here to save lives!"

He was immediately seconded by several other Frenchmen.

The interpreter was frightened and did not dare translate what they said. So the twenty Americans on the podium looked on once more with smiles full of good will, many nodding agreement. One of them even lifted his fist in the air because he knew Europeans liked to raise their fists in times of collective euphoria.

# 16

How can it be that leftist intellectuals (because the doctor with the mustache was nothing if not a leftist intellectual) are willing to march against the interests of a Communist country when Communism has always been considered the left's domain?

When the crimes of the country called the Soviet Union became too scandalous, a leftist had two choices: either to spit on his former life and stop marching or (more or less sheepishly) to reclassify the Soviet Union as an obstacle to the Grand March and march on.

Have I not said that what makes a leftist a leftist is the kitsch of the Grand March? The identity of kitsch comes not from a political strategy but from images, metaphors, and vocabulary. It is therefore possible to break the habit and march against the interests of a Communist country. What is impossible, however, is to substitute one word for others. It is possible to threaten the Vietnamese army with one's fist. It is impossible to shout "Down with Communism!" "Down with Communism!" is a slogan belonging to the enemies of the Grand March, and anyone worried about losing face must remain faithful to the purity of his own kitsch.

The only reason I bring all this up is to explain the misunderstanding between the French doctor and the American actress, who, egocentric as she was, imagined herself the victim of envy or misogyny. In point of fact, the French doctor displayed a finely honed aesthetic sensibility: the phrases "President Carter," "our traditional values," "the barbarity of Communism" all belong to the vocabulary of *American kitsch* and have nothing to do with the kitsch of the Grand March.

## 17

The next morning, they all boarded buses and rode through Thailand to the Cambodian border. In the evening, they pulled into a small village where they had rented several houses on stilts. The regularly flooding river forced the villagers to live above ground level, while their pigs huddled down below. Franz slept in a room with four other professors. From afar came the oinking of the swine, from up close the snores of a famous mathematician.

In the morning, they climbed back into the buses. At a point about a mile from the border, all vehicular traffic was prohibited. The border crossing could be reached only by means of a narrow, heavily guarded road. The buses stopped. The French contingent poured out of them only to find that again the Americans had beaten them and formed the vanguard of the parade. The crucial moment had come. The interpreter was recalled and a long quarrel ensued. At last everyone assented to the following: the parade would be headed by one American, one Frenchman, and the Cambodian interpreter; next would come the doctors, and only then the rest of the crowd. The American actress brought up the rear.

The road was narrow and lined with minefields. Every so often it was narrowed even more by a barrier—two cement blocks wound round with barbed wire—passable only in single file.

About fifteen feet ahead of Franz was a famous German poet and pop singer who had already written nine hundred thirty songs for peace and against war. He was carrying a long pole topped by a white flag that set off his full black beard and set him apart from the others.

All up and down the long parade, photographers and cameramen were snapping and whirring their equipment, dashing up to the front, pausing, inching back, dropping to their knees, then straightening up and running even farther ahead. Now and then they would call out the name of some celebrity, who would then unwittingly turn in their direction just long enough to let them trigger their shutters.

## 18

Something was in the air. People were slowing down and looking back.

The American actress, who had ended up in the rear, could no longer stand the disgrace of it and, determined to take the offensive, was sprinting to the head of the parade. It was as if a runner in a five-kilometer race, who had been saving his strength by hanging back with the pack, had suddenly sprung forward and started overtaking his opponents one by one.

The men stepped back with embarrassed smiles, not wishing to spoil the famous runner's bid for victory, but the women yelled, "Get back in line! This is no star parade!"

Undaunted, the actress pushed on, a suite of five photographers and two cameramen in tow.

Suddenly a Frenchwoman, a professor of linguistics, grabbed the actress by the wrist and said (in terrible-sounding English), "This is a parade for doctors who have come to care for mortally ill Cambodians, not a publicity stunt for movie stars!"

The actress's wrist was locked in the linguistics professor's grip; she could do nothing to pry it loose. "What the hell do you think you're doing?" she said (in perfect English). "I've been in a hundred parades like this! You won't get anywhere without stars! It's our job! Our moral obligation!"

*"Merde!"* said the linguistics professor (in perfect French).

The American actress understood and burst into tears.

"Hold it, please," a cameraman called out and knelt at her feet. The actress gave a long look into his lens, the tears flowing down her cheeks.

## 19

When at last the linguistics professor let go of the American actress's wrist, the German pop singer with the black beard and white flag called out her name.

The American actress had never heard of him, but after being humiliated she was more receptive to sympathy than usual and ran over to him. The singer switched the pole to his left hand and put his right arm around her shoulders.

They were immediately surrounded by new photographers and cameramen. A well-known American photographer, having trouble squeezing both their faces and the flag into his viewfinder because the pole was so long, moved back a few steps into the ricefield. And so it happened that he stepped on a mine. An explosion rang out, and his body, ripped to pieces, went flying through the air, raining a shower of blood on the European intellectuals.

The singer and the actress were horrified and could not budge. They lifted their eyes to the flag. It was spattered with blood. Once more they were horrified. Then they timidly ventured a few more looks upward and began to smile slightly. They were filled with a strange pride, a pride they had never known before: the flag they were carrying had been consecrated by blood. Once more they joined the march.

## 20

The border was formed by a small river, but because a long wall, six feet high and lined with sandbags to protect Thai sharpshooters, ran alongside it, it was invisible. There was only one breach in the wall, at the point where a bridge spanned the river. Vietnamese forces lay in wait on the other side, but they, too, were invisible, their positions perfectly camouflaged. It was clear, however, that the moment anyone set foot on the bridge, the invisible Vietnamese would open fire.

The parade participants went up to the wall and stood on tiptoe. Franz peered into the gap between two sandbags, trying to see what was going on. He saw nothing. Then he was shoved away by a photographer, who felt that he had more right to the space.

Franz looked back. Seven photographers were perching in the mighty crown of an isolated tree like a flock of overgrown crows, their eyes fixed on the opposite bank.

Just then the interpreter, at the head of the parade, raised a large megaphone to her lips and called out in Khmer to the other side: These people are doctors; they request permission to enter the territory of Cambodia and offer medical assistance; they have no political designs whatsoever and are guided solely by a concern for human life.

The response from the other side was a stunning silence. A silence so absolute that everyone's spirits sank. Only the cameras clicked on, sounding in the silence like the song of an exotic insect.

Franz had the sudden feeling that the Grand March was coming to an end. Europe was surrounded by borders of silence, and the space where the Grand March was occurring was now no more than a small platform in the middle of the planet. The crowds that had once pressed eagerly up to the platform had long since departed, and the Grand March went on in solitude, without spectators. Yes, said Franz to himself, the Grand March goes on, the world's indifference notwithstanding, but it is growing nervous and hectic: yesterday against the American occupation of Vietnam, today against the Vietnamese occupation of Cambodia; yesterday for Israel, today for the Palestinians; yesterday for Cuba, tomorrow against Cuba—and always against America; at times against massacres and at times in support of other massacres; Europe marches on, and to keep up with events, to leave none of them out, its pace grows faster and faster, until finally the Grand March is a procession of rushing, galloping people and the platform is shrinking and shrinking until one day it will be reduced to a mere dimensionless dot.

# 21

Once more the interpreter shouted her challenge into the megaphone. And again the response was a boundless and endlessly indifferent silence.

Franz looked in all directions. The silence on the other side of the river had hit them all like a slap in the face. Even the singer with the white flag and the American actress were depressed, hesitant about what to do next.

In a flash of insight Franz saw how laughable they all were, but instead of cutting him off from them or flooding him with irony, the thought made him feel the kind of infinite love we feel for the condemned. Yes, the Grand March was coming to an end, but was that any reason for Franz to betray it? Wasn't his own life coming to an end as well? Who was he to jeer at the exhibitionism of the people accompanying the courageous doctors to the border? What could they all do but put on a show? Had they any choice?

Franz was right. I can't help thinking about the editor in Prague who organized the petition for the amnesty of political prisoners. He knew perfectly well that his petition would not help the prisoners. His true goal was not to free the prisoners; it was to show that people without fear still exist. That, too, was playacting. But he had no other possibility. His choice was not between playacting and action. His choice was between playacting and no action at all. There are situations in which people are *condemned* to playact. Their struggle with mute power (the mute power across the river, a police transmogrified into mute microphones in the wall) is the struggle of a theater company that has attacked an army.

Franz watched his friend from the Sorbonne lift his fist and threaten the silence on the other side.

## 22

For the third time the interpreter shouted her challenge into the megaphone.

The silence she again received in response suddenly turned Franz's depression into rage. Here he was, standing only a few steps from the bridge joining Thailand to Cambodia, and he felt an overwhelming desire to run out onto it, scream blood-curdling curses to the skies, and die in a great clatter of gunfire.

That sudden desire of Franz's reminds us of something; yes, it reminds us of Stalin's son, who ran to electrocute himself on the barbed wire when he could no longer stand to watch the poles of human existence come so close to each other as to touch, when there was no longer any difference between sublime and squalid, angel and fly, God and shit.

Franz could not accept the fact that the glory of the Grand

March was equal to the comic vanity of its marchers, that the exquisite noise of European history was lost in an infinite silence and that there was no longer any difference between history and silence. He felt like placing his own life on the scales; he wanted to prove that the Grand March weighed more than shit.

But man can prove nothing of the sort. One pan of the scales held shit; on the other, Stalin's son put his entire body. And the scales did not move.

Instead of getting himself shot, Franz merely hung his head and went back with the others, single file, to the buses.

## 23

We all need someone to look at us. We can be divided into four categories according to the kind of look we wish to live under.

The first category longs for the look of an infinite number of anonymous eyes, in other words, for the look of the public. That is the case with the German singer, the American actress, and even the tall, stooped editor with the big chin. He was accustomed to his readers, and when one day the Russians banned his newspaper, he had the feeling that the atmosphere was suddenly a hundred times thinner. Nothing could replace the look of unknown eyes. He thought he would suffocate. Then one day he realized that he was constantly being followed, bugged, and surreptitiously photographed in the street. Suddenly he had anonymous eyes on him and he could breathe again! He began making theatrical speeches to the microphones in his wall. In the police, he had found his lost public.

The second category is made up of people who have a vital need to be looked at by many known eyes. They are the tireless hosts of cocktail parties and dinners. They are happier than the people in the first category, who, when they lose their public, have the feeling that the lights have gone out in the room of their lives. This happens to nearly all of them sooner or later. People in the second category, on the other hand, can always come up with the eyes they need. Marie-Claude and her daughter belong in the second category.

Then there is the third category, the category of people who need to be constantly before the eyes of the person they love. Their situation is as dangerous as the situation of people in the first category. One day the eyes of their beloved will close, and the room will go dark. Tereza and Tomas belong in the third category.

And finally there is the fourth category, the rarest, the category of people who live in the imaginary eyes of those who are not present. They are the dreamers. Franz, for example. He traveled to the borders of Cambodia only for Sabina. As the bus bumped along the Thai road, he could feel her eyes fixed on him in a long stare.

Tomas's son belongs in the same category. Let me call him Simon. (He will be glad to have a Biblical name, like his father's.) The eyes he longed for were Tomas's. As a result of his embroilment in the petition campaign, he was expelled from the university. The girl he had been going out with was the niece of a village priest. He married her, became a tractor driver on a collective farm, a practicing Catholic, and a father. When he learned that Tomas, too, was living in the country, he was thrilled: fate had made their lives symmetrical! This encouraged him to write Tomas a letter. He did not ask him to write back. He only wanted him to focus his eyes on his life.

# 24

Franz and Simon are the dreamers of this novel. Unlike Franz, Simon never liked his mother. From childhood he searched for his father. He was willing to believe his father the victim of some sort of injustice that predated and explained the injustice his father had perpetrated on him. He never felt angry with his father, because he did not wish to ally himself with his mother, who continually maligned the man.

He lived with her until he was eighteen and had finished secondary school; then he went off to Prague and the university. By that time Tomas was washing windows. Often Simon would wait long hours to arrange an accidental encounter with Tomas. But Tomas never stopped to talk to him.

The only reason he became involved with the big-chinned former editor was that the editor's fate reminded him of his father's. The editor had never heard of Tomas. The Oedipus article had been forgotten. It was Simon who told him about it and asked him to persuade Tomas to sign the petition. The only reason the editor agreed was that he wanted to do something nice for the boy, whom he liked.

Whenever Simon thought back to the day when they had met, he was ashamed of his stage fright. His father couldn't have liked him. He, on the other hand, liked his father. He remembered his every word, and as time went on he saw how true they were. The words that made the biggest impression on him were "Punishing people who don't know what they've done is barbaric." When his girlfriend's uncle put a Bible in his hands, he was particularly struck by Jesus' words "Forgive them, for they know not what they do." He knew that his father was a nonbeliever, but in the similarity of the two phrases he saw a secret sign: his father agreed with the path he had taken.

During approximately his third year in the country, he received a letter from Tomas asking him to come and visit. Their meeting was a friendly one. Simon felt relaxed and did not stammer a bit. He probably did not realize that they did not understand each other very well. About four months later, he received a telegram saying that Tomas and his wife had been crushed to death under a truck.

At about that time, he learned about a woman who had once been his father's mistress and was living in France. He found out her address. Because he desperately needed an imaginary eye to follow his life, he would occasionally write her long letters.

## *25*

Sabina continued to receive letters from her sad village correspondent till the end of her life. Many of them would remain unread, because she took less and less interest in her native land.

The old man died, and Sabina moved to California. Farther

west, farther away from the country where she had been born.

She had no trouble selling her paintings, and liked America. But only on the surface. Everything beneath the surface was alien to her. Down below, there was no grandpa or uncle. She was afraid of shutting herself into a grave and sinking into American earth.

And so one day she composed a will in which she requested that her dead body be cremated and its ashes thrown to the winds. Tereza and Tomas had died under the sign of weight. She wanted to die under the sign of lightness. She would be lighter than air. As Parmenides would put it, the negative would change into the positive.

## 26

The bus stopped in front of the Bangkok hotel. No one any longer felt like holding meetings. People drifted off in groups to sightsee; some set off for temples, others for brothels. Franz's friend from the Sorbonne suggested they spend the evening together, but he preferred to be alone.

It was nearly dark when he went out into the streets. He kept thinking about Sabina, feeling her eyes on him. Whenever he felt her long stare, he began to doubt himself: he had never known quite what Sabina thought. It made him uncomfortable now as well. Could she be mocking him? Did she consider the cult he made of her silly? Could she be trying to tell him it was time for him to grow up and devote himself fully to the mistress she herself had sent to him?

Picturing the face with big round glasses, he suddenly realized how happy he was with his student-mistress. All at once, the Cambodia venture struck him as meaningless, laughable. Why had he come? Only now did he know. He had come to find out once and for all that neither parades nor Sabina but rather the girl with the glasses was his real life, his only real life! He had come to find out that reality was more than a dream, much more than a dream!

Suddenly a figure emerged out of the semi-darkness and said something to him in a language he did not know. He gave the intruder a look that was startled but sympathetic. The man bowed and smiled and muttered something with great urgency. What was he trying to say? He seemed to be inviting him somewhere. The man took him by the hand and started leading him away. Franz decided that someone needed his help. Maybe there *was* some sense in his coming all that distance. Wasn't he being called to help somebody?

Suddenly there were two other men next to the first, and one of them asked him in English for his money.

At that point, the girl with the glasses vanished from his thoughts and Sabina fixed her eyes on him, unreal Sabina with her grand fate, Sabina who had made him feel so small. Her wrathful eyes bored into him, angry and dissatisfied: Had he been had once again? Had someone else abused his idiotic goodness?

He tore his arm away from the man, who was now holding on to his sleeve. He remembered that Sabina had always admired his strength. He seized the arm one of the other men was lifting against him, and, tightening his grip, tossed him over his shoulder in a perfect judo flip.

Now he was satisfied with himself. Sabina's eyes were still on him. She would never see him humiliate himself again! She would never see him retreat! Franz was through with being soft and sentimental!

He felt what was almost a cheerful hatred for these men. They had thought to have a good laugh at him and his naivete! He stood there with his shoulders slightly hunched and his eyes darting back and forth between the two remaining men. Suddenly, he felt a heavy blow on his head, and he crumpled immediately. He vaguely sensed being carried somewhere. Then he was thrown into emptiness and felt himself falling. A violent crack, and he lost consciousness.

He woke up in a hospital in Geneva. Marie-Claude was leaning over his bed. He wanted to tell her she had no right to be there. He wanted them to send immediately for the girl with the glasses. All his thoughts were with her. He wanted to shout that he couldn't stand having anyone but her at his side. But he realized with horror that he could not speak. He looked up at Marie-Claude with infinite hatred and tried to turn away from her. But he could not move his body. His head, perhaps? No, he could not even move his head. He closed his eyes so as not to see her.

## 27

In death, Franz at last belonged to his wife. He belonged to her as he had never belonged to her before. Marie-Claude took care of everything: she saw to the funeral, sent out the announcements, bought the wreaths, and had a black dress made—a wedding dress, in reality. Yes, a husband's funeral is a wife's true wedding! The climax of her life's work! The reward for her sufferings!

The pastor understood this very well. His funeral oration was about a true conjugal love that had withstood many tests to remain a haven of peace for the deceased, a haven to which he had returned at the end of his days. The colleague of Franz's whom Marie-Claude asked to speak at the graveside services also paid homage primarily to the deceased's brave wife.

Somewhere in the back, supported by a friend, stood the girl with the big glasses. The combination of many pills and suppressed sobs gave her an attack of cramps before the ceremony came to an end. She lurched forward, clutching her stomach, and her friend had to take her away from the cemetery.

## 28

The moment he received the telegram from the chairman of the collective farm, he jumped on his motorcycle. He arrived in time to arrange for the funeral. The inscription he chose to go under his father's name on the gravestone read: HE WANTED THE KINGDOM OF GOD ON EARTH.

He was well aware that his father would not have said it in those words, but he was certain they expressed what his father actually thought. The kingdom of God means justice. Tomas had longed for a world in which justice would reign. Hadn't Simon the right to express his father's life in his own vocabulary? Of course he had: haven't all heirs had that right from time immemorial?

A RETURN AFTER LONG WANDERINGS was the inscription adorning the stone above Franz's grave. It can be interpreted in religious terms: the wanderings being our earthly existence, the return our return to God's embrace. But the insiders knew that it had a perfectly secular meaning as well. Indeed, Marie-Claude talked about it every day:

Franz, dear, sweet Franz! The mid-life crisis was just too much for him. And that pitiful little girl who caught him in her net! Why, she wasn't even pretty! (Did you see those enormous glasses she tried to hide behind?) But when they start pushing fifty (don't we know it!), they'll sell their souls for a fresh piece of flesh. Only his wife knows how it made him suffer! It was pure moral torture! Because, deep down, Franz was a kind and decent man. How else can you explain that crazy, desperate trip to wherever it was in Asia? He went there to find death. Yes, Marie-Claude knew it for an absolute fact: Franz had consciously sought out death. In his last days, when he was dying and had no need to lie, she was the only person he asked for. He couldn't talk, but how he'd thanked her with his eyes! He'd fixed his eyes on her and begged to be forgiven. And she forgave him.

## 29

What remains of the dying population of Cambodia?

One large photograph of an American actress holding an Asian child in her arms.

What remains of Tomas?

An inscription reading HE WANTED THE KINGDOM OF GOD ON EARTH.

What remains of Beethoven?

A frown, an improbable mane, and a somber voice intoning "*Es muss sein!*"

What remains of Franz?

An inscription reading A RETURN AFTER LONG WANDERINGS.

And so on and so forth. Before we are forgotten, we will be turned into kitsch. Kitsch is the stopover between being and oblivion.

# PART SEVEN

# Karenin's Smile

# 1

The window looked out on a slope overgrown with the crooked bodies of apple trees. The woods cut off the view above the slope, and a crooked line of hills stretched into the distance. When, towards evening, a white moon made its way into the pale sky, Tereza would go and stand on the threshold. The sphere hanging in the not yet darkened sky seemed like a lamp they had forgotten to turn off in the morning, a lamp that had burned all day in the room of the dead.

None of the crooked apple trees growing along the slope could ever leave the spot where it had put down its roots, just as neither Tereza nor Tomas could ever leave their village. They had sold their car, their television set, and their radio to buy a tiny cottage and garden from a farmer who was moving to town.

Life in the country was the only escape open to them, because only in the country was there a constant deficit of people and a surplus of living accommodations. No one bothered to look into the political past of people willing to go off and work in the fields or woods; no one envied them.

Tereza was happy to abandon the city, the drunken barflies molesting her, and the anonymous women leaving the smell of their groins in Tomas's hair. The police stopped pestering them, and the incident with the engineer so merged with the scene on Petrin Hill that she was hard put to tell which was a dream and which the truth. (Was the engineer in fact employed by the secret police? Perhaps he was, perhaps not. Men who use borrowed flats for rendezvous and never make love to the same woman twice are not so rare.)

In any case, Tereza was happy and felt that she had at last reached her goal: she and Tomas were together and alone. Alone? Let me be more precise: living "alone" meant breaking with all their former friends and acquaintances, cutting their life in two like a ribbon; however, they felt perfectly at home in the company of the country people they worked with, and they sometimes exchanged visits with them.

The day they met the chairman of the local collective farm at the spa that had Russian street names, Tereza discovered in herself a picture of country life originating in memories of books she had read or in her ancestors. It was a harmonious world; everyone came together in one big happy family with common interests and routines: church services on Sundays, a tavern where the men could get away from their womenfolk, and a hall in the tavern where a band played on Saturdays and the villagers danced.

Under Communism, however, village life no longer fit the age-old pattern. The church was in the neighboring village, and no one went there; the tavern had been turned into offices, so the men had nowhere to meet and drink beer, the young people nowhere to dance. Celebrating church holidays was forbidden, and no one cared about their secular replacements. The nearest cinema was in a town fifteen miles away. So, at the end of a day's work filled with boisterous shouting and relaxed chatter, they would all shut themselves up within their four walls and, surrounded by contemporary furniture emanating bad taste like a cold draft, stare at the refulgent television screen. They never paid one another visits besides dropping in on a neighbor for a word or two before supper. They all dreamed of moving into town. The country offered them nothing in the way of even a minimally interesting life.

Perhaps it was the fact that no one wished to settle there that caused the state to lose its power over the countryside. A farmer who no longer owns his own land and is merely a laborer tilling the soil forms no allegiance to either region or work; he has nothing to lose, nothing to fear for. As a result of such apathy, the countryside had maintained more than a modicum of autonomy and freedom. The chairman of the collective farm was not brought in from outside (as were all high-level managers in the city); he was elected by the villagers from among themselves.

Because everyone wanted to leave, Tereza and Tomas were in an exceptional position: they had come voluntarily. If the other villagers took advantage of every opportunity to make day trips to the surrounding towns, Tereza and Tomas were content to remain where they were, which meant that before long they knew the villagers better than the villagers knew one another.

The collective farm chairman became a truly close friend. He had a wife, four children, and a pig he raised like a dog. The pig's name was Mefisto, and he was the pride and main attraction of the village. He would answer his master's call and was always clean and pink; he paraded about on his hoofs like a heavy-thighed woman in high heels.

When Karenin first saw Mefisto, he was very upset and

circled him, sniffing, for a long time. But he soon made friends with him, even to the point of preferring him to the village dogs. Indeed, he had nothing but scorn for the dogs, because they were all chained to their doghouses and never stopped their silly, unmotivated barking. Karenin correctly assessed the value of being one of a kind, and I can state without compunction that he greatly appreciated his friendship with the pig.

The chairman was glad to be able to help his former surgeon, though at the same time sad that he could do nothing more. Tomas became the driver of the pickup truck that took the farm workers out to the fields and hauled equipment.

The collective farm had four large cow sheds as well as a small stable of forty heifers. Tereza was charged with looking after them and taking them out to pasture twice a day. Because the closer, easily accessible meadows would eventually be mowed, she had to take her herd into the surrounding hills for grazing, gradually moving farther and farther out and, in the course of the year, covering all the pastureland round about. As in her small-town youth, she was never without a book, and the minute she reached the day's pasture she would open it and read.

Karenin always kept her company. He learned to bark at the young cows when they got too frisky and tried to go off on their own; he did so with obvious zest. He was definitely the happiest of the three. Never before had his position as keeper of the clock been so respected. The country was no place for improvisation; the time in which Tereza and Tomas lived was growing closer to the regularity of his time.

One day, after lunch (a time when they both had an hour to themselves), they took a walk with Karenin up the slope behind their cottage.

"I don't like the way he's running," said Tereza.

Karenin was limping on a hind leg. Tomas bent down and

carefully felt all along it. Near the hock he found a small bump.

The next day he sat him in the front seat of the pickup and drove, during his rounds, to the neighboring village, where the local veterinarian lived. A week later, he paid him another visit. He came home with the news that Karenin had cancer.

Within three days, Tomas himself, with the vet in attendance, had operated on him. When Tomas brought him home, Karenin had not quite come out of the anesthesia. He lay on the rug next to their bed with his eyes open, whimpering, his thigh shaved bare and the incision and six stitches painfully visible.

At last he tried to stand up. He failed.

Tereza was terrified that he would never walk again.

"Don't worry," said Tomas. "He's still under the anesthetic."

She tried to pick him up, but he snapped at her. It was the first time he'd ever tried to bite Tereza!

"He doesn't know who you are," said Tomas. "He doesn't recognize you."

They lifted him onto their bed, where he quickly fell asleep, as did they.

At three o'clock that morning, he suddenly woke them up, wagging his tail and climbing all over them, cuddling up to them, unable to have his fill.

It was the first time he'd ever got them up, too! He had always waited until one of them woke up before he dared jump on them.

But when he suddenly came to in the middle of the night, he could not control himself. Who can tell what distances he covered on his way back? Who knows what phantoms he battled? And now that he was at home with his dear ones, he felt compelled to share his overwhelming joy, a joy of return and rebirth.

# 2

The very beginning of Genesis tells us that God created man in order to give him dominion over fish and fowl and all creatures. Of course, Genesis was written by a man, not a horse. There is no certainty that God actually did grant man dominion over other creatures. What seems more likely, in fact, is that man invented God to sanctify the dominion that he had usurped for himself over the cow and the horse. Yes, the right to kill a deer or a cow is the only thing all of mankind can agree upon, even during the bloodiest of wars.

The reason we take that right for granted is that we stand at the top of the hierarchy. But let a third party enter the game—a visitor from another planet, for example, someone to whom God says, "Thou shalt have dominion over creatures of all other stars"—and all at once taking Genesis for granted becomes problematical. Perhaps a man hitched to the cart of a Martian or roasted on the spit by inhabitants of the Milky Way will recall the veal cutlet he used to slice on his dinner plate and apologize (belatedly!) to the cow.

Walking along with her heifers, driving them in front of her, Tereza was constantly obliged to use discipline, because young cows are frisky and like to run off into the fields. Karenin kept her company. He had been going along daily to the pasture with her for two years. He always enjoyed being strict with the heifers, barking at them, asserting his authority. (His God had given him dominion over cows, and he was proud of it.) Today, however, he was having great trouble making his way, and hobbled along on three legs; the fourth had a wound on it, and the wound was festering. Tereza kept bending down and stroking his back. Two weeks after the operation, it became clear that the cancer had continued to spread and that Karenin would fare worse and worse.

Along the way, they met a neighbor who was hurrying off to a cow shed in her rubber boots. The woman stopped long enough to ask, "What's wrong with the dog? It seems to be limping." "He has cancer," said Tereza. "There's no hope." And the lump in her throat kept her from going on. The woman noticed Tereza's tears and nearly lost her temper: "Good heavens! Don't tell me you're going to bawl your head off over a dog!" She was not being vicious; she was a kind woman and merely wanted to comfort Tereza. Tereza understood, and had spent enough time in the country to realize that if the local inhabitants loved every rabbit as she loved Karenin, they would be unable to kill any of them and they and their animals would soon starve to death. Still, the woman's words struck her as less than friendly. "I understand," she answered without protest, but quickly turned her back and went her way. The love she bore her dog made her feel cut off, isolated. With a sad smile, she told herself that she needed to hide it more than she would an affair. People are indignant at the thought of someone loving a dog. But if the neighbor had discovered that Tereza had been unfaithful to Tomas, she would have given Tereza a playful pat on the back as a sign of secret solidarity.

Be that as it may, Tereza continued on her path, and, watching her heifers rub against one another, she thought what nice animals they were. Calm, guileless, and sometimes childishly animated, they looked like fat fifty-year-olds pretending they were fourteen. There was nothing more touching than cows at play. Tereza took pleasure in their antics and could not help thinking (it is an idea that kept coming back to her during her two years in the country) that man is as much a parasite on the cow as the tapeworm is on man: We have sucked their udders like leeches. "Man the cow parasite" is probably how non-man defines man in his zoology books.

Now, we may treat this definition as a joke and dismiss it with a condescending laugh. But since Tereza took it seriously, she found herself in a precarious position: her ideas were dangerous and distanced her from the rest of mankind. Even though Genesis says that God gave man dominion over all animals, we can also construe it to mean that He merely entrusted them to man's care. Man was not the planet's master, merely its administrator, and therefore eventually responsible for his administration. Descartes took a decisive step forward: he made man "*maître et propriétaire de la nature.*" And surely there is a deep connection between that step and the fact that he was also the one who point-blank denied animals a soul. Man is master and proprietor, says Descartes, whereas the beast is merely an automaton, an animated machine, a *machina animata.* When an animal laments, it is not a lament; it is merely the rasp of a poorly functioning mechanism. When a wagon wheel grates, the wagon is not in pain; it simply needs oiling. Thus, we have no reason to grieve for a dog being carved up alive in the laboratory.

While the heifers grazed, Tereza sat on a stump with Karenin at her side, his head resting in her lap. She recalled reading a two-line filler in the papers ten or so years ago about how all the dogs in a certain Russian city had been summarily shot. It was that inconspicuous and seemingly insignificant little article that had brought home to her for the first time the sheer horror of her country's oversized neighbor.

That little article was a premonition of things to come. The first years following the Russian invasion could not yet be characterized as a reign of terror. Because practically no one in the entire nation agreed with the occupation regime, the Russians had to ferret out the few exceptions and push them into power. But where could they look? All faith in Communism and love for Russia was dead. So they sought people who wished to get back at life for something, people with revenge on the brain. Then they had to focus, cultivate, and maintain those people's aggressiveness, give them a temporary substitute to practice on.

The substitute they lit upon was animals.

All at once the papers started coming out with cycles of features and organized letters-to-the-editor campaigns demanding, for example, the extermination of all pigeons within city limits. And the pigeons would be exterminated. But the major drive was directed against dogs. People were still disconsolate over the catastrophe of the occupation, but radio, television, and the press went on and on about dogs: how they soil our streets and parks, endanger our children's health, fulfill no useful function, yet must be fed. They whipped up such a psychotic fever that Tereza had been afraid that the crazed mob would do harm to Karenin. Only after a year did the accumulated malice (which until then had been vented, for the sake of training, on animals) find its true goal: people. People started being removed from their jobs, arrested, put on trial. At last the animals could breathe freely.

Tereza kept stroking Karenin's head, which was quietly resting in her lap, while something like the following ran through her mind: There's no particular merit in being nice to one's fellow man. She had to treat the other villagers decently, because otherwise she couldn't live there. Even with Tomas, she was *obliged* to behave lovingly because she needed him. We can never establish with certainty what part of our relations with others is the result of our emotions—love, antipathy, charity, or malice—and what part is predetermined by the constant power play among individuals.

True human goodness, in all its purity and freedom, can come to the fore only when its recipient has no power. Mankind's true moral test, its fundamental test (which lies deeply buried from view), consists of its attitude towards those who are at its mercy: animals. And in this respect mankind has suffered a fundamental debacle, a debacle so fundamental that all others stem from it.

One of the heifers had made friends with Tereza. The

heifer would stop and stare at her with her big brown eyes. Tereza knew her. She called her Marketa. She would have been happy to give all her heifers names, but she was unable to. There were too many of them. Not so long before, forty years or so, all the cows in the village had names. (And if having a name is a sign of having a soul, I can say that they had souls despite Descartes.) But then the villages were turned into a large collective factory, and the cows began spending all their lives in the five square feet set aside for them in their cow sheds. From that time on, they have had no names and become mere *machinae animatae*. The world has proved Descartes correct.

Tereza keeps appearing before my eyes. I see her sitting on the stump petting Karenin's head and ruminating on mankind's debacles. Another image also comes to mind: Nietzsche leaving his hotel in Turin. Seeing a horse and a coachman beating it with a whip, Nietzsche went up to the horse and, before the coachman's very eyes, put his arms around the horse's neck and burst into tears.

That took place in 1889, when Nietzsche, too, had removed himself from the world of people. In other words, it was at the time when his mental illness had just erupted. But for that very reason I feel his gesture has broad implications: Nietzsche was trying to apologize to the horse for Descartes. His lunacy (that is, his final break with mankind) began at the very moment he burst into tears over the horse.

And that is the Nietzsche I love, just as I love Tereza with the mortally ill dog resting his head in her lap. I see them one next to the other: both stepping down from the road along which mankind, "the master and proprietor of nature," marches onward.

# 3

Karenin gave birth to two rolls and a bee. He stared, amazed, at his own progeny. The rolls were utterly serene, but the bee staggered about as if drugged, then flew up and away.

Or so it happened in Tereza's dream. She told it to Tomas the minute he woke up, and they both found a certain consolation in it. It transformed Karenin's illness into a pregnancy and the drama of giving birth into something both laughable and touching: two rolls and a bee.

She again fell prey to illogical hopes. She got out of bed and put on her clothes. Here, too, her day began with a trip to the shop for milk, bread, rolls. But when she called Karenin for his walk that morning, he barely raised his head. It was the first time that he had refused to take part in the ritual he himself had forced upon them.

She went off without him. "Where's Karenin?" asked the woman behind the counter, who had Karenin's roll ready as usual. Tereza carried it home herself in her bag. She pulled it out and showed it to him while still in the doorway. She wanted him to come and fetch it. But he just lay there motionless.

Tomas saw how unhappy Tereza was. He put the roll in his mouth and dropped down on all fours opposite Karenin. Then he slowly crawled up to him.

Karenin followed him with his eyes, which seemed to show a glimmer of interest, but he did not pick himself up. Tomas brought his face right up to his muzzle. Without moving his body, the dog took the end of the roll sticking out of Tomas's mouth into his own. Then Tomas let go of his end so that Karenin could eat it all.

Still on all fours, Tomas retreated a little, arched his back, and started yelping, making believe he wanted to fight over the roll. After a short while, the dog responded with some yelps of his own. At last! What they were hoping for! Karenin feels like playing! Karenin hasn't lost the will to live!

Those yelps were Karenin's smile, and they wanted it to last as long as possible. So Tomas crawled back to him and tore off the end of the roll sticking out of Karenin's mouth. Their faces were so close that Tomas could smell the dog's breath, feel the long hairs on Karenin's muzzle tickling him. The dog gave out another yelp and his mouth twitched; now they each had half a roll between their teeth. Then Karenin made an old tactical error: he dropped his half in the hope of seizing the half in his master's mouth, forgetting, as always, that Tomas was not a dog and had hands. Without letting his half of the roll out of his mouth, Tomas picked up the other half from the floor.

"Tomas!" Tereza cried. "You're not going to take his roll away from him, are you?"

Tomas laid both halves on the floor in front of Karenin, who quickly gulped down the first and held the second in his mouth for an ostentatiously long time, flaunting his victory over the two of them.

Standing there watching him, they thought once more that he was smiling and that as long as he kept smiling he had a motive to keep living despite his death sentence.

The next day his condition actually appeared to have improved. They had lunch. It was the time of day when they normally took him out for a walk. His habit was to start running back and forth between them restlessly. On that day, however, Tereza picked up the leash and collar only to be stared at dully. They tried to look cheerful (for and about him) and pep him up a bit, and after a long wait he took pity on them, tottered over on his three legs, and let her put on the collar.

"I know you hate the camera, Tereza," said Tomas, "but take it along today, will you?"

Tereza went and opened the cupboard to rummage for the long-abandoned, long-forgotten camera. "One day we'll be glad to have the pictures," Tomas went on. "Karenin has been an important part of our life."

"What do you mean, 'has been'?" said Tereza as if she had been bitten by a snake. The camera lay directly in front of her on the cupboard floor, but she would not bend to pick it up. "I won't take it along. I refuse to think about losing Karenin. And you refer to him in the past tense!"

"I'm sorry," said Tomas.

"That's all right," said Tereza mildly. "I catch myself thinking about him in the past tense all the time. I keep having to push it out of my mind. That's why I won't take the camera."

They walked along in silence. Silence was the only way of not thinking about Karenin in the past tense. They did not let him out of their sight; they were with him constantly, waiting for him to smile. But he did not smile; he merely walked with them, limping along on his three legs.

"He's just doing it for us," said Tereza. "He didn't want to go for a walk. He's just doing it to make us happy."

It was sad, what she said, yet without realizing it they were happy. They were happy not in spite of their sadness but thanks to it. They were holding hands and both had the same image in their eyes: a limping dog who represented ten years of their lives.

They walked a bit farther. Then, to their great disappointment, Karenin stopped and turned. They had to go back.

Perhaps that day or perhaps the next Tereza walked in on Tomas reading a letter. Hearing the door open, he slipped it in among some other papers, but she saw him do it. On her way out of the room she also noticed him stuffing the letter into his pocket. But he forgot about the envelope. As soon as she was alone in the house, she studied it carefully. The address was written in an unfamiliar hand, but it was very neat and she guessed it to be a woman's.

When he came back later, she asked him nonchalantly whether the mail had come.

"No," said Tomas, and filled Tereza with despair, a despair all the worse for her having grown unaccustomed to it. No, she did not believe he had a secret mistress in the village. That was all but impossible. She knew what he did with every spare minute. He must have kept up with a woman in Prague who meant so much to him that he thought of her even if she could no longer leave the smell of her groin in his hair. Tereza did not believe that Tomas meant to leave her for the woman, but the happiness of their two years in the country now seemed besmirched by lies.

An old thought came back to her: Her home was Karenin, not Tomas. Who would wind the clock of their days when he was gone?

Transported mentally into the future, a future without Karenin, Tereza felt abandoned.

Karenin was lying in a corner whimpering. Tereza went out into the garden. She looked down at a patch of grass between two apple trees and imagined burying Karenin there. She dug her heel into the earth and traced a rectangle in the grass. That was where his grave would be.

"What are you doing?" Tomas asked, surprising her just as she had surprised him reading the letter a few hours earlier.

She gave no answer. He noticed her hands trembling for the first time in many months. He grabbed hold of them. She pulled away from him.

"Is that a grave for Karenin?"

She did not answer.

Her silence grated on him. He exploded. "First you blame

me for thinking of him in the past tense, and then what do you do? You go and make the funeral arrangements!"

She turned her back on him.

Tomas retreated into his room, slamming the door behind him.

Tereza went in and opened it. "Instead of thinking about yourself all the time, you might at least have some consideration for him," she said. "He was asleep until you woke him. Now he'll start whimpering again."

She knew she was being unfair (the dog was not asleep); she knew she was acting like the most vulgar of women, the kind that is out to cause pain and knows how.

Tomas tiptoed into the room where Karenin was lying, but she would not leave him alone with the dog. They both leaned over him, each from his own side. Not that there was a hint of reconciliation in the move. Quite the contrary. Each of them was alone. Tereza with her dog, Tomas with his.

It is thus divided, each alone, that, sad to say, they remained with him until his last hour.

## 4

Why was the word "idyll" so important for Tereza?

Raised as we are on the mythology of the Old Testament, we might say that an idyll is an image that has remained with us like a memory of Paradise: life in Paradise was not like following a straight line to the unknown; it was not an adventure. It moved in a circle among known objects. Its monotony bred happiness, not boredom.

As long as people lived in the country, in nature, surrounded by domestic animals, in the bosom of regularly recurring seasons, they retained at least a glimmer of that paradisiac idyll. That is why Tereza, when she met the chairman of the collective farm at the spa, conjured up an image of the countryside (a countryside she had never lived in or known) that she found enchanting. It was her way of looking back, back to Paradise.

Adam, leaning over a well, did not yet realize that what he saw was himself. He would not have understood Tereza when she stood before the mirror as a young girl and tried to see her soul through her body. Adam was like Karenin. Tereza made a game of getting him to look at himself in the mirror, but he never recognized his image, gazed at it vacantly, with incredible indifference.

Comparing Adam and Karenin leads me to the thought that in Paradise man was not yet man. Or to be more precise, man had not yet been cast out on man's path. Now we are longtime outcasts, flying through the emptiness of time in a straight line. Yet somewhere deep down a thin thread still ties us to that far-off misty Paradise, where Adam leans over a well and, unlike Narcissus, never even suspects that the pale yellow blotch appearing in it is he himself. The longing for Paradise is man's longing not to be man.

Whenever, as a child, she came across her mother's sanitary napkins soiled with menstrual blood, she felt disgusted, and hated her mother for lacking the shame to hide them. But Karenin, who was after all a female, had his periods, too. They came once every six months and lasted a fortnight. To keep him from soiling their flat, Tereza would put a wad of absorbent cotton between his legs and pull a pair of old panties over it, skillfully tying them to his body with a long ribbon. She would go on laughing at the outfit for the entire two weeks of each period.

Why is it that a dog's menstruation made her lighthearted and gay, while her own menstruation made her squeamish? The answer seems simple to me: dogs were never expelled from Paradise. Karenin knew nothing about the duality of body and soul and had no concept of disgust. That is why Tereza felt so free and easy with him. (And that is why it is so dangerous to turn an animal into a *machina animata,* a cow into an automaton for the production of milk. By so doing, man cuts the thread binding him to Paradise and has nothing left to hold or comfort him on his flight through the emptiness of time.)

From this jumble of ideas came a sacrilegious thought that Tereza could not shake off: the love that tied her to Karenin was better than the love between her and Tomas. Better, not bigger. Tereza did not wish to fault either Tomas or herself; she did not wish to claim that they could love each other *more.* Her feeling was rather that, given the nature of the human couple, the love of man and woman is a priori inferior to that which can exist (at least in the best instances) in the love between man and dog, that oddity of human history probably unplanned by the Creator.

It is a completely selfless love: Tereza did not want anything of Karenin; she did not ever ask him to love her back. Nor had she ever asked herself the questions that plague human couples: Does he love me? Does he love anyone more than me? Does he love me more than I love him? Perhaps all the questions we ask of love, to measure, test, probe, and save it, have the additional effect of cutting it short. Perhaps the reason we are unable to love is that we yearn to be loved, that is, we demand something (love) from our partner instead of delivering ourselves up to him demand-free and asking for nothing but his company.

And something else: Tereza accepted Karenin for what he was; she did not try to make him over in her image; she agreed from the outset with his dog's life, did not wish to deprive him of it, did not envy him his secret intrigues. The reason she trained him was not to transform him (as a husband tries to reform his wife and a wife her husband), but to provide him with the elementary language that enabled them to communicate and live together.

Then too: No one forced her to love Karenin; love for dogs is voluntary. (Tereza was again reminded of her mother, and regretted everything that had happened between them. If her mother had been one of the anonymous women in the village, she might well have found her easygoing coarseness agreeable. Oh, if only her mother had been a stranger! From childhood on, Tereza had been ashamed of the way her mother occupied the features of her face and confiscated her "I". What made it even worse was that the age-old imperative "Love your father and mother!" forced her to agree with that occupation, to call the aggression love! It was not her mother's fault that Tereza broke with her. Tereza broke with her not because she was the mother she was but because she was a mother.)

But most of all: No one can give anyone else the gift of the idyll; only an animal can do so, because only animals were not expelled from Paradise. The love between dog and man is idyllic. It knows no conflicts, no hair-raising scenes; it knows no development. Karenin surrounded Tereza and Tomas with a life based on repetition, and he expected the same from them.

If Karenin had been a person instead of a dog, he would surely have long since said to Tereza, "Look, I'm sick and tired of carrying that roll in my mouth every day. Can't you come up with something different?" And therein lies the whole of man's plight. Human time does not turn in a circle; it runs ahead in a straight line. That is why man cannot be happy: happiness is the longing for repetition.

Yes, happiness is the longing for repetition, Tereza said to herself.

When the chairman of the collective farm took his Mefisto out for a walk after work and met Tereza, he never failed to say, "Why did he come into my life so late, Tereza? We could have gone skirt chasing, he and I! What woman could resist these two little pigs?" at which point the pig was trained to grunt and snort. Tereza laughed each time, even though she knew beforehand exactly what he would say. The joke did not lose its charm through repetition. On the contrary. In an idyllic setting, even humor is subject to the sweet law of repetition.

# 5

Dogs do not have many advantages over people, but one of them is extremely important: euthanasia is not forbidden by law in their case; animals have the right to a merciful death. Karenin walked on three legs and spent more and more of his time lying in a corner. And whimpering. Both husband and wife agreed that they had no business letting him suffer needlessly. But agree as they might in principle, they still had to face the anguish of determining the time when his suffering was in fact needless, the point at which life was no longer worth living.

If only Tomas hadn't been a doctor! Then they would have been able to hide behind a third party. They would have been able to go back to the vet and ask him to put the dog to sleep with an injection.

Assuming the role of Death is a terrifying thing. Tomas insisted that he would not give the injection himself; he would have the vet come and do it. But then he realized that he could grant Karenin a privilege forbidden to humans: Death would come for him in the guise of his loved ones.

Karenin had whimpered all night. After feeling his leg in the morning, Tomas said to Tereza, "There's no point in waiting."

In a few minutes they would both have to go to work. Tereza went in to see Karenin. Until then, he had lain in his corner completely apathetic (not even acknowledging Tomas when he felt his leg), but when he heard the door open and saw Tereza come in, he raised his head and looked at her.

She could not stand his stare; it almost frightened her. He did not look that way at Tomas, only at her. But never with such intensity. It was not a desperate look, or even sad. No, it was a look of awful, unbearable trust. The look was an eager question. All his life Karenin had waited for answers from Tereza, and he was letting her know (with more urgency than usual, however) that he was still ready to learn the truth from her. (Everything that came from Tereza was the truth. Even when she gave commands like "Sit!" or "Lie down!" he took them as truths to identify with, to give his life meaning.)

His look of awful trust did not last long; he soon laid his head back down on his paws. Tereza knew that no one ever again would look at her like that.

They had never fed him sweets, but recently she had bought him a few chocolate bars. She took them out of the foil, broke them into pieces, and made a circle of them around him. Then she brought over a bowl of water to make sure that he had everything he needed for the several hours he would spend at home alone. The look he had given her just then seemed to have tired him out. Even surrounded by chocolate, he did not raise his head.

She lay down on the floor next to him and hugged him. With a slow and labored turn of the head, he sniffed her and gave her a lick or two. She closed her eyes while the licking went on, as if she wanted to remember it forever. She held out the other cheek to be licked.

Then she had to go and take care of her heifers. She did not return until just before lunch. Tomas had not come home yet. Karenin was still lying on the floor surrounded by the chocolate, and did not even lift his head when he heard her come in. His bad leg was swollen now, and the tumor had burst in another place. She noticed some light red (not blood-like) drops forming beneath his fur.

Again she lay down next to him on the floor. She stretched one arm across his body and closed her eyes. Then she heard someone banging on the door. "Doctor! Doctor! The pig is here! The pig and his master!" She lacked the strength to talk to anyone, and did not move, did not open her eyes. "Doctor! Doctor! The pigs have come!" Then silence.

Tomas did not get back for another half hour. He went straight to the kitchen and prepared the injection without a word. When he entered the room, Tereza was on her feet and Karenin was picking himself up. As soon as he saw Tomas, he gave him a weak wag of the tail.

"Look," said Tereza, "he's still smiling."

She said it beseechingly, trying to win a short reprieve, but did not push for it.

Slowly she spread a sheet out over the couch. It was a white sheet with a pattern of tiny violets. She had everything carefully laid out and thought out, having imagined Karenin's death many days in advance. (Oh, how horrible that we actually dream ahead to the death of those we love!)

He no longer had the strength to jump up on the couch. They picked him up in their arms together. Tereza laid him on his side, and Tomas examined one of his good legs. He was looking for a more or less prominent vein. Then he cut away the fur with a pair of scissors.

Tereza knelt by the couch and held Karenin's head close to her own.

Tomas asked her to squeeze the leg because he was having trouble sticking the needle in. She did as she was told, but did not move her face from his head. She kept talking gently to Karenin, and he thought only of her. He was not afraid. He licked her face two more times. And Tereza kept whispering, "Don't be scared, don't be scared, you won't feel any pain there, you'll dream of squirrels and rabbits, you'll have cows there, and Mefisto will be there, don't be scared . . ."

Tomas jabbed the needle into the vein and pushed the plunger. Karenin's leg jerked; his breath quickened for a few seconds, then stopped. Tereza remained on the floor by the couch and buried her face in his head.

Then they both had to go back to work and leave the dog laid out on the couch, on the white sheet with tiny violets.

They came back towards evening. Tomas went into the garden. He found the lines of the rectangle that Tereza had drawn with her heel between the two apple trees. Then he started digging. He kept precisely to her specifications. He wanted everything to be just as Tereza wished.

She stayed in the house with Karenin. She was afraid of burying him alive. She put her ear to his mouth and thought she heard a weak breathing sound. She stepped back and seemed to see his breast moving slightly.

(No, the breath she heard was her own, and because it set her own body ever so slightly in motion, she had the impression the dog was moving.)

She found a mirror in her bag and held it to his mouth. The mirror was so smudged she thought she saw drops on it, drops caused by his breath.

"Tomas! He's alive!" she cried, when Tomas came in from the garden in his muddy boots.

Tomas bent over him and shook his head.

They each took an end of the sheet he was lying on, Tereza the lower end, Tomas the upper. Then they lifted him up and carried him out to the garden.

The sheet felt wet to Tereza's hands. He puddled his way into our lives and now he's puddling his way out, she thought, and she was glad to feel the moisture on her hands, his final greeting.

They carried him to the apple trees and set him down. She leaned over the pit and arranged the sheet so that it covered him entirely. It was unbearable to think of the earth they would soon be throwing over him, raining down on his *naked* body.

Then she went into the house and came back with his collar, his leash, and a handful of the chocolate that had lain untouched on the floor since morning. She threw it all in after him.

Next to the pit was a pile of freshly dug earth. Tomas picked up the shovel.

Just then Tereza recalled her dream: Karenin giving birth to two rolls and a bee. Suddenly the words sounded like an epitaph. She pictured a monument standing there, between the apple trees, with the inscription *Here lies Karenin. He gave birth to two rolls and a bee.*

It was twilight in the garden, the time between day and evening. There was a pale moon in the sky, a forgotten lamp in the room of the dead.

Their boots were caked with dirt by the time they took the shovel and spade back to the recess where their tools stood all in a row: rakes, watering cans, hoes.

# 6

He was sitting at the desk where he usually read his books. At times like these Tereza would come up to him from behind, lean over, and press her cheek to his. On that day, however, she gave a start. Tomas was not reading a book; he had a letter in front of him, and even though it consisted of no more than five typed lines, Tomas was staring at it long and hard.

"What is it?" Tereza asked, full of sudden anguish.

Without turning his head, Tomas picked up the letter and handed it to her. It said that he was obliged to report that day to the airfield of the neighboring town.

When at last he turned to her, Tereza read her own new-felt horror in his eyes.

"I'll go with you," she said.

He shook his head. "I'm the one they want to see."

"No, I'm going with you," she repeated.

They took Tomas's pickup. They were at the airfield in no time. It was foggy. They could make out only the vaguest outlines of the few airplanes on the field. They went from one to the next, but the doors were all closed. No admittance. At last they found one that was open, with a set of movable stairs leading up to it. They climbed the stairs and were greeted by a steward at the door. It was a small airplane—one that sat barely thirty passengers—and completely empty. They walked down the aisle between the seats, holding on to each other and not paying much attention to their surroundings. They took two adjoining seats, and Tereza laid her head on Tomas's shoulder. The first wave of horror had passed and been replaced by sadness.

Horror is a shock, a time of utter blindness. Horror lacks every hint of beauty. All we can see is the piercing light of an unknown event awaiting us. Sadness, on the other hand, assumes we are in the know. Tomas and Tereza knew what was awaiting them. The light of horror thus lost its harshness, and the world was bathed in a gentle, bluish light that actually beautified it.

While reading the letter, Tereza did not feel any love for Tomas; she simply realized that she could not now leave him for an instant: the feeling of horror overwhelmed all other emotions and instincts. Now that she was leaning against him (as the plane sailed through the storm clouds), her fear subsided and she became aware of her love, a love that she knew had no limit or bounds.

At last the airplane landed. They stood up and went to the door, which the steward opened for them. Still holding each other around the waist, they stood at the top of the stairs. Down below they saw three men with hoods over their heads and rifles in their hands. There was no point in stalling, because there was no escape. They descended slowly, and when their feet reached the ground of the airfield, one of the men raised his rifle and aimed it at them. Although no shot rang out, Tereza felt Tomas—who a second before had been leaning against her, his arm around her waist—crumple to the ground.

She tried pressing him to her but could not hold him up, and he fell against the cement runway. She leaned over him, about to fling herself on him, cover him with her body, when suddenly she noticed something strange: his body was quickly shrinking before her eyes. She was so shocked that she froze and stood stock still. The more Tomas's body shrank, the less it resembled him, until it turned into a tiny little object that started moving, running, dashing across the airfield.

The man who had shot him took off his mask and gave Tereza a pleasant smile. Then he turned and set off after the little object, which was darting here and there as if trying desperately to dodge someone and find shelter. The chase went on for a while, until suddenly the man hurled himself to the ground. The chase was over.

The man stood up and went back to Tereza, carrying the object in his hand. It was quaking with fear. It was a rabbit. He handed it to Tereza. At that instant her fear and sadness subsided and she was happy to be holding an animal in her arms, happy that the animal was hers and she could press it to her body. She burst into tears of joy. She wept, wept until blinded by her tears, and took the rabbit home with the feeling that she was nearly at her goal, the place where she wanted to be and would never forsake.

Wandering the streets of Prague, she had no trouble finding her house, the house where she had lived with Mama and Papa as a small girl. But Mama and Papa were gone. She was greeted by two old people she had never seen before, but whom she knew to be her great-grandfather and great-grandmother. They both had faces as wrinkled as the bark of a tree, and Tereza was happy she would be living with them. But for now, she wanted to be alone with her animal. She immediately found the room she had been given at the age of five, when her parents decided she deserved her own living space.

It had a bed, a table, and a chair. The table had a lamp on it, a lamp that had never stopped burning in anticipation of her return, and on the lamp perched a butterfly with two large eyes painted on its widespread wings. Tereza knew she was at her goal. She lay down on the bed and pressed the rabbit to her face.

# 7

He was sitting at the desk where he usually read his books, an open envelope with a letter in it lying in front of him. "From time to time I get letters I haven't told you about," he said to Tereza. "They're from my son. I've tried to keep his life and mine completely separate, and look how fate is getting even with me. A few years ago he was expelled from the university. Now he drives a tractor in a village. Our lives may be separate, but they run in the same direction, like parallel lines."

"Why didn't you ever tell me about the letters?" Tereza asked, with a feeling of great relief.

"I don't know. It was too unpleasant, I suppose."

"Does he write often?"

"Now and then."

"What about?"

"Himself."

"And is it interesting?"

"Yes, it is. You remember that his mother was an ardent Communist. Well, he broke with her long ago. Then he took up with people who had trouble like ours, and got involved in political activities with them. Some of them are in prison now. But he's broken with them, too. In his letters he calls them 'eternal revolutionaries.'"

"Does that mean he's made his peace with the regime?"

"No, not in the least. He believes in God and thinks that that's the key. He says we should all live our daily lives according to the dictates of religion and pay no heed to the regime, completely ignore it. If we believe in God, he claims, we can take any situation and, by means of our own behavior, transform it into what he calls 'the kingdom of God on earth.' He tells me that the Church is the only voluntary association in our country which eludes the control of the state. I wonder whether he's joined the Church because it helps him to oppose the regime or because he really believes in God."

"Why don't you ask him?"

"I used to admire believers," Tomas continued. "I thought they had an odd transcendental way of perceiving things which was closed to me. Like clairvoyants, you might say. But my son's experience proves that faith is actually quite a simple matter. He was down and out, the Catholics took him in, and before he knew it, he had faith. So it was gratitude that decided the issue, most likely. Human decisions are terribly simple."

"Haven't you ever answered his letters?"

"He never gives a return address," he said, "though the postmark indicates the name of the district. I could just send a letter to the local collective farm."

Tereza was ashamed of having been suspicious of Tomas, and hoped to expiate her guilt with a rush of benevolence towards his son. "Then why not drop him a line, invite him to come and see us?"

"He looks like me," said Tomas. "When he talks, his upper lip curls just like mine. The thought of watching my own lips go on about the kingdom of God—it seems too strange."

Tereza burst out laughing.

Tomas laughed with her.

"Don't be such a child, Tomas!" said Tereza. "It's ancient history, after all, you and your first wife. What's it to him? What's he got to do with it? Why hurt the boy just because you had bad taste when you were young?"

"Frankly, I have stage fright at the thought of meeting him. That's the main reason I haven't done anything about it. I don't know what's made me so headstrong and kept me from seeing him. Sometimes you make up your mind about something without knowing why, and your decision persists by the power of inertia. Every year it gets harder to change."

"Invite him," she said.

That afternoon she was on her way back from the cow sheds when she heard voices from the road. Coming closer, she saw Tomas's pickup. Tomas was bent over, changing a tire, while some of the men stood about looking on and waiting for him to finish.

She could not tear her eyes away from him: he looked like an old man. His hair had gone gray, and his lack of coordination was not that of a surgeon turned driver but of a man no longer young.

She recalled a recent talk with the chairman of the collective farm. He had told her that Tomas's pickup was in miserable condition. He said it as a joke, not a complaint, but she could tell he was concerned. "Tomas knows the insides of the body better than the insides of an engine," he said with a laugh. He then confessed that he had made several visits to the authorities to request permission for Tomas to resume his medical practice, if only locally. He had learned that the police would never grant it.

She had stepped behind a tree trunk so that none of the men by the pickup could see her. Standing there observing him, she suffered a bout of self-recrimination: It was her fault that he had come back to Prague from Zurich, her fault that he had left Prague, and even here she could not leave him in peace, torturing him with her secret suspicions while Karenin lay dying.

She had always secretly reproached him for not loving her enough. Her own love she considered above reproach, while his seemed mere condescension.

Now she saw that she had been unfair: If she had really loved Tomas with a great love, she would have stuck it out with him abroad! Tomas had been happy there; a new life was opening for him! And she had left him! True, at the time she had convinced herself she was being magnanimous, giving him his freedom. But hadn't her magnanimity been merely an excuse? She knew all along that he would come home to her! She had summoned him farther and farther down after her like the nymphs who lured unsuspecting villagers to the marshes and left them there to drown. She had taken advantage of a night of stomach cramps to inveigle him into moving to the country! How cunning she could be! She had summoned him to follow her as if wishing to test him again and again, to test his love for her; she had summoned him persistently, and here he was, tired and gray, with stiffened fingers that would never again be capable of holding a scalpel.

Now they were in a place that led nowhere. Where could they go from here? They would never be allowed abroad. They would never find a way back to Prague: no one would give them work. They didn't even have a reason to move to another village.

Good God, had they had to cover all that distance just to make her believe he loved her?

At last Tomas succeeded in getting the tire back on. He climbed in behind the wheel, the men jumped in the back, and the engine roared.

She went home and drew a bath. Lying in the hot water, she kept telling herself that she had set a lifetime of her weaknesses against Tomas. We all have a tendency to consider strength the culprit and weakness the innocent victim. But now Tereza realized that in her case the opposite was true! Even her dreams, as if aware of the single weakness in a man otherwise strong, made a display of her suffering to him, thereby forcing him to retreat. Her weakness was aggressive and kept forcing him to capitulate until eventually he lost his strength and was transformed into the rabbit in her arms. She could not get that dream out of her mind.

She stood up from her bath and went to put on some nice

clothes. She wanted to look her best to please him, make him happy.

Just as she buttoned the last button, in burst Tomas with the chairman of the collective farm and an unusually pale young farm worker.

"Quick!" shouted Tomas. "Something strong to drink!"

Tereza ran out and came back with a bottle of slivovitz. She poured some into a liqueur glass, and the young man downed it in one gulp.

Then they told her what had happened. The man had dislocated his shoulder and started bellowing with pain. No one knew what to do, so they called Tomas, who with one jerk set it back in its socket.

After downing another glass of slivovitz, the man said to Tomas, "Your wife's looking awfully pretty today."

"You idiot," said the chairman. "Tereza is always pretty."

"I know she's always pretty," said the young man, "but today she has such pretty clothes on, too. I've never seen you in that dress. Are you going out somewhere?"

"No, I'm not. I put it on for Tomas."

"You lucky devil!" said the chairman, laughing. "My old woman wouldn't dream of dressing up just for me."

"So that's why you go out walking with your pig instead of your wife," said the young man, and he started laughing, too.

"How is Mefisto, anyway?" asked Tomas. "I haven't seen him for at least"—he thought a bit—"at least an hour."

"He must be missing me," said the chairman.

"Seeing you in that dress makes me want to dance," the young man said to Tereza. And turning to Tomas, he asked, "Would you let me dance with her?"

"Let's all go and dance," said Tereza.

"Would you come along?" the young man asked Tomas.

"Where do you plan to go?" asked Tomas.

The young man named a nearby town where the hotel bar had a dance floor.

"You come too," said the young man in an imperative tone of voice to the chairman of the collective farm, and because by then he had downed a third glass of slivovitz, he added, "If Mefisto misses you so much, we'll take him along. Then we'll have both little pigs to show off. The women will come begging when they get an eyeful of those two together!" And again he laughed and laughed.

"If you're not ashamed of Mefisto, I'm all yours." And they piled into Tomas's pickup—Tomas behind the wheel, Tereza next to him, and the two men in the back with the half-empty bottle of slivovitz. Not until they had left the village behind did the chairman realize that they had forgotten Mefisto. He shouted up to Tomas to turn back.

"Never mind," said the young man. "One little pig will do the trick." That calmed the chairman down.

It was growing dark. The road started climbing in hairpin curves.

When they reached the town, they drove straight to the hotel. Tereza and Tomas had never been there before. They went downstairs to the basement, where they found the bar, the dance floor, and some tables. A man of about sixty was playing the piano, a woman of the same age the violin. The hits they played were forty years old. There were five or so couples out on the floor.

"Nothing here for me," said the young man after surveying the situation, and immediately asked Tereza to dance.

The collective farm chairman sat down at an empty table with Tomas and ordered a bottle of wine.

"I can't drink," Tomas reminded him. "I'm driving."

"Don't be silly," he said. "We're staying the night." And he went off to the reception desk to book two rooms.

When Tereza came back from the dance floor with the young man, the chairman asked her to dance, and finally Tomas had a turn with her, too.

"Tomas," she said to him out on the floor, "everything bad that's happened in your life is my fault. It's my fault you ended up here, as low as you could possibly go."

"*Low?* What are you talking about?"

"If we had stayed in Zurich, you'd still be a surgeon."

"And you'd be a photographer."

"That's a silly comparison to make," said Tereza. "Your work meant everything to you; I don't care what I do, I can do anything, I haven't lost a thing; you've lost everything."

"Haven't you noticed I've been happy here, Tereza?" Tomas said.

"Surgery was your mission," she said.

"Missions are stupid, Tereza. I have no mission. No one has. And it's a terrific relief to realize you're free, free of all missions."

There was no doubting that forthright voice of his. She recalled the scene she had witnessed earlier in the day when he had been repairing the pickup and looked so old. She had reached her goal: she had always wanted him to be old. Again she thought of the rabbit she had pressed to her face in her childhood room.

What does it mean to turn into a rabbit? It means losing all strength. It means that one is no stronger than the other anymore.

On they danced to the strains of the piano and violin. Tereza leaned her head on Tomas's shoulder. Just as she had when they flew together in the airplane through the storm clouds. She was experiencing the same odd happiness and odd sadness as then. The sadness meant: we are at the last station. The happiness meant: we are together. The sadness was form, the happiness content. Happiness filled the space of sadness.

They went back to their table. She danced twice more with the collective farm chairman and once with the young man, who was so drunk he fell with her on the dance floor.

Then they all went upstairs and to their two separate rooms.

Tomas turned the key and switched on the ceiling light. Tereza saw two beds pushed together, one of them flanked by a bedside table and lamp. Up out of the lampshade, startled by the overhead light, flew a large nocturnal butterfly that began circling the room. The strains of the piano and violin rose up weakly from below.